Shelby's Bridge

Randall Probert

Shelby's Bridge
by Randall Probert

www.randallprobertbooks.net
email: randentr@megalink.net

Art and Photography credits:

Cover photo from iStock.com

Author's photo, page 288, by Patricia Gott

Disclaimer:This book is a work of fiction.

ISBN: 979-8668317332

Printed in the United States of America

Published by
Randall Enterprises
P.O. Box 862
Bethel, Maine 04217

Acknowledgements

I would like to thank Laura Ashton of Woodland, Georgia, for her help in formatting this book for printing, and Amy Henley of Newry, Maine, for typing the manuscript and for her help with editing.

More Books by Randall Probert

Shelby's Bridge

Prologue

Armand Martin and his wife, Rebecca, lived near the coast in Rockford, Maine, and Armand had worked in the granite quarry since he was twelve years old, first just shoveling up the scraps and crushed stones. Then, as he grew older, he started cutting the granite slabs. After five years of this, he was fed up with the heavy, dusty work and he quit and started fishing with a friend.

After a month he had had enough of handling stinking fish, so he went back to the granite quarry. Tex Gilman owned the quarry and at first he didn't want to rehire Armand.

Armand stood five-eleven, weighed one-eighty and was extremely strong and rugged. There were other, larger workers, but Armand was a bully and he put the fear of God in the other workers. But he was a good worker. Begrudgingly, Mr. Gilman rehired him.

For the next year Armand stopped bullying, he met Rebecca Stencil and they were soon married. Nine months later Shelby was born.

Armand was jealous with all of the attention he was not getting from his wife, Rebecca, but his new son was. He began spending much of his free time drinking with the few friends he had at the local bar. And one night he watched as a stranger put a roll of money back in his pocket after paying for his drinks.

Armand left the bar early and waited for the stranger. He didn't have long to wait. When the stranger walked by him, he stepped out from the shadows and came up behind the stranger and hit him on the top of the head with his fist. The stranger collapsed and Armand dragged him into the shadows and took his money and ran home.

He put the roll of money in a jar and sealed it and buried it in some sawdust behind the shed. He would count it later.

* * * *

While Rebecca was making Sunday dinner, Armand uncovered his money jar in the sawdust and counted the bills he had stolen two nights ago. He had fifty-three dollars that he added to his life savings in the jar.

Armand was a frugal man and he didn't spend money foolishly. He now had close to eight-hundred dollars. He never had much faith with the banks. He didn't want someone else holding his money.

Two weeks later he robbed another stranger that had been drinking at the bar. He decided this was a good way to make money and he began alternating nights when he would rob someone, always a stranger who was passing through.

He had always wanted his own farm with a few head of cattle and a wood lot to supplement the farm. There was no way he was ever going to be able to save enough money from working in the quarry. But now with what he was stealing, he could see the end to working in the quarry.

His robbery attacks went on for four years and not one victim was able to identify the attacker or describe his physical appearance or his voice. He had been questioned once by the local sheriff and asked to explain his skinned knuckles. "I did that, Sheriff, in the quarry yesterday. It happens often."

When Sheriff Burley left, Armand knew it was time to leave. He now had eleven-hundred dollars in his money jar and he made arrangements with the land agent to purchase his house. "Where will you go, Mr. Martin?"

8

"I've been thinking about New Hampshire."

"How soon can you be out, Mr. Martin? I think I might have someone who might be interested."

"Will three days be soon enough?" Armand asked.

"That'll be fine, Mr. Martin."

Armand went home and told his wife. "Rebecca, I have sold the house and we have to be out of here in three days."

"Why, Armand? Where are we going?"

"I'll tell you once we are on the road. Until then we have much that we must do." That was the only explanation that he gave her.

He left and returned in time for supper with a new large wagon and two beautiful work horses.

"If anyone asks where we are going, tell them New Hampshire."

After he paid off the house lien he had two hundred dollars, and the two horses, wagon, harness and canvas cost him the two hundred dollars.

On the third morning, with all of their possessions loaded—and eleven hundred fifty dollars—they left Rockford and headed north. "Okay, Armand, we have left Rockford behind. Where are we going?"

"We are going to the town of Flagstaff in northern Franklin County. It'll take us four or five days."

"Why, Armand?"

"I have always wanted my own farm and wood lot, and Flagstaff will give us a new start."

"Okay, Armand." That's all she said—all she dared to say.

"Will we have to live in a log cabin with a dirt floor?" Rebecca asked.

"I'm sure there might be a few log cabins in Flagstaff, but there is a sawmill and a grist mill. There is a general store, hotel and restaurant. And I'm sure we'll be able to find suitable land for a farm."

Shelby was only four years old and he had no idea where they were going.

"There is something else Rebecca." She waited for Armand to continue. "We will be close to the Quebec border and I'd like to change our name from Martin to Martinique. The name is French and being this close to Quebec we might be accepted easier."

Rebecca was thinking that there was probably a more sinister reason for changing the name. Perhaps this move will give us a new start, she was thinking. Hoping.

Armand was only too happy to be leaving before the sheriff came looking for him.

* * * *

The road to Augusta was in excellent condition, and that first night they made camp just on the other side of the city.

Rebecca couldn't help but notice how happy and cheerful Armand had been all day. This wasn't like him, to be this happy. But he was and he was following his dream. And now with enough money to see the dream come into reality.

"Armand, have you ever been to this Flagstaff?" Rebecca asked

"No."

"How come you decided to go there?"

He wasn't about to admit to his wife that he had been responsible for all of the muggings and robberies. "I overheard two workers talking about it in the bar one night. I asked some questions and liked what I heard."

"We only have enough food, Armand, to have breakfast tomorrow."

"Then we'll find a place after breakfast and buy some food. No problem," he said.

And this certainly surprised her, too. *Maybe he has changed*, she began to think.

Armand pushed on that first day until an hour before sunset. While Rebecca was preparing food, Armand stretched the canvas over the wagon and brought the edge over the side so they would have protection from the rain that he was sure would come. Then he fed and watered the two horses.

"Why did you fix the canvas like that?" Rebecca asked.

"I think it'll rain later."

Their son, Shelby, lay down for the night as soon as he had eaten and he was soon asleep.

They were awake at daylight the next morning, Armand started the fire and Rebecca put the coffee on to make. While she was doing that, he fed and watered the horses and then hooked the harness.

Breakfast was leftover beef stew. It was hot and nourishing. Armand was not trying to rush them. Instead, he sat down beside Rebecca and poured himself another cup of coffee. "I'm getting excited now, Armand."

"You ready?" he asked.

"Let's go."

It only rained enough during the night to put a layer of dew on the grass.

By mid-morning they came into some steep hills and Armand would have to stop and rest the team for a few minutes on top of each of the three hills. "These hills are going to slow us down today. I was hoping we might reach Farmington today."

When they started up the first long hill, Shelby jumped off the wagon. "What are you doing, Shelby?" his mother asked.

"I'm tired of sitting. I want to walk some." It was a difficult job for a four-year-old boy to sit still all day.

"That's a good idea. Rebecca, why don't you jump down, too. It'll take that much weight off the load for the team," Armand said.

Shelby was too young to be able to help his dad much, so it became his job to collect firewood for his mother each day.

By mid-afternoon they were on the north side of the hills and they came to a sharp corner; the road went through a farm yard. There was a man walking towards the barn and Armand stopped and asked, "Excuse me, mister, is there any place beyond here where we might be able to buy some food?"

"Three more miles to New Sharon. There's a general store there. What are you needing? Maybe the Mrs. and I can help you. My name is Karl Barns."

"I'm Armand Martinique and my wife, Rebecca, and this is our son, Shelby."

Rebecca asked, "Would you have bacon, beans, flour, ham, eggs and maybe some milk for Shelby?"

"I think we can fix you up. Hey Sayde!" he hollered.

"Stop that hollering Karl. What do you want?"

"Come here I want you to meet … this is Armand and Rebecca Martinique and their son, Shelby. This is my wife, Sayde. They would like to buy some food, Sayde. Why don't you climb down, Mrs. Martinique, and go with Sayde into the house."

Armand climbed down also and helped Shelby. "Would you have a bag of grain for the horses?"

"Sure, will one bag be enough?"

"It should be."

"Where you folks traveling?"

"Flagstaff."

"Ah, I wish I could go with you. I hear there is plenty of black, rich soil. The ground around here is awful rocky."

"Well, you seem to do okay, Mr. Barns."

"We're doing okay now, but the first ten years were difficult. Me and the boys have finally cleared the fields of rocks."

Fifteen minutes later the two women came out carrying armloads of food. "This should see you through to Flagstaff, Mr. Martinique," Sayde said.

"How much do I owe you?" Armand asked.

"With the bag of grain—how's five dollars?"

Armand paid him and they were on their way. "Have a good trip."

They crossed the Sandy River in New Sharon and made camp in a field next to the road on the other side of town.

After they had laid down for the night, Rebecca said, "I was completely surprised that the Barns were so friendly and helpful. I liked them."

It was an easy day of travel the next day. There were no long or steep hills and by 5 p.m. they were at the turnoff to the Great Works in New Portland. They went another mile and stopped for the day next to the Carrabassett River.

"Look how clear the water is, Armand. We can use it for cooking and drinking."

"We had an easy day today, but tomorrow, I think might be a long one," Armand said.

"Why?"

"I think we need to reach Bigelow Village before sunset tomorrow. From Bigelow Village we'll be only one more day."

Both Armand and Rebecca were awake and up before daylight the next morning, and they were able to get an early start on the day's travel. They went through Kingfield at 8 a.m. and the streets were full of wagons and people on the sidewalks.

"Is this the same river, Armand?"

"Yes, the Carrabassett."

"It sure is beautiful up through here."

"Look, Dad," Shelby said, "there are men working on the other side of the river."

"It looks like they're clearing the right of way for a road," Armand said.

Once they were beyond Kingfield, they had the road to themselves again.

"I think we are getting into the mountains. The road is continually going uphill."

When they came to the Jerusalem Flats, the Bigelow Mountain Range was in front of them. "Wow, look at those mountains," Shelby said. "We never had mountains like those back home."

Once they were across the flats, the road had been carved out of the side of a hill, still following the river. And still climbing.

"We have made good time today, Rebecca, I think we'll reach Bigelow Village before sunset."

They went around a sharp bend in the road and there was another tall mountain. "That must be Sugarloaf Mountain."

They had traveled a great distance this day and the team was tired. Then they saw a sign that said, Bigelow Village one mile ahead.

"We're almost there."

As they turned off the road at the village a looming steep hill was in front of them. "At least the team will be well rested when we have to climb that hill in the morning," Armand said.

Armand brought the team to a stop in front of a general store and a man walked over to them. "Hello, I'm Frank Bigelow. Can I help you?"

"We're just looking for a place to camp for the night."

"In the field across the road is okay. Where are you folks headed?" Frank asked.

"Flagstaff."

"That's about six hours from here by wagon. That's a nice looking team."

"Thank you. We noticed four different crews working on something across the river. What is there, another road going in?"

"No, a railroad. The Franklin and Megantic Railroad."

"How far is it going?"

"It'll stop here. There's no way around this hill or the swamp. There's another railroad being built that will go from Strong to Rangeley and through the Green Farm to the Skunk

Brook Lumber Camps. This is an exciting time here in the wilderness."

"When will this railroad be completed?" Armand asked.

"In two years. Might you be interested in freighting supplies into Stratton and Flagstaff from here? You sure do have the team and wagon for it."

"I sure would."

"Okay, you come back and see me on July 1st two years from now. What is your name?"

"Armand Martinique and this is my wife, Rebecca, and our son, Shelby."

"I'll remember you. And I'll be right here in two years."

"Thank you very much, Mr. Bigelow. Now, we've had a long day and need to make camp."

"Help yourselves to the field. Oh, where have you come from?"

"We left Rockford four days ago."

"You have made good time."

Shelby had to go the length of the field before he found enough firewood for his mother. Armand gave the horses extra grain and then he brushed them down. "We have a steep hill in the morning, fellas. I hope you'll be up to it."

It had been a long day for them and they went to sleep early. The next morning was a repeat of the previous day and they were soon on their way.

The team, having a good night rest and extra grain, had no problem with Bigelow Hill. "I'm surprised," Rebecca said, "I would have thought Shelby and I might have to walk up the hill."

"The team surprised me, too," Armand said.

Rebecca was happy with the sudden change with Armand's temperament. She had half expected him to use a whip to get the team to work. She was hoping he would remain like this.

They pulled into Stratton before noon and continued on

towards Flagstaff. "It won't be long now," Armand said. "We are almost there."

"This has been quite a trip."

"You did real well, Rebecca."

A half mile before they reached the town of Flagstaff, they saw a man nailing up a for sale sign. Armand stopped and asked, "What are you selling?"

"The house and land. You interested?"

"Can we have a look? I'm Armand Martinique and this is my wife, Rebecca, and our son, Shelby."

"I'm Fred Stevens. Bring your wagon right in. There's room to turn."

"Where are you going, Mr. Stevens?" Rebecca asked.

"Home, Augusta area." Mrs. Stevens came outside then. "This is my wife, Hilda."

"Ma'am."

"Why are you leaving?" Armand asked.

"My mother is sick and in bed and father needs help taking care of her. Besides, I've never liked it way up here," Hilda said.

"How long were you here?" Armand asked.

"Two years."

"You certainly have cleared a lot of land in two years," Armand said.

"The previous owner cleared most of it."

"May we see the inside of the house?" Rebecca asked.

"Certainly."

There were two bedrooms on the ground floor and two upstairs, a woodshed connecting the house to the barn and a hand pump at the kitchen sink.

"How much land, Mr. Stevens?" Armand asked.

"Fifty acres, with ten acres cleared."

"Any animals go with it?"

"Two pigs, two goats and two milking cows. I was going to sell them all to the butcher in town, but if you are interested,

I'll let them go with the farm."

"How much?"

"Nine-hundred dollars."

"Do you hold the mortgage or does a bank?"

"We own it free and clear. There's a clear title that goes with it."

"Mr. Stevens, I can give you six-hundred dollars cash right now, if you'll agree to that price." Stevens didn't seem to like that offer.

"Eight-hundred and you have a deal," Armand said.

"I hate to sell for eight-hundred, but Hilda and I would like to get out of here as soon as we can. I guess if you have the money, we have a deal."

* * * *

Fred had a wagon like Armand and they loaded on as much as they could, but there was some that would have to be left behind. They were able to leave at noon on the second day.

Armand was beginning to feel like a rich man. He had his farm that he had always wanted; with livestock to boot and still with almost six-hundred dollars in his pocket—never once thinking about those men he had robbed. He didn't have a conscience. In his mind, the money he had, he had worked hard for it.

Rebecca had a nicer house than they had had in Rockford and Armand had been so pleasant since leaving their old home. Yes, life was being good to Rebecca.

Shelby would go to the barn with his father and watch him milk the two cows and feed the animals. He was only four years old, but he was big for his age and his father showed him how to feed the animals.

Once they were settled into their new house, Armand went to the Eustis sawmill and asked Charles Eustis for a job. "You look like a big rugged fellow and I could use you on the deck rolling logs onto the saw carriage; my regular man quit two weeks ago and moved back home. Can you start today?"

"Yes, Mr. Eustis, I can."

"What's your name?"

"Armand Martinique."

"Oh yeah, you bought the Stevens farm. Fred was the deck man that quit. He was a good man.

"There'll be times when we shut the sawmill down and start up the grist mill. But that usually isn't until the fall harvest of wheat or oats are in."

* * * *

Armand was having to get up real early each morning now, so he could milk the two cows before going to work. He'd be glad when Shelby was old enough to do some of the milking.

At the supper table Monday evening, Armand said, "I'm not sure if I can farm, tend the animals and work at the mill too. And I don't think there'll be enough hay in the ten acre field for two cows and two horses."

"What are you thinking, Armand?"

"Well, Frank Bigelow offered me that job of hauling freight, so I'll need the team and wagon, so I suppose the two cows will have to go. I'll talk with Mr. Adalbert at the general store and see if he will buy one cow for meat to sell in his store. The other one, we butcher for ourselves. I was hoping so much that I could make a living from farming. But ten acres of field surely won't support much of a herd. And I'll have to start cutting the hay before it all goes to seed.

"I found a mowing machine behind the barn and it'll work okay. But I'll have to hire help to bring it in. If Shelby was older, I wouldn't have to worry."

The next day after work, Armand stopped at Adalbert's store and he offered to pay Armand forty dollars if he'd wait until October and cooler weather, and he had to clean, skin and quarter it.

He also talked with the young fella on the green chain, Tommy Phillips, and Tommy said he would be glad to help out.

"What about the pigs, Armand?" Rebecca asked.

"After I have butchered one cow, I'll do one pig and if Mr. Adalbert needs more meat, I'll do the other cow and pig. The pig … I think I'll smoke the hams and bacon myself."

* * * *

That weekend Armand and Tommy were able to put all of the hay in the barn. The last load was finished at sunset. At the mill, Tommy was paid a dollar a day. Armand gave him three dollars for two days of work. Tommy was happy.

In October, cool weather came and Armand butchered the cow first and hauled it to Adalbert's store. "Yes I'll buy your pork, ham and bacon too. You smoke it and I'll give you fifty dollars."

The ham and pork sold out so fast, Adalbert asked Armand if he would butcher the other pig. "I can sell you half for twenty-five dollars. I'll need the other half for my family."

Adalbert agreed. When the second pig was taken care of, Armand butchered the remaining cow. He hung some of it up in the cool cellar and some still hung in the barn where it would freeze.

"I'll have to can some of the beef, Armand, and I'll need a canner and canning jars.

"Next spring, Armand, I'd like to get a couple dozen baby chickens. It would be awful nice if we could have our own eggs."

"Okay. By then Shelby should be old enough to take care of them and collect the eggs when they start laying."

With both cows butchered, he kept half of the cow, also, and the pigs, and the only food Rebecca had to buy that winter was flour, milk and eggs.

One day at the supper table, Rebecca said, "Armand, I'm glad we moved here. You have a good job at the mill and I never liked you working in the quarry. We are better off and this is a better place for Shelby to grow up. And the people here are friendlier. In case you haven't noticed, Armand, I'm pregnant."

"Since when?"

"I'm due in May."

"No, I haven't noticed. I've been so busy."

Rebecca ordered her two dozen chicks and two roosters from Mr. Adalbert and they would be in with the first freight wagon in the middle of May.

Shelby turned five years old in April and he was already taller and stronger than other boys of the same age. When the snow was gone he helped his dad fence in an area for the chickens beside the barn and cut an opening in the side of the barn so they could come and go. Every time Shelby would do something, whether he was right or not, his dad would find fault and correct him.

Armand sectioned off part of the cow tie-up for a hen house and a smaller section for the two roosters. There was still room in the tie-up for two cows if he wanted.

He brought home sawdust for the laying nests. "These chickens, Shelby, will be your responsibility. And when your mother has the new baby, I'll expect you to help out a lot around the house."

There was a medical building on Main Street and one day while Armand was at work, she knew she was about to deliver, so she had Shelby harness one of the work horses to the wagon and he drove her into town. Two hours later she gave birth to another son and she named him Raul.

On weekends that spring and summer, Shelby helped his dad with a large garden and working up firewood for the winter. Because of Shelby's size and strength his dad expected more from him than a normal-sized five-year-old.

That fall, Shelby started school and each morning before he left home, he had chores to do. Feed and water the horses, clean their stalls out, and shovel the manure outside. He had to open the small door, so the chickens could go outside and scratch for food.

He liked school and he made friends easily. He was as tall as the boys in the fifth grade. One day some of the older boys started teasing him by saying he had to be older than five and that he had probably stayed back in school a couple of years. Instead of getting angry like his dad most certainly would have, he just let the comments roll off his back, like he was now used to doing when his dad would find fault with everything he did. He just walked away.

When there was fresh snow on the ground, before Shelby could walk to school, he would have to shovel a path to the barn. But he didn't care.

* * * *

In July of the following year Rebecca gave birth to a girl and she named her Sis. In June, Armand had given his notice at the mill. There were no hard feelings and Mr. Eustis said, "If the freighting job doesn't work out, Armand, you can always come back to work here."

"Thank you, Mr. Eustis."

He left home before the sun was up in order to be back by 6 p.m. The wagon was unloaded the next day, and the next day, he was back on the road to Bigelow Village. Because he had his own team and wagon, he was paid ten dollars a trip.

One week making three trips and the next week four trips, this was a lot more money than he had been earning at the mill.

Raul and the new baby, Sis, moved into Shelby's bedroom so Rebecca could hear them during the night. Shelby moved upstairs. He didn't mind at all.

Life was good now for the Martinique family. Armand came home tired every day like he had from the quarry, but he was no longer angry all the time. And Rebecca had a little girl to bring up. She, in particular, couldn't be happier.

Chapter 1

Shelby was now twelve years old and he stood as tall as many adult men—and he was more rugged than most. But unlike his dad, he always had a happy disposition. Even with the frequent criticizing, he remained happy. He simply had accepted the fact that his dad was never going to praise him for anything. So, he tried to avoid him whenever possible.

Raul was eight and he was not as big as his brother, Shelby, although he tried to do the same work as his brother.

Sis was seven and she and Raul were best friends. She was a pretty seven-year-old girl, and both Sis and Raul looked up to their big brother. And neither of them had any problems at school with the other students bullying them. Shelby protected them.

When Shelby and Raul had any spare time they would go fishing in Dead River and sometimes they would meet up with friends from town. Armand didn't mind the boys taking the time to fish. They always brought home enough for the family. Sometimes Sis would tag along, but Shelby had to bait her hook. Their fish poles were an alder branch with string tied to one end.

Shelby and Raul were doing most of the work now around home. They were even working up the winter's firewood. This was just good exercise for Shelby, and Raul wanted to be just like his big brother.

One evening while Armand was having supper with his family, he said, "You know I have never eaten any better pork or bacon than that first winter here. Our own pig. I think I'll buy two piglets from Jim Reed at the Green Farm. And buy another pig that we can butcher later this year." There was no arguing from Rebecca; she also liked the pork and bacon.

That following Saturday, Armand and Rebecca took a load of sawn lumber to the Green Farm depot. Sis went with them. The boys had to stay and rebuild the outside pigpen.

That summer Shelby cleared out a mile-loop trapline. He knew his dad would never give him money to buy traps, so he made a deal with Mr. Adalbert at the general store. He could pay Mr. Adalbert for the gear after he sold his fur. He would also need a gun to shoot the animals in his traps, so he also picked out a Colt .22 caliber revolver and a holster. And, as part of the agreement, Shelby was to sell his fur to Mr. Adalbert.

Raul wanted to go with Shelby while he cleared his trapline, but he said, "No, Raul, I'm going to do this for myself."

His mother was proud of him. He didn't say anything to his dad.

The Sandy River and Rangeley Lakes Railroad had finished all the way to the Skunk Brook lumber camp in Coplin Plt. and most of the freight was now being delivered to the Green Farm depot. Armand no longer had to haul up and over Bigelow Hill in Wyman Twp. And he only needed one horse to haul the freight wagon. Some days, if he got an early start, he might make two trips and get home about 8 p.m. It made for a long day, but the money was good.

In the evenings, after he and Raul had finished firewood for the day, Shelby would make wooden stretchers for the fur pelts.

Four days before the start of the school year, Shelby filled his packbasket with traps, and with his ax, he started making trap sets along his trapline and hanging the traps in trees. He wanted to set a few but he knew it was too early yet. The fur wouldn't be prime.

He saved the dead chickens for bait that had died of old age, instead of throwing them away. And he thought maybe a couple of putrefied eggs might be a good attracter.

At the furthest corner on his trapline was a big beaver colony. He knew from listening to other trappers that beaver castor was an excellent lure.

His mother, brother and sister all knew about Shelby's plans to trap and they didn't say anything to Armand about it. Armand was good with Raul and Sis but she could never understand why her husband was always so eager to find fault with Shelby. Being the oldest son, it should have been him that the father should have favored.

Shelby liked school and he had always been a good student. He was eager to learn. But the anticipation of being a trapper was more alluring. He kept up with his studies but he'd lay awake at night dreaming about how to set each trap.

* * * *

Shelby decided to set traps the first weekend in October. His dad was busy hauling freight that weekend. As soon as the morning chores were done he shouldered his packbasket and strapped on his revolver and struck out. He was feeling like a real trapper. A man.

His first set was at the edge of the field and he dug a bait hole and put one of the bad eggs in it. Then he set the trap and when he was satisfied with everything he broke the end of the egg. "Oh man! That stinks. It should bring a fox in, though."

His next set was for a mink in a small stream that ran to Dead River.

Not far from the mink set there was a natural covey under a spruce root. He decided to use the last egg before it broke in his pack.

His next set was a large dead leaning tree. He used a chicken wing here. It already smelled as bad as the eggs.

He set three more traps before he reached the beaver colony. And just like he had heard other trappers talk about, he made a trough in the top of the dam and laid in his trap. He also had a covey set he had earlier dug into the bank about fifty feet away from the pond. Before he was finished with that trap he heard his beaver set go off and the beaver thrashing in the water. "Holy dang! Already?"

He waited until the beaver stopped thrashing and then he pulled in a large beaver. This surprised him and he reset the trap and began skinning, fleshing as he skun—like he was told to do.

Before he finished he had another beaver, as large as the first one. The flowage went dead then. He was two hours skinning both beaver and cutting out the castors, and he decided to take the hind legs home. There was a lot of meat there.

He used a beaver head in that covey set and put some castor on a stick and stuck that in the ground above the covey hole.

He wrapped up the meat in the two hides and the castors and some of the carcass to use as bait. He was ecstatic to think he had two beaver already.

He circled the pond and made another water set in a small inlet stream then another covey set under a root system and baited that with beaver meat and castor as before.

He had ten traps out and although he wanted to continue, he decided ten was enough to tend every day after school.

Shelby was back before his dad and he took the fresh beaver into the house. "Hey, Mom, look what I brought back," and he held out the meat to her.

"What is it?"

"It's beaver meat."

"Can you eat it?" she asked.

"I listened to an old trapper in town who says it is the best tasting meat there is."

"I'll clean it up and fry it for supper and see if your father says anything."

25

Shelby and Raul went out to the barn and Raul helped him nail the hides to drying boards.

When Armand got home he was in a good mood. Shelby took care of the wagon and horse and Armand went into the house to clean up.

Shelby wasn't long and he washed up. "Supper is ready," Rebecca said.

"Hmm, that smells good," Armand said. He filled his plate and started eating. They were all watching and waiting for him to say something.

When he didn't, Shelby said, "How do you like the meat, Dad?"

"It's delicious. Sweet and tender."

"It's beaver, Dad."

"Hmm, I never would have supposed. Where did you get beaver meat?"

"I'm running a trapline, Dad."

"Hmm, where did you get the traps?"

"I worked out a deal with Mr. Adalbert."

"Good, maybe if you earn enough you can start paying board."

"Me pay board," Shelby said straight forward, "and work my ass off every day for you for nothing—not hardly."

Everyone stopped eating and held their breath except for Armand. Rebecca was expecting him to get angry. Shelby had never spoken to his father like that.

Shelby was only twelve years old, but he was already taller than his father and almost as rugged. This time it was Armand who didn't answer. Rebecca breathed a sigh of relief.

* * * *

"There's a load of lumber I could haul to the Green Farm. Would you like to ride over with me, Rebecca?" Armand asked.

"I didn't think you worked on Sunday."

"I usually don't, but this is an extra trip and we could use the money. And maybe Mr. Reed will have a load to come back."

"Sure, I'd like to get out of the house for a day. What about Sis?"

"She can stay with the boys today."

"Okay."

After morning chores Shelby left to tend his traps. There was a red fox in the field set and he smelled of rotten egg. He reset it using beaver meat and castor for a lure.

The next trap where he had used a second egg for bait, he had a big fisher cat.

The rest of his traps had not been touched, except the beaver trap on the dam. It had been pulled into the water and when he pulled it in, the beaver in it was much bigger than the two he caught the day before.

He reset the trap and took the beaver ashore and started skinning. When he finished the beaver, he skun the fox and fisher cat. He cut off the hind legs off the beaver, and the castors, and went further up the side hill until he found a hollow rotten log lying on the ground. He put the beaver carcass inside, blocked off the end of the log and set a number 3 trap in front of the log. He smeared a little castor on the end of the log.

He put some dead leaves on the disturbed ground and trap, to make it appear more natural. When he was satisfied, he went back to the pond.

The trap was gone again and he pulled in another super-large beaver.

The pond had gone quiet, so he put everything in his packbasket and headed for home. His pack was full and heavy but he was able to shoulder it without any problem.

He finished stretching the hides before his folks returned and he took the beaver meat in the house.

When they got home, Armand said, "You and Raul take care of the horse, I'll have to leave the wagon loaded and in the barn tonight."

The only comment Armand made about Shelby's trapping was, "This beaver meat sure is better than beef."

* * * *

After school the next day Shelby ran home, changed his clothes, fed the pig, horse and chickens, and headed for his trapline.

He didn't have anything until he got to the pond and the trap was pulled off the dam. He pulled in another large beaver and he didn't reset the trap this time. He might be able to skin and flesh one beaver but not two.

The other traps were empty and he headed home. He'd wait for the weekend to set traps on the dam again. Besides he wasn't sure how many more beaver there would be.

He no more than had finished nailing that hide to the drying board and his father arrived home. He jumped off the wagon and without speaking walked into the house, expecting Shelby and Raul to take care of the horse. Raul had already taken the beaver meat inside.

As they were eating supper, Rebecca asked, "How many more beaver do you think you might catch, Shelby?"

"Maybe two. I don't want to take the small ones."

"I'll keep the meat in the cold storage until there's enough to can it."

The next morning after Armand left, Rebecca asked, "How is your trapping going, Shelby?"

"Good, but I wish I didn't have to go to school. I have seven animals so far."

That afternoon was a repeat of the day before. When his chores were done he rushed out to his trapline. There was another fox in the first set. He shot it in the ear and reset the trap and baited it and left the fox there. He'd pick it up when he came back. There was a martin in the next two sets and he had a big gray wolf. "Holy cow! I didn't know there were any gray wolves here."

It was a big male. The other traps were empty so he started back. He draped the wolf over the top of his packbasket and shoulders. As he was hiking back, he smiled and said, "I like this kind of life."

In the barn he skinned the two martin and fox and left the wolf until after supper.

At the supper table his dad said, "What, no beaver meat tonight?"

"No beaver, but I did get a big wolf."

"Wolf?" Armand questioned, "You sure it ain't someone's dog? I didn't know there were any wolves in Maine." That was his only comment. Raul went out to the barn to help his brother.

Shelby learned that a wolf was not as easy to skin as a fox. The hide held tight against the meaty flesh. He was almost an hour skinning it. Then he had to stretch it. "This fur is so pretty, Shelby. It looks like a German Shepherd dog."

"Yeah, it does. But, believe me, they are far more vicious.

"Raul, I don't want you telling anyone about me trapping, okay?"

* * * *

Until Saturday, he only picked up one more. Then on Saturday morning after Armand left and the morning chores were done, he changed clothes and headed for his trapline.

Leaves had turned color, most of them had fallen and there was a cool breeze in the air. Winter was coming.

He had a nice mink in the first water set and nothing until the pond. He dug out the trough again and set the trap and he made another trough and set another trap. Then he checked the other traps and had an otter in the inlet stream.

The otter was a feisty creature; hell, he was mad and every time Shelby would get close enough for a shot in the ear the otter would snarl, growl and lunge at him. After many attempts he finally succeeded. He took the time to skin it there before going

29

back to the dam.

He couldn't simply leave the otter carcass or the other animals would be lured to that and not his traps, so he looked for another covey set. He didn't find what he wanted so he tucked it in a very thick bunch of blackberry bushes. There was only one way an animal could get at it and he set the only trap he had left, a number 3. Then he went back to the pond. Both traps were in the water.

The first one was another large beaver and the next one was a small beaver. He decided then to pull both traps. He wasn't long skinning those two beaver and cutting off the meat and castors. He threw the remains of the carcass into the pond.

He shouldered the packbasket and started for home. It had warmed up a little, but still cool. Just before the field there was a year old bull moose standing broadside in his trail and looking towards the field, about thirty feet away. Without even having to think about it, he withdrew his handgun and waited until he had a fine bead right behind the left ear. Shelby fired and the moose collapsed in the trail.

He walked up to the moose with his gun held ready—just in case. But the moose was dead. He would need help with this, so he hurried home.

He put his packbasket in the barn and went in the house. Excitedly he said, "I shot a moose! Raul, I'm going to need your help."

"How are the two of you going to get it back here?" Rebecca asked.

"We'll have to use the work horse. Come on, Raul, change your clothes."

Rebecca sat at the kitchen table, smiling. Shelby was only twelve years old and already a man.

Raul followed Shelby behind the work horse. He was more excited than his brother. "Is it a big moose, Shelby?"

"No, a small bull."

Raul held the moose on its back while Shelby cleaned it . "How do you know how to do this, Shelby?"

"Well, it's no different than butchering a cow or pig really." He was blood up to his elbows by the time they started back to the barn.

They dragged the moose inside and used block and tackle supported from a beam to hoist the moose enough so they could skin it, when their father got home from work.

"What the hell is that?" he asked in surprise.

"I shot a moose, Dad."

Armand looked the moose over and asked, "What did you use? I don't see a bullet wound. Did you take my rifle out without asking?"

"No, Dad, I used my .22 revolver."

"Where did you get a handgun?"

"From Mr. Adalbert's, along with the other trapping supplies. It was part of the deal I made with him."

"You killed this with only a .22 revolver?"

"Yes."

"How close were you?"

"About thirty feet."

"Where did you hit it?"

"Behind the left ear. He dropped dead in his tracks."

"What are you going to do with the hide?"

"I'll see if Mr. Adalbert will buy it."

Raul wanted to be part of this conversation so he said, "Mom is frying liver and onions for supper tonight."

Without a word of appreciation, Armand turned and walked to the house.

That was the longest conversation he could ever remember having with his dad.

Shelby and Raul went back to work. "After supper, Raul, we'll have to nail this up on the side of the barn. If Mr. Adalbert will give me anything for the hide, I'll give it to you, brother, for your help." This made Raul smile, the idea of having his own money.

Before they could finish with the hide they had to take care of the horse, harness and wagon. For now they turned both horses out into the pasture. They would grain them later.

At the supper table, Rebecca asked, "Did you bring home any more beaver meat?"

"Yes, and it'll be the last. I pulled those traps."

"You certainly have provided the family with a lot of meat. It'll see us through the winter."

"Mom?" Raul asked, "Is all this meat liver?"

"No, I fried up some heart with it. We'll have eggs, fried potato and the rest of the heart for breakfast tomorrow morning."

After supper, Shelby and Raul went back out to the barn.

"Look how fast these piglets are growing," Raul said. "A nice roast pork would go good about now."

"Raul, you are always thinking of food," Shelby laughed.

During the night the temperature dropped and there was hoar frost where the weight of the moose had been dragged across the field in some places where the grass had been scraped down to dirt.

There was a bear track in the dirt where his trap had been, that had been flicked out of the set. He smoothed the dirt out and reset the trap with new bait and more castor.

The gut pile from the moose was completely gone and there were four piles of bear crap. One of the piles was huge. Probably a mother with a cub or two. He stood still and looked around him. He wasn't quite sure he wanted to face a mother bear with cub with only a .22 revolver. Hopefully the bear had their bellies full and had gone off to sleep somewhere.

There was a noisy martin in his next trap and a bobcat in the lower set at the beaver pond. The bobcat had torn up the ground some but was pretty calm now—until he started to walk towards it, then it began to snarl and growl and bite the trap. He finally was able to shoot it—a big male and his front teeth had been worn down to nubs. "I did you a favor, fella."

He put it in his packbasket and would skin it at home. The hollow log set was untouched, another mink in the water set in the small inlet stream and at the new set, in the snarl of blackberry bushes, he had another wolf. This one was smaller and not fighting. It was snarled up pretty bad with blackberry thornes.

He was some time trying to unsnag it from the bushes. He reset the trap and draped the wolf over his shoulders and headed for home.

It was getting time for the animals to start feeding again, so he began talking to himself and hoping it would be enough to keep the bear away. When he reached the field, he breathed a sigh of relief.

Raul saw him coming across the field and ran out to meet him. "How'd you do today, Shelby?"

"Good—one bobcat, wolf, martin and a mink."

The bodies were still warm and the hides came off easy, except for the wolf. "This wolf isn't as big," Raul said.

"No, it's a female and probably the mate to that big male."

After he had everything skun and on stretchers, he and Raul brought the horses in and gave them some grain. They had had enough grass so they didn't need any hay. "How many eggs did you get this morning, Raul?"

"Fifteen."

"And we have another ten now. That's pretty good."

For supper that night they had moose liver and onions again. Shelby hadn't eaten since breakfast and he ate enough for two men.

To everyone's surprise, Armand said, "It'll storm tonight and as cool as the air is now, it'll probably be snow."

"How do you know a storm is coming, Armand?" Rebecca asked.

"When I left the Green Farm, the cows were all standing and facing the sun."

The next morning there was twelve inches of new snow. Shelby and Raul harnessed both horses that morning for Armand. "I may be late tonight because of the snow. Tell your mother."

They finished their chores, then ate breakfast and now it was time to walk to school. Shelby walked ahead dragging his feet in the snow to make a trail and easier walking for Raul and Sis. Because of the cold air, the snow was dry and fluffy.

Shelby had difficulty concentrating on his studies that day; with the snow, he was debating whether or not to pull all of his traps. He had twenty pieces plus the moose hide and for his first year he figured he had done good. As he was walking home with Raul and Sis, he decided to pull everything and call it a year.

"Raul, can you feed the pigs and chickens and collect the eggs? I'm going to pull all of my traps and the sun is setting early."

"I can do it," he said.

He found fresh bear tracks where the gut pile had been. He probably had spooked the bear hiking across the field. He followed the tracks for a short ways and according to the tracks the bear was running. "Good."

From there all the way to his last trap in the blackberry bushes, he never saw any tracks in the snow. Except, that is, for red squirrel tracks. This wasn't taking him as long as he thought it would. But the last two traps he pulled in the moonlight.

Armand didn't get home until seven o'clock that evening. "How was the road, Dad?" Shelby asked.

"Coming back it was pretty good. There had been enough wagons to beat the snow down. Tonight a crew and horses will haul a snow roller all the way to the Green Farm and the roads in town."

Armand didn't ask or maybe didn't care how his son was doing with his trapline. Or it never occurred to him.

* * * *

It snowed again three days later and before the freight wagons could run the road to the Green Farm, it had to be rolled to allow it to freeze. Armand was busy for two days with his team helping to roll-pack the snow to the farm. Shelby was glad he had pulled his traps when he did.

Rebecca was getting more eggs now than the family could use, so once a week she took a basket of eggs to the Adalbert General Store. He was happy to buy them. This money Rebecca kept for herself.

November came in with unusually warm weather and all the snow melted. But Shelby was still glad he had pulled his trapline.

By the middle of the month more normal temperatures returned, without the snow. On Saturday, Shelby bundled his pelts together and took them to Adalbert. Raul wanted to tag along.

Mr. Adalbert took the boys and the fur pelts out back and he gave Shelby a list of prices for the different species. "You sure have taken good care of these, Shelby. There's nothing I can deduct for mishandling."

"How much for the moose hide, Mr. Adalbert? You don't have that on the list."

Adalbert unfolded the pelt looking for the bullet holes. "Hmm, no wounds. Where did you shoot it?"

"Behind the left ear."

"That explains it. Seven dollars for the moose hide. If you accept these prices, I'll give you $470.00. Do you want me to deduct what you owe me for the gun and traps?"

"Yes."

"Here's your bill," and he marked it paid. Then he gave Shelby $400.00. "You did real well, son, for your first year. But I'm surprised you aren't still trapping."

Shelby didn't answer.

"Raul, here is your $7.00," Shelby said, "Would you like a candy bar?"

"Would I? Holy cow, yes!"

Shelby bought four of the biggest ones he could find. "I think we should get one for Mom and Sis, too."

Before leaving town, Shelby and Raul stopped at the bank. "Mr. Edwards, I would like to start a savings account."

"And how much would you like to deposit?"

"$390.00."

"Wow, that's a lot for someone so young."

"I've been working hard. Now this will be in my name correct?"

"Correct."

"So there is no way my father could touch it?"

"Not without your permission."

"Good. Do it."

On the way home, Shelby said, "Raul, I don't want you to mention to anyone how much money I sold my fur for or anything about the savings account, okay?"

"Okay."

"Now why don't you go find Sis and give her a candy bar."

Shelby gave the other one to his mother.

* * * *

Armand noticed Shelby's fur pelts were gone from the barn, but he never asked about them.

Shelby had ended his trapping season early and now his fur pelts were gone and life had more or less returned to normal for him. He did hang up the beaver castors to dry.

On weekends Sis would help her mother canning some of the moose meat. For Thanksgiving dinner that year they had fresh moose steaks and apple pie for dessert.

The weather going into December seemed abnormally cold because there was very little snow on the ground. Since the warm spell there had only been a couple inches of snow come at a time, not enough to require rolling. Armand was still able to make two trips most days.

There was so much meat that needed canning, the three children would help their mother every day after school. It would be another year before their pig was ready to butcher so Armand did buy a half a pig from Jim Reed at the Green Farm. It became Shelby and Raul's chore to smoke the ham and bacon. None of the pig was wasted.

As Christmas was approaching, Shelby wanted to do something special for the family. He skipped afternoon class one day. He wanted to buy gifts without Raul or Sis being there. He bought a pair of snowshoes for himself and a pair for Raul. He got two green plaid wool shirts for himself and his father. A warm hat and fur lined mittens for Sis and a new winter coat for his mother. "How much for everything Mr. Adalbert?"

"Fifty-one dollars."

"Will you wrap everything, except the snowshoes of course."

"The Mrs. will"

"I'll have to go to the bank, Mr. Adalbert, while she wraps the gifts." He was back in fifteen minutes.

"Thank you for wrapping the gifts, Mrs. Adalbert."

He hurried home and put everything upstairs in his room under the bed.

There was twelve inches of new snow Christmas morning. After breakfast they exchanged gifts and all were surprised with the gift from Shelby. "Mom, this is from Raul and Sis, also."

Even Armand was surprised with his gift and said, "Thank you, Shelby. This is nice." Those were the first kind words his dad had ever said to him.

"Wow, Shelby, these snowshoes are almost as tall as me."

"You'll grow into 'em."

When the chores were done, Shelby and Raul went

snowshoeing. They followed along his trapline trail. "This is where I set traps, Raul."

Wherever there had been a set, the snow and ground was now all torn up by animals after what was left of the bait.

The snow was dry and fluffy and although Shelby was breaking trail, Raul had to stop often to rest. "We can turn around anytime, Raul."

There were fresh wolf tracks on the beaver pond and these made Raul uneasy. "Will they attack people Shelby?"

"They have been known to attack, but I wouldn't worry none, Raul."

"I think it's time to go back, Shelby."

"Okay." Raul liked being with his big brother, but he simply didn't feel comfortable in the woods. He didn't think he could ever be a trapper.

Chapter 2

January thaw that winter was unusually warm. Some days the temperature would rise to sixty degrees. The roads would soften during the day but the temperature would drop enough at night to freeze them again. What little snow there was settled and when the thaw was over the snow froze solid enough for moose to walk on top without punching through.

It was a cold job sitting on the wagon seat and sometimes going into the wind. If this job didn't pay so well, Armand would rather have worked at the mill.

Come spring breakup, the road to the Green Farm became so muddy that it was closed until it dried.

* * * *

When the roads did dry, Armand got a job grading the roads in town, the road to the Green Farm and the road to Bigelow Village. There were many nights when he couldn't make it home. There were small cabins on both roads for anyone to use who was traveling along the two roads, for emergencies.

The nights he was away, Rebecca and the children picked dandelion greens and fiddleheads. It was more work cleaning them than picking them. But when they had finished she had several quarts of each, plus meals of fresh, crispy fiddleheads.

That summer Shelby cleared another trapline around the left side of the ridge out back. When he came to the river, he followed that for a while. There were two feeder streams and each one had peeled beaver wood in the bottom. He stayed with his main trail for now and would come back to the two streams later. He couldn't do all he wanted in one day, because of his chores at home.

But after a week, he had a mile-long trapline that circled some around the ridge and trails up alongside both streams to the beaver colonies. Both dams were about three feet tall and they backed up a lot of water. He liked what he was seeing for the trapping possibilities.

He bought more traps, form wire and a new, smaller trapper's ax made for cutting limbs and small bushes. He honed the blade until it was as sharp as a straight razor.

"Do you boil your traps, Shelby?" Mr. Adalbert asked.

"No, are you supposed to?"

"Well, it gets rid of the greasy smell. A lot of trappers do."

"Maybe I'd better, too.

"Mr. Adalbert, last year I came real close to stumbling upon a mother bear and cub. All I carry with me is a .22 revolver for dispatching the caught animals. I've been thinking a lot about getting something bigger."

Mr. Adalbert reached under the counter and brought out a new revolver. "This is a new Remington .44 caliber revolver. It doesn't have quite the punch of a .45, but it is big enough for anything we have around here. It is much safer than the .45 too. The cartridges are a little smaller diameter allowing for a little thicker cylinder walls, so this gun is not as likely to explode in your hand. There's another advantage, also; this handgun uses the same cartridges as a .44 rifle. That way you wouldn't have to always be carrying two different calibers."

"How much for the revolver, a box of cartridges and holster?"

"Forty dollars."

"I have to go to the bank. I'll be right back."

Adalbert wouldn't normally sell a handgun to a thirteen year old. But Shelby was as big as many men in town and he showed a lot of savvy and responsibility. Besides he was a good customer.

"I'll wait on the rifle, Mr. Adalbert." Shelby said.

It was getting close to trapping season and Shelby decided to boil his traps. He had earlier purchased another dozen. He also put some green cedar boughs in the water, to give the traps a woodsy smell.

While he watched the water come to a boil, he thought about what Mr. Adalbert had said about the .44 rifle. It sounded like a good idea, but for now he'd put it on the back burner.

When he figured the traps had boiled long enough, he hung them up on the outside of the barn in the fresh air. He also put a half dozen eggs aside to ferment.

Charles Eustis saw Armand come into the yard, and he walked over to talk with him. "Armand, I'd like you to purchase one of the log sleds to haul the dimensional lumber. With the long iron runners they won't rud the snow and ice road so much. The center of gravity is lower and you'll be able to haul more per load. And the iron runners will not wear out as fast as the wheels. Even with a heavier load, it'll still be easier for your team to haul. And I'll give you another dollar per load."

"It sounds good, Mr. Eustis. Where do I find one of these?"

"We'll make it in the blacksmith shop."

"Okay."

"I'll deduct it from your pay each week over four weeks."

"When you have it made, is it okay if I leave it here until I need it?"

"No problem."

Shelby was chomping at the bit, wanting to start laying traps. But he'd wait another week. He had his packbasket loaded and ready to go. He packed his eggs with sawdust in a gallon paint can. He set that on top of his packbasket. He also put in his

.22 revolver. He'd wear his .44 revolver in case of a bear or wolf.

The fall chores were all done around the farm and Saturday of the following week he left right after morning chores. His first stop was at the edge of the field where his new trapline began. Fifty feet off to the right was an old, inactive, raised ant hill. He dug in the side of the hill facing the field about halfway up.

He set the rotten egg in about six inches, set his trap and buried it, and with a stick reached in and broke a small hole in the egg. He had to hold his breath and he shouldered his packbasket.

Not far in from the field was a leaning dead tree. He wired a chicken wing to the tree so it would move in the wind and then he set his trap and applied some beaver castor.

His next set was another leaning tree. And near that was a small spring freshlet and he set a water set for either a mink or otter. Probably a mink.

Two hundred yards beyond the water set he made a hollow log set and used another rotten egg for bait. The other end was open so he had to pile rocks up to block it off.

There was an opening beyond the log set that had grown up thick with blackberry bushes. His trail went around the clearing.

He reached into the thickest bunch of bushes and wired a chicken head above the ground so it would be visible and then he set his trap and lure.

His trail was now following the river and he found a perfect place for a covey set in amongst the roots of a fir tree. He used another rotten egg for bait.

He made two more leaning tree sets before he came to the first stream that came out of a beaver pond about a hundred yards upstream.

He went upstream to the pond and set two trough sets on the dam and then an otter water set below the dam. Before he had that trap set one of the dam sets went off with a lot of water splashing. He knew he had a beaver.

He pulled in a huge beaver and reset the trap and went

ashore and began skinning.

He no more than finished that beaver and the other trap went off and was pulled into the water. While this beaver was drowning, he took the beaver head and trap and he found a huge spruce and he nailed the head to it and set a number 3 trap and smeared castor on the tree.

He pulled the second beaver in and reset the trap and went ashore and began skinning. The pond went quiet and when he had finished the beaver, he wrapped all the meat and castors and went up to the inlet and set for a mink in the water.

Then he took one of the beaver carcasses and followed the small inlet until he came to a rocky ledge area. He found a natural covey between two ledges and he was able to force the carcass in and set another number 3. He didn't think he'd have to use castor here. The smell of fresh beaver meat should be lure enough.

He went back to the pond and one trap was pulled off the dam. This one was an extra-large beaver; only a little smaller than the first two.

The pond had gone quiet again, so he decided to leave. He didn't think he had any more room to carry back another beaver hide and meat.

He shouldered his packbasket and picked up one carcass and tossed it into the pond and took the third one with him back to the river where he made another covey set using wood to form the covey.

He was hungry, but as he worked his way back to the field he double checked each set. He was particularly excited about his first set in the ant hill. *It will be exciting to check tomorrow.*

At home he took about fifteen pounds of beaver meat in to his mother and then went back out to the barn. He had one beaver hide nailed to the drying board before his dad got home. He left the horse and wagon for his two sons to take care of.

"Shelby," Raul said, "this beaver is much bigger than even your biggest one last year."

43

"It is nice, isn't it? There's another one just like it.

"You collect eggs, brother, and I'll feed the pigs," Shelby said. Shelby also had time to feed and water the horses.

Armand saw the beaver meat on the sideboard and said, "Are you going to cook up some of this or can it, Rebecca?"

"I was thinking of canning it. You'll probably bring more home tomorrow won't you, Shelby?"

"More than likely."

After supper Shelby and Raul went back out to the barn and Sis helped her mom in the kitchen.

After the last two beaver hides were put on the drying boards, Shelby and Raul stayed in the barn for a while talking.

"When you finish school, Shelby, what are you going to do? Stay on the farm?"

"I haven't thought much about it. I like trapping and being in the woods. I don't know if I could support myself by trapping or not."

"I know I'm younger than you, but I like the farm."

* * * *

When the morning chores were done, Shelby left to tend traps. He was surprised when he saw his ant hill set. The trap was sprung and the ant hill was flattened. And, of course, the rotten egg was gone. Not even a scrap of egg shell could be seen. The ground had been torn up so much he was not able to see any clear tracks.

He made another set in the middle of the disturbed ground and used another egg for bait. He stood back scratching his head and wondering what animal had done this.

Nearby in the leaning tree he had a nice male martin. The next leaning tree was untouched. In the first waterset, he had a female mink.

Something had scratched the ground in front of the trap at the hollow log, but had not sprung the trap. And the bait was still there. He left it and moved on.

He was again surprised when he reached the blackberry set. He had an angry bobcat. And like the bobcat caught in the same blackberry set last year, this one was just as tangled up in the bushes. It was no problem to shoot it, but it took time to untangle it.

He reset in another thicket of blackberry bushes and he used another chicken head and wired it just as he had before.

His next set was the covey in the fir tree roots and he had another martin. He rebaited with another rotten egg. He had only one left.

The next two leaning tree sets were empty. As was the water set below the beaver dam. But both traps were pulled off the dam. He pulled in another extra-large and another super large beaver. He took those ashore and then he reset both traps.

He took care of the hides and meat before checking any more sets. The pond was quiet.

The beaver head set was untouched, so he continued on to the inlet stream. He had a mink in the water set and that was it. Something had scratched the ground near the ledge covey set but had not gone near. He went back to the beaver pond. He still had a bobcat, two martin and a mink to skin.

He set back away from the dam so he wouldn't spook the beaver and he began skinning. The martin and mink were like peeling a banana. But he had to be more careful with the bobcat.

At least his packbasket was not as heavy now. He walked down close enough so he could see the dam. One trap was not there. It was in the water and snapped closed. He reset it and then he smeared a little castor on a stick at the outer edge of the dam.

It was mid-afternoon and he was hungry.

Rebecca had almost as much beaver meat to can as he had brought back the day before. "I'm counting on you to bring back beaver meat tomorrow for supper, Shelby," his mother said.

"I'll do what I can."

* * * *

The next morning the ant hill set was again torn up. The trap was sprung closed, the egg was gone and no visible tracks in the sand. Shelby stood back looking at the torn up set and scratched his head.

He used the last egg he had and set the trap like he had done before. Only this time he placed three more traps. One behind the bait. "Well that's all I can do here, I guess."

He picked up two more martin on his trapline down to the beaver pond outlet stream. There was a fisher cat in the tree root covey there and nothing in the water set below the dam.

Both traps were again pulled off the dam and he pulled in two extra-large beaver. That made seven beaver from this pond and he pulled those two traps.

Up on the high ground near the dam where he had the beaver head for bait, he had another fisher cat. Another large male.

At the inlet stream he could see an animal in the water set and at first he thought it was another mink. But it was a female martin; very dark colored.

There was only the ledge covey set to check now. Some animal had been there and had again scratched up the dirt in front of the trap without touching it. The bait had not been touched. He left it alone and went back to the pond and began skinning his catch for the day.

As he was skinning the beaver he said, "Well, Mom, I have your beaver meat for supper tonight."

He finished and packed everything in his packbasket, plus the two beaver heads and one beaver carcass. The rest he threw into the pond. "I doubt if I catch any otter or mink here with all these carcasses in the pond. Oh, well."

It was only 11:30 in the morning, so when he was at the

river he continued setting traps along his trapline up to the next beaver pond. There wasn't enough time left to set the pond up so he headed for home. He had managed to set four traps. One being in another blackberry thicket, where he used one of the beaver heads.

"Only two beaver today, Shelby?" his brother asked. "Do you want me to take these in to Mom?"

"Yes, that'll save me a trip."

Shelby went to work first putting the beaver hides on the drying boards and then the other pieces.

At the supper table, Shelby said, "I don't know if I'll have any beaver meat to bring home tomorrow or not. I pulled my beaver traps today and I hoped to be able to set up on another flowage tomorrow, if I have the time."

"That's okay, Shelby, Sis and I canned what beaver meat we had today. Tomorrow we'll use up the last of the canned moose meat. We could use another moose, son, if you see one."

"I've seen a few tracks but that's all."

* * * *

Shelby didn't sleep much that night. At first he kept thinking about the ant hill set. *What animal is doing this? To level the mound and dig out and spring the trap, all without leaving any visible tracks.* He tried to think of a different way to set the traps. He finally decided he would have to wait until morning when he would tend his traps.

He put those thoughts out of his mind and started thinking about his future. What did he really want to do? After studying about the many places in the world in world geography, he would like to travel and see some of these places. And then another idea crossed his mind—what he had said to Raul about being a trapper. That idea really appealed to him. But one thing for sure, he was not going to live under his father's roof.

Then he began dreaming about his own log cabin where he

could trap, fish and live off the land. With these thoughts running through his mind he eventually went to sleep.

In the morning, Shelby hurried through the chores. "Go tend your traps, Shelby, all we have left is the chickens and I'll do that. Go on."

There was hoarfrost in places and he thought that was strange. It didn't feel that cold. He was more interested with the ant hill set than the rest of his trapline. And sure enough the ground was torn up again and all but one trap dug out and sprung. He walked around looking for tracks. There were none.

So this time he dug a hole about a foot deep and put in some beaver scraps and a little castor and one trap close to the hole and one about a foot in front.

He shrugged his shoulders and moved on.

In the next two leaning trees he had a martin in each. And not wanting to take too many he pulled those two traps. The water set was empty, as too was the hollow log. At the blackberry set he had another bobcat and like the other one, this was twisted up in the bushes. He pulled that trap, too.

At the fir root covey, he had another martin and he pulled that trap. The next two leaning tree sets were untouched, as was the water set below the beaver dam.

He had pulled the two dam traps yesterday, so he went up hill where he had nailed a beaver head to a tree and there he had a red wolf and it was much smaller than last year's gray wolf. But it sure was a fighting little bugger. He had never seen or even heard of red wolves before.

It fit in his packbasket and he'd sink it when he reached the second beaver pond.

At the inlet set he had another mink and he decided to pull that trap also.

His last set was at the ledges and there he had a cat. It looked like a bobcat, but it was a little bigger. Perhaps a lynx. He wouldn't know for sure until he shot it and looked at its feet.

It was fighting more than any bobcat he had caught so far. After a little bit of work, he was finally able to shoot it. The paws were like mittens, there was so much hair. It was a lynx.

It would be a load, but after resetting the trap he shouldered his packbasket and lay the cat over the top. There was still plenty of the beaver carcass left.

He had never been over this ridge to the second flowage, but to walk around would take too long.

After crowning the top of the ridge, he could look down on the flowage. But he kept up a good pace.

He set his packbasket down near the dam and went to work making two troughs on the dam and placing a trap in each.

Then he went ashore to begin skinning the lynx, wolf and fisher cat. He looked up the pond and a beaver was already coming to investigate why water was flowing over the dam. And sure enough, without any hesitation he swam into the trough and was caught.

He waited five minutes before the beaver drowned. It was a super large beaver.

He skun the wolf first, knowing the hide would come off drier than the other animals.

When he had finished the wolf, the traps on the dam were still quiet. So he started skinning the lynx, then the bobcat and fisher and still the dam traps were quiet. He wrapped everything up and put it all in his packbasket and started out, checking the traps he had set yesterday. He only had another martin.

He gave each trap a cursory glance as he worked his way home. Even the ant hill set. On his way out, he had decided that once he had what he figured were all the large beaver from the second pond, he would pull everything.

Halfway across the field he looked over towards the mouth of his other trapline and there was a cow moose just coming to the opening. The wind was blowing across the field towards her and she must have scented Shelby as she suddenly turned and ran back.

Shelby was just as glad. He was tired—too tired to bother with a moose now.

* * * *

Each morning the ant hill set would be torn apart, the bait gone and traps sprung with no clear track in the sand to identify the beast. Shelby was beginning to lose his patience, but at the same time he would like to know what animal kept outsmarting him.

He caught five from the second beaver flowage and he decided to pull those traps. At the ledge covey, he caught another lynx.

On the last day of tending he picked up another red wolf and probably the mate to the first one. He also picked up a martin in the second blackberry set. He had pulled many of his traps and this day he pulled everything. As he was approaching the field he saw a large raccoon digging at the ant hill set. The trap had already been pulled.

The raccoon was so intent at digging trying to find another meal he was unaware of Shelby's approach. Shelby had lost all patience with whatever had been outsmarting him with this set and he said softly, "You bastard, I'll show you," And he drew his revolver and aimed at the biggest part of the raccoon. The bullet hit its mark and the force of the shot practically blew the raccoon into pieces. "There, see if you ever rob anymore of my traps."

Then he began to feel bad, not just shooting the raccoon, but destroying the pelt—and all for revenge.

He had thirteen more pieces this year and he hoped the prices would be as good.

"When are you going to get that moose your mother asked you to get?" Armand asked.

"I'm all through trapping for this season, so I'll have more time now to look for a moose."

"It's about time. I want to butcher that pig next week," Armand said.

The next day was Monday and while walking home from school, Shelby asked, "Raul, will you do my share of chores before supper? I need to look for a moose."

"Sure enough, Shelby."

Shelby put his warm clothes on and strapped on his new handgun and headed for his old trapline. He hadn't seen any moose tracks at all on the newer trail. About halfway to the beaver pond there was a swale hole and he had often seen moose tracks there last year. And sure enough there were moose tracks all over the area. He found a short plump fir tree to sit behind and he began calling. The rut was over, so instead of calling like a cow in heat he tried to imitate the sound a bull moose makes. Even though the rut was over bull moose are very territorial and often fight with other bulls. Sometimes deadly.

He didn't see or hear anything until he started to leave. Off to his left he heard a very faint grunt. He was about to grunt back, but the sun had already set and in five minutes he'd lose all visible light. He had no choice but to start for home.

* * * *

On the way to school the next day, "Raul, Sis, I'm skipping classes this afternoon so I can look for a moose. So don't wait for me after class."

Shelby had lunch with his mother and then put on his hunting clothing and headed for the same alder swale. After he was about halfway to the swale, he heard something and stopped. The noise also stopped. He waited and just as he started walking he heard it again. But he wasn't sure what he heard. He started walking very slow and trying not to make any more noise than necessary. There it was again. He still wasn't sure what it was. He kept walking. The noise was coming more often now. It was beginning to sound like someone was banging something against trees. As he got close he could hear grunting now mixed with the banging noise. He still had no idea what was up ahead.

In the distance, he could see the tops of two hardwood trees thrashing back and forth, but there was no wind. The grunting noise now sounded like a bull moose, but what was the other noise?

He withdrew his .44 revolver, just in case. He kept stealing closer, one foot at a time. The noise was almost steady now. He was only maybe a hundred feet away and whoops! He stopped dead in his tracks. There was something coming through the alders now making a lot of noise. And mixed with this new noise there was obviously another bull moose grunting.

Then he heard the unmistakable clash of antlers. But the noise was still coming from the same location, not moving. He was puzzled and as he kept going; he was beginning to get concerned.

He could see movement now through the trees and he could see two bulls fighting. There was one back-to to him and it was down on its front knees while fighting with the other moose. The two tree tops were really thrashing now, and Shelby understood why. The moose that was down on its front knees had gotten its antlers lodged between two hardwood trees and was unable to free itself.

There was no mistaking it now; this poor moose was going to be killed by the other one. There was only one thing he could do. He had to shoot the one caught between the trees and hope the other one would run off.

He got into a better position and waited until they were not moving so much and he sighted in behind the moose's ear and pulled the trigger. The other moose's head went up and he stood there looking around. Shelby fired another shot hoping to scare it off. It worked as the other one turned and ran off where it had come from. Shelby fired another shot to help it along.

His moose was down and still. Before starting to clean it, he walked around the forked hardwood tree. The bull didn't have a huge trophy rack. He might be four years old. The other moose was bigger and had a bigger rack.

He holstered his gun and began cleaning the moose. When he had finished he looked at the trees briefly and then started for home. He would have to bring an ax back with him to cut down at least one of the trees.

At home he harnessed the horse and brought along a long chain. He wished Raul was home. "Mom, are you busy?"

"Not particularly. What do you need?"

"I could use your help with this moose."

"Okay, I'll just leave a note for Sis and change my clothes."

On the way out he told his mother the whole story about the two bull moose and how nervous he had been.

"If you'll hold the horse here, Mom, I'll cut one of those two trees."

Shelby was proud of his mother. She didn't seem the least nervous. But she was keeping a watchful eye of their surroundings. He cut the tree as close to the ground as he could.

"Can you turn the horse around, Mom?"

"Come on big boy, you can do this," she encouraged.

"The chain won't quite reach. Can you make him back up two or three feet?"

Rebecca first spoke softly to the horse and then she pulled his head down a little and pulled back slightly. The horse responded just like she wanted.

Shelby hooked the chain through both gambles. "Okay, Mom, when you're ready. I need to lift the head as you start going."

Once the moose was beyond any trees, the antlers could get tangled in, he shortened the chain and walked behind the moose in case he had to help it around some object. His mom was doing a good job with the horse. "You're doing good, Mom. Head for the barn."

She was proud to be helping. She stayed and helped him hang it with block and tackle off the floor. Raul and Sis came out to see. "Holy cow, Shelby, that's a big moose."

"There's a good story with this fella, too, and I'll tell everyone at the supper table."

Rebecca and Sis went back to the house and Raul stayed to help. They cut the head and antlers off first. "While the body is still warm the hide will come off easier." Shelby started skinning while Raul helped by pulling the hide away from the body.

"This is easier to skin than a beaver or wolf," Shelby said.

"Go ask Mom for a big pan that we can put the heart, liver and backstraps in."

While he was gone Shelby cut away both backstraps and laid them over a ladder rung. Then he split the brisket and removed the heart and liver. "Here, Raul, put those backstraps in and take the pan in for Mom."

Shelby waited to tell his story of the two moose until everyone had eaten.

"Shelby," Raul said, "When are you going to tell us about shooting the moose?"

"Right now. I probably will never see this again as long as I live and I doubt if there are many who have seen such a scene." Even Armand was interested now.

He told them the story, starting with yesterday's hunt trying to call in a moose. He told his story slowly not leaving out a single detail. When he had finished his dad said, "You mean you saw the two bulls fighting even with one caught in the two trees? Unbelievable."

"It's a wonder you weren't hurt, son," Rebecca said.

"That must have been scary," Raul said.

"It would have been if that bull had come after me instead of running off."

"Tomorrow, liver and onions, Rebecca,"—not a question—Armand said.

"This weekend we'll can what we can," Rebecca said.

* * * *

That weekend Armand and his two sons butchered the pig and started the smoker for the hams and bacon. He decided to keep both sides of bacon, but he would sell one pork loin and one front leg and one hind leg, smoked.

After Thanksgiving, Shelby bundled up his fur pelts and carried them to Mr. Adalbert's store.

"My, Shelby, these look awful nice. The mink dropped two dollars, I can only give you thirty dollars for each wolf—the red wolf is not as valuable as the gray wolf—and fisher cats are up a couple of dollars. For your beaver twenty dollars across the board."

"No, Mr. Adalbert, not this year. There are no small beaver and five are over eighty inches, the other eight are seventy-five to eighty. I want thirty dollars each."

"I can't do thirty each, Shelby, but I'll give you thirty for the five and twenty-five for the other eight. How's that?"

"Okay. What about the moose hide? It is bigger this year."

"Eight dollars. That comes to $780.00. Will you take a check?"

"Certainly. From here I'm going to the bank."

"How much of this are you going to deposit, Shelby?" Mr. Edwards asked.

"Seven hundred and fifty. The rest I'll take."

"With your interest and this new deposit, you have a total of $1,070.00."

He split the $8.00 between Raul and Sis.

Chapter 3

There was a lot of snow that winter and Armand spent half of his time rolling snow, both in town and to the Green Farm.

Shelby and Raul did all the work around the farm that summer. Raul was in his glory. He liked farming even though the only animals were the two works horses, two pigs and chickens. There just weren't enough cleared fields to support any more.

When trapping season came, Shelby set traps along his first, or number one, trail and this trail didn't produce as well as the number two trail did the previous year. But he was able to deposit another four hundred dollars into his savings account.

The last day that he trapped he pulled all of his traps. At supper that night Armand said, "Shelby, I have bought another horse, not quite as big as the two we now have, and I am hiring a new man to drive the freight wagon and sledge, Tom Henderson. You and I are going to harvest some lumber this winter and you'll have to quit school."

"But, Dad—I like school."

"You've been through the eighth grade. I can't see why you would need anymore. That's more school than I ever had."

Shelby knew it was useless to argue with him.

"This is Monday; I'll need your help starting next Monday."

He still didn't say anything. He got up and went out to the barn to finish chores.

* * * *

When Monday morning arrived, Armand and Shelby headed out back to cut trees. There was just enough snow to make twitching the logs easier for the horse team. That morning they felled a pine and a spruce tree and logged them.

In the afternoon, they twitched them to a landing and rolled the logs onto the log sledge. The team could only haul the logs from one tree at a time. It took all afternoon to haul the two trees to Eustis' sawmill.

As each day passed they were able to freeze down a nice twitching trail for the team.

Shelby was still upset with his father and he was trying to work his father to the ground, until he was ready to call for a break.

"Come on, old man, can't you keep up?" and he'd laugh.

With every log they cut, Shelby was getting stronger and stronger. He now had a set of shoulders broader than his father's. He was fifteen years old.

He could lift the butt end of a sixteen foot pine log off the ground. His father could not. Shelby one day held the log up and stood up looking at his father and grinned.

At spring breakup, Armand went back to hauling freight and Shelby went back to being fifteen years old.

* * * *

That fall Shelby trapped along his number two line and that first week his land sets weren't producing at all. He did well with beaver, otter and mink. Then towards the end of the second week he began catching a number of red wolves, and animal tracks started appearing in the light snow cover and he started catching the land fur bearers. By the end of the season he had six red wolves.

"Shelby, I want you to start in the woods with me Monday."

"No. I have two more weeks of trapping. Then I will."

His father didn't argue.

At the end of trapping that year, Mr. Adalbert paid him six hundred and twenty-five dollars. He put six hundred in his account.

Even that was better wages than most men in the mill would earn all year.

* * * *

That winter Armand and Shelby harvested mostly spruce and huge fir. Armand wanted to leave the pine for later and better prices.

Armand and Shelby worked side by side every day and the only time either one of them spoke to the other was for a warning of a falling tree.

Shelby had adjusted fairly well to the yearly routine. Each spring after the breakup, he had chores around the farm. Trapping in the fall was his wonderland. He enjoyed being in the woods by himself. And he never tried to trap too many of any of the fur animals.

Then after the trapping season he would work with his father in the woods. This routine went on unbroken for three more years and Shelby had deposited all of his money for those four years, a total of just over two thousand dollars. He now had forty-one hundred dollars in the bank.

All that winter he had been making plans to leave home forever and find a place away from town where he could homestead some land and trap. He was twenty years old now and he figured it was time for him to be on his own.

Raul was sixteen and Sis was fifteen, and very pretty.

When they were done cutting, Shelby went to talk with Mr. Eustis at his mill.

"Come in, Shelby. What can I do for you?"

"I understand your carpenters are building canoes."

"Yes, that is correct. Cedar canoes, covered with a special canvas and a special coating that hardens the canvas. Are you wanting to purchase one?"

"Yes, eighteen feet long by forty inches wide, seats on both ends and two paddles."

"We don't have anything that size on hand. It'll have to be a special order."

"How long would it take the men?"

"It'll take them a week."

"Will you require a deposit?"

"Not necessary."

"How much?"

"Fifty dollars for the canoe and ten for the two paddles."

"Fair enough. Say in ten days?"

"Okay," Charles Eustis said.

For the next several days Shelby would buy what he would be needing for tools, and Mr. Adalbert agreed he would keep everything together in the back storage room. "I'm going to need a rifle now, too, Mr. Adalbert. Instead of the .44, I've decided on the Winchester .30-30, and two boxes of bullets."

He purchased clothes and some non-perishable food and the basics of cooking utensils, rope, a large enough piece of canvas for making a temporary shelter, boxes of bridge spikes and nails. He asked Mr. Adalbert for the window dimensions and ordered five. "Will you hold the windows here Mr. Adalbert until I'm ready for them? I'll pay you for the windows when I pay you for everything."

He kept his plans from his family. At first he thought about taking what he would need for tools from the farm, but that would be like rubbing salt in a wound when he told his father he was leaving.

He helped Raul with the garden and repairs to the pig pens and horse stalls.

* * * *

The time had come to leave. It was mid-May and the woods

and ground had dried after the spring breakup. He would leave early Monday morning.

After supper that Sunday evening Shelby said, "I have an announcement to make." Everyone waited. "I'll be leaving here in the morning, forever."

"Why, you can't do that!" Armand said. "What about the work on the farm? You can't expect Raul to do it all. And what about cutting timber? I can't do that alone. No, Shelby, you can't go. I won't have it. You can't go, Shelby. And that's all there is. No."

"Well, Dad, I am going and you can't stop me."

"But why?" Armand almost pleaded.

"All my life you have ridiculed and criticized me with everything I did. I worked six years with you cutting timber and you have not paid me a thin dime. To you I am only a slave. You put a roof over my head and that's all. I have had enough. And I'm changing my name back to Martin.

"And you better start treating Raul and Sis better or they'll leave too. You're a bully. And if you ever lay a hand on Mom, Raul or Sis—well I'm bigger and stronger than you and I'll fix you for good."

With that said he left and went out to the barn to finish chores. Raul joined him in a few minutes. "Are you really going, Shelby?"

"Yes, I've been planning this all winter. I have to leave. Don't you see?"

"I suppose I do—but I'll miss my big brother, Shelby."

"Will you help me harness the horse? I'm taking a few things from here."

"Sure."

Shelby loaded all of his trapping equipment and the beaver castors, his trapping ax, pliers, wire and stretchers. "Will you ride down with me, Raul, so you can bring the wagon back?"

As they were walking to the house, Shelby said, "This

farm will be yours someday Raul. Go with Dad some, so you can learn the freighting business. If he makes you work in the woods with him, make sure he pays you and don't quit school to be his slave."

"I'll be okay, Shelby, and I'll protect Sis."

"Mom?" Shelby asked, "If I could, I would like to take some food."

"What do you have in mind?"

"As many eggs as you can spare. A side of bacon and two loaves of bread."

"Raul, pack as many eggs as you can in a small keg and cushion them with sawdust. Sis, go downstairs and bring up the bacon and bread."

When they were gone, Rebecca turned to Shelby and said, "Don't feel bad about leaving, son. I'm surprised you stayed home this long. I do not understand why Armand treated you like he did and I won't make any excuses for him. When you talked back to him last night—well, I don't think anyone had ever talked to your father like that. He took you serious and I think he is a little afraid of you.

"Where will you go son?"

"I don't know exactly. Down river somewhere. I'll have to come back for lumber at the mill, and when I do, I'll stop."

He hugged his mother then and they each had tears running down their cheeks.

Sis came up with the bacon and bread and Rebecca wrapped them.

Shelby hugged Sis and said, "You sure are pretty for a fifteen-year-old. You won't have any problem finding yourself a good man. I love you both.

"Goodbye Mom—Sis," he said and went outside. Raul had drawn the wagon up. "You ready, Shelby?" he asked.

"Let's go. We have to go to the mill first and pick up my canoe."

Then they pulled out back of Adalbert's Store and loaded everything Shelby had bought.

"Down to the river, Raul."

As big as the canoe was, he could have taken the windows, too. "I wish you could go with me, Raul, for the summer to help build a cabin."

"I could, you know."

"No—that would only give Dad something else to be mad about and then he might take it out on the three of you."

"I guess you're right. I'll miss you, Shelby," and they hugged.

Shelby climbed into the canoe while Raul steadied it. Then he pushed him off. Raul stood on the riverbank watching until Shelby disappeared around the first bend. He hollered out, "I don't blame you for going, brother!"

Chapter 4

Shelby heard his brother and that brought a lump to his throat. He swallowed, coughed and leaned into his paddle. He had no idea how far he could go today, but he would like to make it to Long Falls.

The weight of his gear balanced his weight and he liked the long and wide canoe. He found it handled very well. He paddled as if he was in a race. In a way, maybe he was, if he wanted to get where he wanted by sunset.

Before the sun was directly overhead he had reached Long Falls. He put-in and dragged his canoe ashore enough so he could unload it. He carried as much as he comfortably could. He knew he would have to make several trips to portage the falls. But what surprised him most was that he didn't have to go downstream from the falls far at all before he came to canoeable waters.

He hurried back for another load and then another and then the canoe. The canoe was heavy but he shouldered it well and didn't have to stop and rest.

He didn't waste any time when he had the canoe with the rest of his gear. He loaded everything and pushed off, this time going slower, looking for an ideal place to homestead and build a cabin.

He liked what he was seeing. This was looking like excellent trapping country, and there was peeled wood washed up against the riverbank in places. For a long way, both sides of the river were too marshy for building. Then about mid-afternoon he found a place where the softwood trees came down to the riverbank.

After putting ashore, he stretched and then began walking around to see what it was like. There were plenty of spruce and fir trees in the general area just right for a log cabin. Off to the left there was a low lying area studded with hardwoods, some of which were dead and still standing. That was good. Now he wanted to see if he could find a spring.

He didn't have to go far. Circling the softwoods at the edge of the hardwoods, he found a trickle of water coming out of the bank. After pulling the moss back, the ground was cool and moist. Everything was looking good. He circled in behind the softwood to see how far back they went. The level land butted up to a rolling hill. He was about four feet above the river. "This is my home!" he bellowed.

First he made a temporary lean-to with the canvas. Then he dug two holes in the ground where he had found the trickle of water. At two feet deep the water started filling the hole. He also dug out a ditch so the water could drain, so it would always stay clear.

The next hole was square and not as deep. This was for cool storage for food. He lined the bottom with green moss. For now his meat and eggs and bread would be kept here.

It was time to build a fire and catch some fish for supper and breakfast in the morning. He started the fire first and when that was going good, he cut an alder pole for a fish pole. He wasn't long catching four, about a pound each. He put two on a spit to roast over the fire and the other two he took back to the storage box. Boy, yeah, he realized he'd have to make a box to sit in the hole, with a wooden cover.

When the fish were cooked he ate the meat off the bone. Fresh trout and bread is a good meal.

He could see for the near future he would be eating a lot of fish and when his bread was gone, he would make some dough with his flour for either pan or stick bread.

He spread out his blanket then sat up watching the fire. For just-in-case, he put some wood, kindling and birch bark under the lean-to, so if it rained during the night he'd be able to start a fire.

In order to have the cabin up and tight to weather and clear-out a trapline before trapping, he had his work cut out for him.

Before going to sleep that first night on his own, he thought of his mother, sister and brother. He would miss them.

* * * *

Like a farmer, he was up at daylight the next morning and after a breakfast of brook trout, eggs, bread and a cup of coffee, he began work. There was a flat, high place, and when he measured it, it was more than big enough for his fourteen-by-sixteen-foot cabin. He dug out the moss and piled it up out of the way, thinking he could use it later for chinking between the logs.

Hemlock would be the best logs to use for a base. Because of the oil in the wood, it did not rot as fast as other softwoods. They couldn't be too big because he would have to drag them back.

There was a nice stand of hemlock towards the ridge to the north. And in the center of the stand were several just the right size.

He wasn't long dropping one. He wanted a porch facing the river, so he cut out a twenty-two foot log. He lifted one end and tucked it under his arm and headed back. The log was heavy but he had no problem.

He felled three more and cut out the length he wanted from the butt ends and dragged those three back. The end cross logs were shorter and not as heavy.

The bark peeled off easy and he leveled the knots and high places with his ax and draw shave. By the time he had them peeled, the sun was overhead and he was hungry. He warmed up a can of beans and fried a thick piece of bacon and a slice of bread, to sop up the gravy. "Boy, a piece of Mom's apple pie would go good now."

Coffee gone, he went back to work positioning the four base logs, and he squared them up using his hundred-foot tape. That done, he now had to have a carrying timber through the middle for nailing down and supporting the floor.

For the carrying timber he went back and brought back the top of one of the hemlock trees. Then he chiseled a square notch in the front and back base logs, measured the distance between, cut the top to fit and peeled it. Then he made square ends that would fit in each end log. Now he was ready for boards.

He took a break and caught more brook trout for supper and breakfast. After eating there was still too much daylight left to waste by not doing anything.

So he made a rack to put his logs on to peel them, so he wouldn't have to bend over so much. With that done, he made another rack for his canoe.

There was still some daylight left but he was tired. He stripped down and washed up. Yes sir, he could eat a whole apple pie now.

The next day, he cut and peeled spruce and fir trees. It would take two spruce trees to weigh as much as one of the hemlocks and he actually had an easy day.

By the end of Friday he figured he had enough. There was nothing to do now until he canoed back for boards for the floor. So he busied his time making a box for his cold storage. He used small cedar trees. Until he had some boards, he covered the top with the tops of the cedar trees and covered that with moss.

When that was done, he made two ladders, a short one and one taller, and then he made two saw horses.

The next day he decided to level the base logs. He was going to wait until he had the floor boarded over, but now he needed something to keep him busy.

The next morning he went for a walk looking for rocks perfectly flat. Downstream up against the ridge, he found what he was looking for.

He found four about three inches thick and about the size of a dishpan. He made two trips carrying two at a time.

By noon he had the logs level with good support under each end and the middle carrying timber also blocked up and supported.

Next he caught a brook trout and put it on a spit to roast. Later in the afternoon, he piled up all of the peeled bark. Maybe when it dried he could use it to either cook with or heat the cabin. For now he would do all of his cooking on the open fire outside. He refixed the canvas tarp so now it extended over his fireplace. Then he built a crude table and hand hewed the small logs for the tabletop, so he would have a fairly flat surface. All he needed now were some chairs. That would have to wait.

He had decided to leave home on Sunday afternoon, make the portage at Long Falls and spend the night there, so he could get an early start on Monday for the sawmill.

Come Saturday he was pretty much caught up, so he took his trapping ax and compass to scout out a trapline. He headed out to the base of the ridge and started to make a circle to the west when he came across a small stream littered with peeled beaver wood. He followed the stream only a short distance and came to an active colony. There were two beaver swimming in the water. The house was huge. He circled the pond and the inlet was a nice stream, too, and he followed that upstream to a much bigger pond. He would have to buy a map from Mr. Adalbert. He went back to the beaver pond and continued with his circle west and he came to another larger stream, and this, too, had peeled wood in it. Since the wood had to have come down with the current, he followed it upstream to another active colony and the house here was as big.

From there he swung to the south up to the base of Flagstaff Mountain then east and eventually north back to the outside of the hardwoods below his cabin. He was real satisfied with what he had seen and anxious to trap.

Sunday morning, just to be on the safe side, after slicing off a thick piece of bacon for the trail, he laid two heavy pieces of hemlock on the top of his storage box to keep out the predators.

If it rained during the night, he would sleep under the overturned canoe. And if it was raining on the way back, he would buy a piece of canvas to cover everything.

He was traveling light and only had to make one trip around the portage.

Rather than walking the road to see his mother, he pulled his canoe ashore on the farm side of the river and walked across the field. He knew Armand would be hauling freight.

She was in the kitchen baking and surprised when she looked up and saw Shelby. "Well this is a surprise. I didn't think you'd call so soon."

"I came after more boards. Ummm, that smells good. Pie by any chance?"

"Yes, two apple pies."

"Any chance I could pay you for those two?"

"No, I won't take your money, but you can have them. Anything else you need?"

"Yes, two loaves of bread. I miss your cooking."

"Where did you settle?"

"Down river a long ways. I'm building a log cabin. I'm free, Mom, and it feels good—to make my decisions each day and live the life I enjoy."

"I'm happy for you, son. But don't forget you always have a home here, if the need should arise."

"I think Dad would have something to say about me coming back."

"You really scared him that night when you talked back to

him. I think that was the first time anyone had ever stood up to him.

"Raul and Sis will be disappointed they missed you."

"And I would like to have seen them also. But I must be going, Mom; I have a long ways to go before nightfall."

She wrapped the pies for him. "I'll be back again soon." He hugged her and walked back across the field to his canoe.

At the Long Falls Portage he had to make three trips to get all of his equipment and food stores across. He was home and it was time for supper.

* * * *

He was back in time to catch enough fish for supper and breakfast. It was a good thing he liked eating fish. After eating that and one slice of apple pie, he put the pies and bread in the cold storage box. There was just enough room.

For something to do to keep busy before dark, he worked up some firewood. He bucked up a few of the hemlock tops and he would use those on his campfire at night. Because of the oil in the wood they would burn too hot for a stove. But outside the coals would still be hot come morning.

For breakfast he had one egg, fish and one slice of bread and a slice of pie with his coffee. Now he was ready to start building.

Before doing any cutting, he laid out all the boards to cover the deck except for the porch area. He might have to use some of those boards for making window and door jambs.

Satisfied, he cut one board at a time and nailed it. With one board nailed securely the rest went down faster and he had finished the floor by mid-morning. Then he started measuring the log lengths, loosely fitting the first course down until he was sure they were square. Then he secured them with the bridge spikes. "There, almost done," and he laughed.

Before he could spike the front log he had to make a door

jamb and stand that up and secure it where he wanted it—about four feet from the right wall standing on the porch and facing the cabin.

The next course was slow work. He had to use his draw-shave and make a flat surface on each log to fit flush and the notches at the end to the other wall were on the bottom of each log so there wouldn't be a pocket to collect water.

By the end of that day he was only up three logs. But it was finally beginning to look like a cabin. After supper he made three window boxes. The other two he'd make in the morning.

The next day before laying any more logs, he made the last two window boxes.

He put on another course of logs before he nailed each window box in place. Two in front, side by each, and one on each of the other three walls. By noon he only had another course of logs. That was okay.

After eating lunch, he stood appraising his work so far. "Not bad. I like it."

By the end of that day he had added two more courses. He was up seven logs now. Maybe two more courses tomorrow.

That evening as he was sitting and watching the fire and listening to the forest sounds, two loons silently swam upstream and remained there for several minutes facing the cabin. In a soft voice, he said, "Hello, fellas. I won't hurt you. I'm going to live here." One of them dove and soon came back to the surface with a fish head and swallowed it. Then the other one dove for the other head.

One of them started flapping his wings enough so he was standing on the water. Then they both swam back downstream.

By the end of Saturday he had the four walls up and had started on the back gable end. First, though, he had to build a makeshift staging to work from. It was an easy job, actually, much easier than he had first thought. He simply laid his tall ladder across the side walls and laid boards on the ladder rungs to work on.

It was time consuming cutting the right angle on each end of each log. He also had to leave cutouts for two purlings on each side of center. The purlings had to be long. He wanted a two foot overhang in back and six feet in front, figuring on a five-foot porch deck with the overhang a foot. Each purling had to be twenty-four feet long and for the center purling, he only had two that were long enough. So after these were set, he cut three more spruce trees, peeled the bark and cut them to length.

He was three days finishing the gable ends and purlings. That evening he figured up what he would need for more boards. There still were three more boards to nail down on the porch.

He doubted if he'd be able to make it in one trip.

As he was falling asleep that night, he was thinking how far he had come on the cabin in such a short time. But there also was more to do and more trips back to Flagstaff for materials.

But he was up before daylight and had a hearty breakfast of fish and two eggs today, bread, coffee and a slice of pie and then he was on his way to Flagstaff.

He arrived before mid-morning and loaded another twenty boards and the five windows and he was back on the river heading home.

Building this log cabin was more tiring than Shelby at first thought it would be, but then again he had been working for more than twelve hours a day and he had come far.

By mid-afternoon he pulled his canoe ashore at home.

There was a lot of climbing up and down to close the roof in. But he wanted every board to fit exactly. By Thursday noon he had run out of boards and he still had half of a roof to close in.

Knowing that he would be needing extra boards for an outhouse and shed, he again hauled a load of twenty boards and four twelve-inch finish boards for building a table and counter and shelves inside the cabin.

The windows he had to tie on top of the boards.

At home he set the windows inside under the enclosed portion of the roof.

By Sunday noon he had the roof enclosed and the windows in. He built a picnic style table and countertop with shelves under it and he framed up a bed.

By Monday evening he had finished the bed frame with two wooden drawers under the bed for clothes.

That night there was a slight rainstorm and the roof leaked in only one spot. He still had to shingle it.

He left Tuesday morning for Flagstaff. He was tired of sleeping on the ground so he intended to bring back a double mattress with sheets and pillows and as many cedar shingle bundles as he could.

* * * *

By the end of June the cabin was finished—as finished as it was going to be for now. He had used extra thick cedar shakes on the roof and one night during a thundering rain storm, there wasn't one leak. The front door and windows were in. He had a medium sized ramdown woodstove for heat and a smaller version of a wood cookstove, each fitted with stove pipe and a cap on top. He was now digging a hole for the outhouse which was already built. All he had to do was to tip it up and secure it. He wished now he had made a back door for access to the outhouse. Maybe next year.

He lay in bed, between clean sheets, in a weather-proof log cabin feeling proud of himself. Alone, he had accomplished a lot in just six weeks. Much sooner than he had originally thought it would take.

He needed to stock up on food now and he owed his Mom another visit. So the next Monday morning he struck out for Flagstaff.

He dragged his canoe ashore in the field and walked to his mother's home. They saw him coming across the field and they all ran out to greet him.

"Raul, you have grown taller and, Sis, you are even prettier. Hello, Mom."

"It is so good to see you. I can tell by the expression on your face that you are happy."

"Yes, Mom, very happy. And the cabin is done. I just need to fill my canoe with food."

"Come in, you must be hungry," Rebecca said.

"I could eat."

Eat? He had four eggs, two thick slices of bacon, almost a whole loaf of fresh bread and coffee.

They visited for two hours and it was time for Shelby to leave. "I have already put up some pie and bread for you."

"Thank you, Mom. I'll be back before the end of summer.

"You take care of Mom and your sister, Raul."

"I will."

Two older men were fighting behind Adalbert's store when Shelby tied up at Adalbert's wharf. The two men were oblivious of Shelby's presence. He walked over and grabbed each man by the front of their shirts and lifted them off the ground. Of course, they each only weighed about a hundred and forty pounds. "Why are you two fighting?"

"Louis took my whiskey bottle and won't give it back," Edsel said.

"Last week he took my bottle, so I was only taking what is rightfully mine."

"Can you two swim?" Shelby asked.

"I can—Louis can't swim a stroke."

"Well, I tell you what. You two are dirtier than pigs and you smell as bad. I think it is time that you two took a bath."

Shelby carried them down the wharf, to the end. "Edsel,"— and Shelby threw him in the river—take a bath and you'll have to save Louis." And he threw him in also.

"Damn you, Shelby! If you weren't so big I'd pound you."

"I said bathe. Don't come out until you have washed off the stink," and he left. He wasn't aware there were people watching him.

"Mr. Adalbert, I need a few things," and he handed him a list.

"How many pails?"

"Three plus a smaller one with a cover." The eggs were put in sawdust in a small keg. There was ham, bacon, beans, salt, sugar and a variety of canned goods, writing paper, pencils and onions.

"A set of dishes. Nothing fancy, but I'm tired of eating out of a tin plate and bowl. A quilt and two blankets and fine mesh screen to cover my windows and for a screen door. A cabbage, squash, turnip, potatoes and flour. And that should do it. Can you put the food into boxes?"

"Sure we can, Shelby," Mrs. Adalbert said. "You have become a good customer. A lot of people in town charge too much."

Mr. Adalbert helped Shelby carry everything down to his canoe.

"Will you be back before winter, Shelby?"

"Yes, I'll have to stock up with enough food to carry me through the winter."

"Goodbye; good luck."

As he canoed out of sight of the village he began to realize he no longer had the same foreboding feeling of abandoning his family. He was now following his own dreams and making his life.

* * * *

Back home, he unloaded his canoe of supplies and soon realized he had made his cabin too small.

It had been a long and busy day and after he had taken care of his supplies he lay on his bed. It was so comfortable. Instead of relaxing, he suddenly saw an idea flash through his mind and he got up and went outside to the left of the cabin. He wished the knoll was a little higher. But as he walked about it, he thought he could make do with it. The top of the knoll was about five feet above the river. He could dig down three feet and build a root cellar and put the fill up around the logs burying it completely. *It just might work,* he was thinking.

But that would have to wait for next year. He still had a lot of work to do before the trapping season began. All in good time.

Instead of working the next day, he went exploring. After studying his map that he now had pinned to a wall, he decided to push across the river in his canoe and make a trapline circle between the river and Basin Mountain to the east.

He went north on the edge of the marsh and he had to clear a lot of alders and bushes for a useable trail. He did find two small beaver colonies, but would leave those for another year. These were probably only two year olds in both colonies. After he had traveled about a mile following the river, he began to circle up on higher ground. Here he didn't have as much clearing to do. He left just enough ax scarfs, so he'd be able to follow the trail next year without too much difficulty.

He liked what he was seeing on this loop. There were many huge beechnut trees and on a beechnut year this would be good deer hunting.

He was all day making the loop back to the river and then downstream where he left his canoe. As nice a trapping area as he thought this would be, he still thought the two traplines he had made earlier would be better fur-producing country.

As he was sitting on his own front porch, he began to think maybe he should pick up another dozen #2 traps, just to be sure he had enough. He doubted if this country had ever been trapped before and he was beginning to feel anxious about starting.

But until then, he had a lot of firewood to work up. And he

began to do that the next day.

For the first two days he cut standing dead and dried hardwood trees in the hardwood grove behind his food storage box. The trees weren't that heavy and he would drag them back to camp one at a time. On the third day he built three saw horses that would support the whole tree and he began bucking them to stove wood length with his bucksaw. The blade was sharp and he wasn't long working up a tree. By the end of that day, he had worked up everything he had brought back.

The next day he piled it on the porch, but not in front of the door and windows. He figured he had a half of a cord piled there. Some of it would need splitting, but he would do that as needed, for now.

He didn't want to cut down all of the dead trees this year, so he started felling green trees. These were larger, heavier and more difficult to drag back to camp. What he needed was a hand cart.

After a week he had worked up and piled two cords of wood.

He woke up one morning and there was a spikehorn deer across the river. He had eaten fish all summer and he instantly had a fancy for some fresh venison. He loaded his .30-30 and leaned up against the door jamb. But he didn't pull the trigger. Instead, he set the rifle down and went out on the porch. The deer just stood there watching him. "You come back in September and I'll have me some fresh venison."

In a brief, lucid moment, he realized most of the meat would spoil in this hot weather. *But not if I had a root cellar.*

He sat down on the railing thinking about that deer. He knew it would be against the law to shoot a deer out of season. There had been a Game Warden Department created a few years ago and he wondered where the nearest game warden would be.

After breakfast he went back to work on firewood. Because the green wood was heavier and harder to handle, he wasn't quite working up a cord a day. He went to bed tired each night and slept good.

By the end of July, he figured he had more than enough firewood split and piled up under the trees. Before winter he'd spread out the canvas over the wood to keep the snow off.

There was a chorus of frogs croaking near Halfway Brook. He and Raul used to catch frogs in the summer and eat their hind legs. So for a day he forgot about firewood and went frogging. He put a bucket and his alder branch fish pole in the canoe and paddled up to the brook. The frogs were still croaking. As he eased the canoe up the brook there were frogs sitting on lily pads everywhere. He put a small piece of black cloth on the fish hook and dangled it just in front of the frog. Thinking it was a bug the frog would jump for it and take the hook.

He wasn't long catching a dozen and that was all he figured he could eat for one meal. The frogs would be around when he wanted another feed.

As he was bringing his canoe into shore back at the cabin, he suddenly decided it would be a good idea if he built a wharf. It wouldn't have to be anything fancy. A few cedar logs nailed together.

After he cleaned the frogs and threw the remains in the river, he went behind the cabin after a couple of cedar trees.

He dragged two about twelve inches thick and about twenty feet long. There were enough short boards he had had to cut off the roofing boards to nail across the tops of the two logs, leaving a two inch gap between the boards to make sure he'd have enough.

He had to get in the water, in order to drag it into the river. It wasn't long and he could see the river current wanted to wash it downstream.

He sharpened a stake and drove it into the river bottom to hold the wharf.

While he was back after the cedar trees, he found a big

one that was dead. *This will make for some good kindling.* Even though it was dead and dry, he still could not drag the whole tree back. So he cut off blocks from the butt end. "These will make good chairs until I can get some."

By the time he had all of the cedar back at the cabin it was time to eat supper. He did bring in two cedar blocks for chairs or stools. "They'll do for now."

The frog legs were delicious and he didn't have any trouble eating them all. And there was only one more slice of pie and it was gone. If he wanted a steady diet of pie, he had two choices: find a wife who can cook or learn to bake. He guessed for now he'd settle with pies from Mr. Adalbert's store.

As he lay in bed that night thinking about what else he had to do or must do, the wind started to blow and he could hear rain hitting the roof. He was glad he had pulled the canoe up on shore and overturned it.

It wasn't a gale force wind, but heavy all the same. He felt safe and secure in his cabin. He was happy.

Just before awaking the next morning he saw images of a smokehouse run through his mind and this woke him and the images were still there.

After breakfast, with an ax he headed out back looking for tall, dead trees. There were many mixed in with the softwoods. He would make a teepee by leaning the dead poles up against each other. When he had this up he cut green trees to fill in the spaces between the dead poles making the shelter practically rainproof and he could store winter food here also. He made an opening and a hinged door, so he could close it off.

Chapter 5

In the dog days of August, the river level was beginning to drop a little. Shelby was counting on the fall rains to bring it back, or it would be a slow trip to Flagstaff to stock up for winter.

In the evenings, he started making a list of things he would get on his next trip to town. There would be beaver meat once he started trapping. He will want more turnip, squash and cabbage. Butter and flour was a certain. He hoped while running his trapline he'd find a deer to shoot. A moose would be too big and most of the meat would probably spoil.

It was time to start collecting bait for his trap. He caught several brook trout and cut their heads off and put them in a bucket and filleted the bodies leaving a hinge at the tail so he could hang the trout over a rod in the smoker. He started a small fire in the smoker and then put a cover on the bait pail and buried it next to the spring to keep it cool.

When those trout were thoroughly smoke-cured, he caught several more and repeated the process. This was a new way for eating fish. He had it for breakfast some mornings.

He put the cured fish in his storage box. He was glad he had made it larger.

* * * *

Before he could make the trip to town, he had to chink the logs before he forgot all about it. He used the old moss he had removed for the cabin space. To keep it in place he nailed in small hardwood saplings.

He was all one day chinking everything. Then there was the gap below the base logs and he had enough spruce and cedar tops to fit tightly under the logs. With both jobs done he now could make the trip to town.

The leaves were beginning to show some color and the river had come back to normal level with rain. It was time to go.

He would take the empty keg with him to get as many eggs as he could.

It was in the middle of the week when he finally decided to make the trip. It was just getting daylight when he pushed off from the wharf. The temperature had dropped during the night making it feel even more like trapping.

First he picked up four more pine finish boards. He could work on projects during the winter. He gave his list of purchases to Mr. Adalbert and then he picked out rubber boots, leather boots, leather mittens and liners, a heavy wool jacket and a lighter one, a knit hat, cotton pants, wool pants, four shirts, two padlocks, magazines, old copies of the newspaper and two boxes of candy. "And how many pies do you have made up?"

"Four," Mrs. Adalbert said.

"I'll take 'em.

"If you can put everything together for me, I'll go visit my mother and then come back."

"We'll have everything ready for you."

He walked the road to the farm. He wasn't afraid of his father, but if he should see him, there might be problems for the family.

As always, Rebecca was happy to see Shelby. "Are you hungry, son?"

"Yes, I left as the sun was coming up. I'm sorry to miss Raul and Sis again, but I don't want to come when dad might be here. He might take it out on you."

"I understand, son."

"Can you spare any eggs, Mom?"

"How many would you like?"

"Two or three dozen, if you have them."

"Did you bring the keg with you?"

"Yes, I left it outside."

He packed three dozen into the sawdust and gave his mother five dollars for the eggs. At first she started to reject the money, but the money would better explain the missing eggs to Armand.

"And, Mom, here's five dollars each for Raul and Sis. Tell them to buy something special for Christmas, and here's five dollars for you, too, Mom. You buy something special for yourself. Okay?"

"Okay."

After two hours, Shelby said, "I have to be going, Mom. I won't be back now until spring."

"You be careful, son."

"I will, Mom. I love you."

To Shelby's surprise, the Adalbert's had bundled everything into a shipping pack, except for the two dozen eggs which were packed in sawdust in a separate box.

Before Shelby had finished business with the Adalberts, Louis and Edsel from last summer walked into the store. When they recognized Shelby, without a word they turned around and went back out.

"What was all that about, Shelby?"

"I had to give them a bath in the river last summer."

"I guess I do remember hearing something about that. Do you have everything, Shelby?"

"I hope, because I won't be back now until spring."

The daylight hours were shorter now and he had to hurry some to make sure he was home before dark.

He carried everything inside for now. He'd sort it out after eating something. It only took two lanterns to illuminate the inside.

As he was unpacking his things it became obvious he was going to have to make a few more shelves. One of the most important items he had on his list was matches. Without fire he'd be dead.

* * * *

While he waited for trapping to begin he'd walk around the cabin making sure everything was done that needed to be before cold weather set in. He knew this first winter alone in the woods was going to be challenging. As long as he could keep busy he believed he would be okay.

Days before trapping began he hung his traps up on the side of the cabin to air out and get rid of any human scent. He figured another four days and he would begin.

Early the next morning when he looked across the river, there was probably the same spikehorn deer. He didn't hesitate this time. As soon as the deer dropped, he was already running to his canoe and putting it in the water and pushed off.

The deer never knew what had hit him. He was hit in the top part of the head.

He dressed the deer there and washed out the cavity in the river before putting it in his canoe.

There was room to hang it up in the smoker teepee. Here he wouldn't have to worry about animals eating it while he was trapping.

He hadn't eaten breakfast yet, so once the fire was going in the cook stove he fried up some heart with eggs.

After breakfast he skun the deer so the meat would cool. The smoker was shadowed by trees and the sun would not heat up the inside. He wished now he had made the cold storage box even larger. With a root cellar he wouldn't have to worry. There was only so much he could do in one summer. All in good time.

The nights were cold now and although the deer meat was not freezing inside the smoker, it was still cold enough to keep the meat fresh.

The deer liver and onions and potatoes were a welcome break from his fish diet.

Not wanting any part of the deer to go to waste, he even stripped the meat off the neck and made a big venison stew.

The hide was a reddish brown color and quite pretty, so he scraped all of the meat and sinew off and nailed it to the side of the cabin to dry. He wouldn't be able to sell it come spring with the rest of his fur pelts because the reddish brown tint of the hair would give it away as a summer killed deer. So he'd use it for a throw rug next to his bed.

It rained hard all the next day and he pretty much had to stay inside. He fixed a cup of coffee and sat down at the table with last June's newspaper. There was one article in particular that interested him.

Apparently a man and woman traveling by wagon to Quebec had been accosted at night while they made camp near Sarampus Falls. When the man tried to fend off the attackers, he was beaten and all they took was what little money he had and some food.

Because the attack had been at night the victims were not able to give a very good description of them. Neither of the attackers had said anything.

Earlier that same spring there had been a similar attack in Wyman Twp. between Flagstaff and Bigelow Village. There was a five hundred dollar reward offered to the capture of these two men.

The next day he put a padlock on his door, for when he had to go to town.

* * * *

The day finally came when Shelby left with all his trapping

gear. He decided to set up the loop to the north of his cabin first—or as he was referring to it, the #1 loop.

Close to the cabin he found two good sets for mink. Then a martin set not far beyond those two traps, and two covey sets before he reached the top of his trapline loop. And there he set another covey.

Turning west now, following his trapline, he was in more hardwood and his first set along the ridge was in an old woodchuck hole that wasn't being used anymore. He used a number 3 trap here.

He set two more covey sets along the hardwood ridge before he came to the intersection of his #2 loop. There was a perfect place for a leaning tree set, once again off the high ground and in the softwoods.

From there he followed the stream up to the beaver flowage and he set two trough sets and then a water set for otter in the inlet.

Just as he was approaching the dam to check the two dam sets, a beaver swam up to one. But he had heard Shelby and he slipped back into the water and disappeared.

Beaver were a favorite food source for many carnivores. They were drawn to beaver flowages because of the scent of castors in the air. So Shelby found a place about a hundred feet away on higher ground, and he dug out a covey, much like a woodchuck hole, and placed a number 3 trap.

The beaver had not returned to the dam so Shelby continued on his trapline.

He only made one set between the two flowages, a ground set in the roots of a fir tree.

At the second, or number 2 flowage, he went to work and made his usual two trough sets and while he was making a ground set on a slight knoll away from the pond, he heard both traps snap close and the beaver splashing in the water.

It was noon and he was hungry, so he built a fire and then

he pulled in both traps—two super large beaver. After resetting both traps he took the beaver ashore to his fire which was quite a ways from the dam.

The first beaver was skun, meat on a stick was roasting over the fire and he had just begun skinning the second beaver, when a trap sprung and he could hear the beaver in the water. Only one trap.

He finished skinning that beaver and ate a piece of meat before pulling in the beaver. An extra-large beaver. He set more meat to roasting and skun the third beaver.

He wrapped the meat and castors in the hides and put them in his packbasket. Then he put the fire out and threw two carcasses in the pond and carried the other one with him to the next set.

He waited until his trail turned to the east before he made another set. There was an out-cropping of rocks and a perfect covey. He put in the whole beaver carcass and put a heavy rock on it.

He made two leaning tree sets in the softwoods before he was back at the river. From there he made a water set for otter in the stream from the beaver ponds. There was otter scat on the bank and he thought this would be a good set. He had twenty-two traps. Not a long trapline, but he expected it to do well.

After finishing the water set, he stood and stretched, shouldered his heavy packbasket and hiked home.

He took care of the meat first, leaving some in the sink and after washing the other legs he hung them up in the smokehouse for now. They'd freeze there and the meat would stay good longer.

There was only a little of daylight left and he put the three beaver hides on the drying boards before picking up and washing up for the night. He left the hides in the smokehouse also. The shelter was proving to be more than just a smokehouse.

Before the sun had disappeared below the horizon, there

was a narrow band of orange light which usually meant a nice day coming.

Before washing up and going to bed, he had a narrow slice of pie and washed it down with water.

He tried to lay awake for a while thinking about the day's trapping, his life here on the river and the life he left behind.

Sleep came too soon as he forgot about everything else.

The first tend on any trapline was always exciting. To see what the line would produce. Trapping was his only livelihood now and he hoped he would be able to live the life of a trapper.

Before leaving to tend traps the next morning, he made sure the door to the smokehouse was securely closed. Then, like a kid on Christmas morning, he hurried along his trapline. The first set produced a mink and nothing in the next one.

The first trap beyond the two water sets held a beautifully colored martin. He was screaming death threats at Shelby as he approached.

At the two covey sets before turning west he had a martin each. And they each were screaming death threats. Shelby knew few trappers tended their lines every day like he did; he just hated the idea of leaving an animal in a trap any longer than necessary.

The woodchuck hole produced a fox, which didn't surprise him. The next two covey sets were empty and another martin in the leaning tree set.

Both traps were gone from the dam at #1 pond and he only pulled in one super large beaver. It was still early and he decided to wait until later to roast meat for lunch.

At the water inlet set he had an otter and he was real feisty and Shelby had to be careful. The trap higher up at that first pond held another red fox. So far this was better success than he had hoped for.

The next two ground sets were empty and both traps were gone from the dam. He pulled in two super large beaver. It was time now to make a fire and cook lunch.

He had become pretty proficient at fleshing beaver while skinning them and he wasn't long before he had both of them done. The pond had gone quiet and he ate his fill of beaver meat before moving on.

He had another fox, a big one, in the bank set there near the #2 pond. And a lynx at the rock covey set and this fella was really agitated and angry.

From there, in the second leaning tree set, he had a female fisher cat. The rest of the traps were empty.

There was still a little daylight left when he got back to the cabin. Before skinning the rest of his catch, he took care of the beaver meat and castor and started a fire in the cook stove. There were eleven animals to skin and they were all easy; even the lynx. Before he had everything on stretchers and drying boards, he was working by lantern light at his outdoor table.

Between his deer and beaver meat and hides, all in the smokehouse, it all represented a lot of work and money. It would be a shame if some animal was to get in and destroy everything.

Before going inside, he placed several hemlock short logs and blocks up against the door. "There, that should keep the animals out."

He was tired again tonight and he didn't try to lay awake thinking. About midnight he was awakened by wolves fighting near the smokehouse. Without getting dressed he pulled his revolver out of the holster and eased the door open. The moon was full and it was bright. The wolves, three of them, were still fighting.

Leaning against the corner of the cabin he took the best aim he could which was more guess work than aiming. He fired and one wolf hy-yied and fell. The other two ran off. Then the third managed to get up and hobble off. He wasn't about to follow it in the dark. It would have to wait for daylight. He doubted if they would be back again that night, so he went back inside.

He went to bed, but he lay awake for most of the remaining night, listening for the wolves to return.

As soon as it was light enough to see, he checked the smokehouse. There were claw marks on the door and on the ground. He couldn't see any blood. But his conscience said he had to see if he could follow it. Last night all three had run off away from the river. Just as he was about to give up there was one spot of blood on a rock. And it had not coagulated yet. As he continued on there were a few more drops of blood. The wolf must have laid down shortly after being shot, and now Shelby had spooked it and it was on the run.

Just as he was about to turn back he heard some bushes rattling. Going more slowly now, he inched forward until he saw the rust colored coat of the wolf. He shot it again.

The wolf was dead alright, but he wasn't going to touch it. It had a bad case of the mange. He had actually done this wolf a favor. He left it there and went back home. It was time for breakfast.

Beaver meat and warmed up bread for breakfast. Before leaving for the day, he drove nails through a board so the sharp end would stick up. It took some time to drive through enough to do the job. Then he laid it on the ground in front of the hemlock logs in front of the smokehouse door.

When he was satisfied, then he left to tend traps.

The first nine traps were all empty. Both traps on the dam of the first pond both had extra-large beaver. He reset and began skinning. Not wanting to catch any small beaver, he decided to pull those traps. The next pond was bigger and he might be able to take a few more.

The trap on the high ground in the bank had another fox. And the traps between the two ponds were once again empty. He pulled in one super and one extra-large beaver at the next pond. He did reset both of those traps.

He had an otter in the water set by the river, and everything else was empty. He was beginning to think the presence of the three wolves probably had something to do with so light a catch today.

He had finished putting everything on stretchers and drying boards before dark. Nothing had attempted to break through to the smokehouse and the food storage box was okay, too.

As he cooked supper, he was thinking about the mangy wolf. Probably the other two also had the mange.

After eating he stepped outside for a minute and there had been a family of otter feeding on the carcasses he had thrown in the river.

By the end of that first week he had three more extra-large beaver from the second pond and he pulled those traps. In one day he caught five more martin, two more mink another fisher and lynx. He thought probably the other two mangy wolves had either died or left the area.

It snowed six inches that Sunday night and all of his traps were empty, but he did rebait a few with a little more castor lure. Two days later there was a warm rain and the snow melted. His deer and beaver meat in the smoke house had frozen before the warm weather and they had not spoiled. He sure was wishing he had some canning jars and a canner. He was afraid some of his meat would spoil before he could use it.

When colder nights returned after the warm up, the fur animals became more active and he picked up five martin, two foxes, one otter and a fisher.

This was a big woods and there probably wasn't any worry about over trapping. But just the same, he had had a remarkable trapping season and he didn't want to take any more than necessary. He had forty-four pieces now.

He would tend one more day and pull the rest of his traps. He thought it strange that there weren't any bobcats.

Instead of going to bed as soon as he had been, he stayed up reading another July issue of the newspaper. There was a short follow-up article about the people that had been victimized and robbed. All three cases had occurred along a roadway and not one victim was able to give the deputy sheriff any kind of description; only that they were two big men.

"I hope someone gets them," he said.

* * * *

During the night the temperature had dropped to zero and all of the shallow water holes were frozen solid. There was still some snow in the shady places and he was surprised to see so many animal tracks. And he was even more surprised when he picked up another lynx and two more martin.

He was back at the cabin before sunset and he began skinning the lynx and martin. There was only a narrow channel in the middle of the river that was still open and when he threw the lynx carcass out it didn't reach the channel. He tied up the two martin in the trees for the birds to feed on.

As he thought back on the trapping season, he had never seen any deer or moose tracks. The area couldn't be devoid of moose and deer. It was a big area and he doubted if any hunters or trappers had ever been in this country before. Perhaps the presence of the three mangy wolves had driven them out of this country. But the country was so big three wolves couldn't cause the deer or moose to leave. He wasn't sure if that early deer would see him through to spring breakup or not. He was glad now that he had so much beaver meat stored in the smoke house.

For something to do, he built more shelves in the smoke house and moved all the food from the storage box. What he didn't want to freeze he brought into the cabin.

With constant wood heat now the logs were drying and sometimes he would wake up at night by a sharp crack as one of the logs cracked from the heat. At times the cracks were as loud as a .22 revolver going off. Almost.

In an odd way it was also a comforting noise. A reminder that he had built a secure and comfortable home.

During the night, wind started howling and he was enjoying listening. In an odd sense of humor, the wind was for him, music more than a disturbing noise. But—it put him to sleep. He slept so well during the wind storm that he had not awoken and put more wood in the ramdown wood stove. Now the cabin was a little cool, and for the first time since leaving the farm, he was enjoying lounging in bed. There was nothing pressing that had to be done. Maybe take some of the hides off the stretchers.

Eventually he had to get up, before the water in the bucket froze. With both fires going, it wasn't long before the inside was too warm and he had to open a window.

As breakfast was making on the stovetop, he looked out the front window. There were two bald eagles eating the lynx carcass he had thrown on the ice. They were beautiful birds. He was beginning to wish he hadn't thrown all of the carcasses into the open water. It would be nice to feed and watch the eagles. Canadian Jays were busy at the two martin carcasses he had hung up in the trees. He smiled thinking, *Nothing has gone to waste.*

The floor was cold and as soon as there was more snow he'd bank the cabin.

After breakfast he went outside and checked on the smokehouse and then out to the cold storage box. Although he had moved all the food to the smokehouse, he wanted to see if any animals had been curious about the smells from the storage box. There were no tracks.

He took everything off the stretchers and bundled them together and hung the bundle up in the smoke house.

Days later, wanting something to do after breakfast, he went exploring. The river ice was solid now. He strapped on his .44 revolver and with his ax, he headed downstream to see what there was.

Not far downstream from his cabin, he found a small feeder stream on the left and he followed that to a beaver flowage. His number 1 trapline passed behind it just out of sight. It was a small house and probably a couple of two year olds. He went back to the river and followed it to Grand Falls. He had not seen any deer or moose tracks and this was puzzling. He turned around and hiked up to Long Falls. There he found a well-used deer trail coming from the right, crossing the river to the left side, or east of the river.

He began following the deer trail and it led him to a semi marshy area that looked like it had burned over a long time ago. Most of the new growth was cedar trees and hazel bushes. There was a concentration of deer in here and this certainly explained the absence of deer tracks elsewhere.

He would remember this area next year when he would be needing some fresh meat.

In the middle of cedar haven, he found another beaver flowage. The water was backed up for a long ways and he found three different beaver houses. "This is where I'll start trapping next year."

The flowage covered a big area and he figured there were probably a dozen of extra or super large beaver. And there'd surely be more next year.

It was time to head back. His legs were tired from hiking all day and he was hungry. As he thought about how hungry he was the idea of fried beaver meat, potatoes and cabbage sounded pretty good. He could almost smell the gravy. He began to walk faster.

Later that evening he began figuring how much the cabin had cost him. He still had most of the receipts. Boards for the roof and flooring was the biggest expense.

For everything, including the rifle, canoe, clothes, traps and food, he had spent four hundred and eighty dollars for the cabin with both stoves and windows. Leaving nearly thirty-six hundred dollars in his bank account.

Chapter 6

Before the end of December Shelby had snow banked up against the cabin as high as the bottom of the windows. And the floor was warmer.

The snow was deep in the woods where the wind couldn't blow it around—dry and fluffy snow which made snowshoeing tiring. He kept a beaten trail out to the spring and to his wood pile, instead of shoveling a path.

This year there wasn't the usual January thaw; instead it snowed and snowed. Snowshoeing was impossible. Snow was up over the windows and he had to shovel snow off the porch and throw the snow as far as he could away from the cabin. For something to do one day before the snow started, he had filled the porch with firewood. The pile under the trees was now buried.

It was tiring trying to snowshoe to each window, but it had to be done. He was low on food but he had to wait for the snow to settle before he could venture out to the smokehouse.

When the snow stopped the wind started to blow, it filled in his snowshoe paths, which were more like tunnels. Most of the snow had blown off the roof and he was glad for that. After a week with little to eat, January thaw came in the middle of February. It stayed in the fifties day and night. It was more like April weather than in the middle of winter. He saw robins and other migratory birds. They had also been fooled by the warm weather.

One day after the snow had settled enough, he donned his snowshoes and ventured to the smokehouse for food. During the height of the snow, it was halfway up to the top of the teepee. The snow had settled a lot, but now he could see some animal had managed to claw a hole through the door. There were tracks all through the snow in front, scats and urine spots.

He was afraid of what he might find inside. As he was taking his snowshoes off two large raccoons shot out through the hole in the door and headed for the trees out back.

After shoveling the snow away from the door, he was able to force it open. Well, his hides were still hanging and they didn't look like they had been touched. It smelled awful inside the smokehouse. A mixture of urine and feces. It looked like the raccoons had been living there. But there was another pungent odor and it was a terrible smell.

The food was gone and what little there was was covered with urine and feces. Even some of the deer bones had been cracked open. Raccoons could not have done that.

He took his hides down and put them in the cabin. Then he took stock of what he had that was edible. There was coffee, tea, salt, pepper, a little butter and a handful of rice. He had been subsisting on a handful of rice with a little butter for several days. Now there was only a handful left.

That evening he ate the rice with butter. It was quite good, but did very little to give him the nutrition that he needed.

The weather turned cold during the night and come daylight there was two inches of new snow.

He poured a cup of coffee and a half spoonful of sugar with it. That's all the sugar there was.

There was nothing else to do. He strapped on his snowshoes and put his .22 revolver in his pocket. He needed food. A squirrel, partridge—or even a mouse, at this point.

The two inches of snow had insulated the wet snow underneath and the snow was still soft. He kept punching through with his snowshoes, tiring him to the point where he had no choice but to turn back.

He stood by the stove trying to get warm. He had no idea what he was going to do. Then in desperation he went back to the smokehouse to see if he could find a morsel or two to eat.

While he was there, he looked at the claw marks on the door. "No raccoon did this. It was a bigger animal." But he still didn't know what. He didn't find anything fit to eat.

He sat at the table thinking about his troubles and trying to think how he could get himself out of this situation. *Things were going so nice. Then the snow almost buried me, then animals ate all of my food. What did I do to deserve this?*

His stomach had shrunk so much now it wouldn't even growl from hunger pains.

Just then a mouse ran down the table towards him. In one swift swoop he scooped up the mouse. It wasn't fighting. "Ay, food! I can fry you and eat you."

Then he looked at the mouse that wasn't even fighting to get away.

"I bet you're hungry, too, aren't you, fella?"

He reached for the empty butter dish and set it down near the mouse and said, "Here, fella, you can lick the butter off the dish. You wouldn't make much of a meal anyhow," and he let the mouse go.

And the mouse licked every bit of butter from the dish. Then he sat down on his haunches looking up at Shelby. They both just sat there for a while just looking at each other. Then the mouse ran back down the table. Shelby looked under the table and he couldn't see the mouse. *Where had he gone? Where did he come from?* That was probably the mouse he had seen earlier inside the cabin. He put more wood in the ramdown stove and he turned the kerosene lantern off and lay down on his bed without taking his clothes off.

* * * *

Shelby lay down thinking. Not feeling sorry for himself. But wondering why all this trouble and would he survive to see tomorrow.

Shelby opened his eyes. The inside of the cabin was as bright as if the sun was shining through the windows. He was bewildered, and there, standing at the foot of his bed, was a beautiful woman. He was too stunned to say anything.

In a soft voice she said, "You will not starve. You will survive." And she was gone.

* * * *

Shelby woke up the next morning. The fire was out, but the cabin was not cold. He swung his legs over the bedside and started to stand up. Then he sat down, "Holy cow! Wow, did I ever have a dream last night."

At that moment he could remember the experience clearly. But the experience started to fade away.

He dressed and started the fires in both stoves. He could at least have a cup of coffee. While the water was heating, he stood looking out the front windows at the river.

"What the heck!?" He went outside. There was a two pound brook trout in his snowshoe trail. He picked it up looking at the puncture wounds on both sides of the trout. It was not frozen, so it had not been lying there very long. He heard a high pitch shriek overhead and looked up. There were two bald eagles circling overhead.

He didn't know why, but he started looking around and found another brook trout in the snow.

He looked up again, waved and said, "Thank you!"

He went back inside and cleaned both trout. He saved the heads to make a fish head soup. The entrails were put in the snowshoe track for the Canadian Jays.

He only ate one trout. He saved the other one for later. As he was eating the mouse ran down the table and stopped about two feet in front of him. "Hello, fella. Are you hungry?" and he put some meat on the table for the mouse. The mouse ate the fish and then ran to the other end of the table.

During the rest of that day he kept thinking about the eagles, brook trout and, yes, the mouse. *What did it all mean?*

For supper he put off eating the second brook trout. Instead he used both fish heads in a soup. He never had eaten fish head soup and knew no one who had. He had heard about it.

To his surprise it was very good. To keep the second trout from going bad, he packed it in snow in the sink.

He was feeling much better in the morning and he ate the second brook trout and the mouse joined him for his little portion.

Feeling much better and stronger he strapped on his snowshoes, and with his .22 revolver, he went hunting. A red squirrel, rabbit or partridge. He decided to hunt his number 1 trail backwards. During the trapping season he had seen many squirrels and partridges. There were tracks in the snow, but that's all. While he was trapping the squirrels would seem to follow him, all the while scolding him. The woods were quiet.

He made the loop around and was halfway back along the river and a partridge was eating alder buds. It was an easy shot.

For supper that night he had partridge breast and the two legs. He threw the carcass out on the river for the eagles. The mouse was waiting for his portion and ate it hurriedly.

Snowshoeing today probably had cost him more protein than what he got from the partridge. He would have to go hunting tomorrow, too.

Again that night as soon as he had closed his eyes the same woman appeared standing at the foot of his bed and the cabin was as bright as daylight.

"Why did the eagles help me?"

"They were starving when you gave them food."

"Why are they helping me?"

"You chose not to eat the mouse. Instead you gave it butter and even now you share your food with the mouse."

"I suppose there is a reason for this dilemma I am experiencing?"

"Think about it. You caused it."

"How?"

"You shot the raccoon because you were angry."

"I did.

"Who are you?"

"I am called Kalipona."

"Where do you go?"

"Go? I am here. And I must leave now."

* * * *

Shelby awoke in the morning feeling better about his dilemma than he had since his troubles had started. At first the experience with Kalipona was sharp and clear. But little by little the memories were fading.

That morning there were two more nice brook trout, both lying in the snowshoe track.

This went on until traveling became easier and Shelby was more able to hunt for his food. But he continued to leave food for the eagles on the ice and each meal the mouse would join him for his lunch.

Kalipona made a last appearance in late March. And once again she helped him to awaken.

"Hello," he said.

"Shelby, you have survived the winter, your hunger and I think you understand why this happened to you. It wasn't by chance."

"Yes. I understand."

"This will be my last visit for a while."

"Where are you going?"

"We will meet again, but not for a while."

When he awoke in the morning the only memory he now had of that experience was a beautiful woman. He tried to see the image of her in his mind. It was difficult to do. Slowly the images of last night faded away.

When the river opened he was able to fish once again. When he first arrived here he had made the comment that he would be eating a lot of fish. At that time he had no idea how true that statement would be.

He would have liked to leave now with his hides, but the river was high and the current was strong. While he waited he decided to animal-proof his cabin.

He made four more nail boards to place on the ground under the windows and one on the doorstep and he still had the one that was at the smoke house that he would put in front of the door and he nailed it to the porch floor so it could not be moved.

He also nailed boards across the windows.

Because of the deep snowpack that year, the water level in the river stayed high and the current swift.

There were only patches of snow left in the more shady places. Wanting something to do he took his .22 revolver and started walking along #1 trapline. He didn't go but a short distance and his trail was too soft and muddy.

Back where the sandy knoll that the cabin sat on, where the knoll met the low lying alders, there was a spring feeder stream. It was too small last fall to think about making a set. There was water seeping out from under a rock on the side of the slight knoll.

He stopped suddenly and took two steps backward while looking at the little stream. "Well I'll be damned." He knelt down and reached into the cold water and picked up a gold colored rock about the size of a green pea. He looked it over carefully. "It is gold."

He started looking at the stream bottom a little closer now and he picked up four more nuggets, all about the size of green peas.

He walked back and forth several times to the river and back and picked up more nuggets. There was enough for a small handful. He was ecstatic. There might be a pound of gold in that small handful; at current prices, Shelby knew he was holding more than two hundred dollars in his hand.

He made a little cloth pouch. There was no way he was going to sell this in Flagstaff. If he did then every mother's son would follow him out here looking for gold. No, he knew he would have to take his fur and gold to Lac Megantic. He had overhead trappers talking about a furrier there that paid good prices for fur.

There was a stagecoach that traveled to Coburn Gore twice a week, Tuesday and Friday.

Not wanting to waste precious time and needing something to keep him busy until he left, he thought about either digging out the hole for the root cellar or cutting and peeling the trees he would need. But he had not regained his strength from being too undernourished in February and March.

That would have to wait. It was May 1st and he decided to leave in four days, on Sunday, planned to camp out one night at the portage, arrive in town and spend Monday night in the hotel and catch the stage Tuesday morning. This would also give him time to visit his family.

"When I do regain my strength, I have a lot of work to do. Hmm—and I thought this would be an easy summer and I could relax and do a lot of exploring."

From the wind storm last winter, there were dead branches littering the ground. He picked them up into a pile. He would use them in the cookstove.

He had not used as much firewood as he would have thought, and now he had at least a cord and a half of dry wood to start the winter.

He was getting anxious to leave. For weeks now all he had had to eat was fish. No vegetables or bread. Just fish and coffee and his companion at each meal, Mr. Mouse. Shelby didn't understand why, but he felt a responsibility for the mouse. The eagles would circle overhead every day or so and shriek their greeting, but they no longer dropped fish at his doorstep.

After breakfast Sunday with Mr. Mouse, he put his canoe in the river and tied it to the wharf. He also cut off a piece of canvas in case it should rain.

He sat on his porch enjoying the sounds of spring. There were two projects he needed to complete this year. The root cellar and a closed-in work shed, also for firewood, attached to the west end of the cabin. Oh yeah, he was going to have to do something about a smoker, too. There was no way he was going to use the teepee that the raccoons urinated and defecated in. It still had a stink to it. He could always use the dried poles for firewood.

He caught enough brook trout for lunch and to take with him for supper and breakfast tomorrow morning. As he sat down to eat, Mr. Mouse joined him and waited for Shelby to give him his portion. "I wish you could talk, Mr. Mouse. I bet you have an interesting story."

When the mouse had finished eating it scurried off and out of sight. "I wonder where you go, Mr. Mouse. I never see you except at meal time."

After cleaning up the cabin, he pulled out his bundle of hides and made a rope harness for the bundle so he could carry it on his back. He had no idea how far it was from the border crossing to Lac Megantic. He might end up having to walk it and the hides would be easier to carry on his back.

He was taking the brook trout with him; he cleaned and wrapped them in a bundle of fresh green grass, to keep them fresh.

He wanted to be on the up hillside of the portage before dark. He took his packbasket to put food in when he came back, and a change of clean clothes. He shaved and wrapped his razor and toiletries in a towel and put that in the packbasket. He put his pouch of gold in the towel also.

It was time to leave. After loading the canoe he walked back and locked the door. "So long, Mr. Mouse. I left you some fish on the table." *Wherever you are.*

A year ago he would have carried everything across in one trip. Although he was feeling good, he realized he had lost some stamina, so he didn't push it. He had plenty of time.

He kindled a fire and roasted both trout. He'd plan on breakfast with his mother in the morning.

The canvas was doubled up and used for a bed under the canoe. Before going to sleep he began thinking about the mouse and what it was about him—*what part did he play in my life.* And there was something in his mind about—*because I did not kill the mouse. Where did that come from and why should I be remembering that now?"*

* * * *

During the trip to town he had decided not to tell anyone about almost starving and then being saved by two eagles who brought him food. No one would believe him anyhow. And he certainly wasn't going to tell anyone about the gold, ever.

Before going to see his family, he got a hotel room and shaved again and washed up. Then he bought passage on Tuesday's stage coach and stopped in to see Mr. Adalbert.

"Hello, Shelby."

"Mr. Adalbert, do you have any wicker rocking chairs? I'm looking for two."

"We do; they're overhead."

"Good, I'm taking my fur this year to Lac Megantic. I have other business there also. I don't know how long I'll be, but here is a list of things I'll be needing. And would it be okay if I left my canoe here, overturned out back?"

"Sure, Shelby, no problem. You going over to see your

mother? She was asking about you at church yesterday."

"I'm heading over now. Thank you."

He left his stuff in his hotel room, pulled his canoe ashore and overturned it.

After the winter he had had, he didn't care if his father would be home or not. He didn't want to cause trouble for his family, but he was through side-stepping around him.

Rebecca was hanging out clothes and saw Shelby walking down the driveway.

"Hello, Mom."

"Oh, Shelby, I've been so worried about you. Let me look at you. You've lost weight son and you definitely need a haircut."

"I was hoping you could cut my hair. But I'm hungry, Mom."

"What would you like?"

"Oh, maybe four eggs and thick slices of bacon and a couple slices of bread."

"How long can you stay?"

"I'm staying at the hotel tonight and tomorrow I'm taking the stage to the border and eventually to Lac Megantic."

"Why Lac Megantic?"

"I can get a better price for my fur there.

"How are Raul and Sis?"

"They're doing good. They miss you. Can you stay long enough this trip to see them?"

"Yes. How has dad been? Has he been any trouble?"

"He still works long hours and he is no more trouble than usual. I never tell him when you have stopped to visit."

"That's a good idea."

Rebecca watched as Shelby shoveled the food in him. "My, you were hungry. When did you leave your cabin?"

"Late yesterday afternoon.

"I've eaten so many fish I think I probably could swim like a fish."

"How short do you want your hair?"

"Like I always did Mom. Short."

"Are you happy living in the wilderness by yourself, son?"

"Yes. There is something different every day. It was hard work to get everything done before cold weather, but I have always worked hard. I'm happy, Mom."

"You should have a wife out there with you, Shelby."

"Maybe someday, Mom, but I'm not likely to meet anyone out there."

"I must say, son, you sound happy, and other than being too thin, you look good."

At lunchtime Shelby was hungry again and they had ham sandwiches with chicken stew.

After lunch, Shelby offered to hang up the washing while Rebecca started making pies and biscuits.

And that was what he was doing when Raul and Sis came walking down the driveway after school. Sis saw him first and ran yelling towards him. Raul was all smiles as he walked.

"Never thought I'd see the day, brother, that you'd be hanging out the wash," Raul said.

"It's good to see you too, brother."

"Go inside; I'll be done here soon.

"You filled out and got tall, Raul. And Sis you are prettier than ever."

"And you're so thin, Shelby," Raul said.

Jokingly, Shelby replied, "My own cooking." He had made up his mind not to say anything to anyone about him almost starving to death.

All four talked and ate fresh hot biscuits. "Change your clothes, Raul, and I'll help you with chores."

Rebecca had tears in her eyes as she watched her two sons walking out to the barn. She was happy and in one way, sad. Her big young son was no longer just a big boy. He was twenty-one now and he carried himself as a big man, capable of taking care of himself. Yes, she was proud of him. And she also knew Armand would never again be able to belittle him.

Shelby didn't leave until 6 o'clock. "I don't know how long I'll be in Lac Megantic, but I will come by when I get back."

He said goodbye and walked the road to town.

Chapter 7

The stagecoach left Flagstaff promptly at 7 a.m. and he had to pay a dollar for hauling his bundle of fur pelts. There was one other passenger besides Shelby, Mr. Henry Bovin from customs.

The stage made four stops at highway work camps to deliver mail.

The gravel road had recently been graded for the first five miles but thereafter it was rough. There were crews repairing culverts and bridges.

"How far is it to the border?" Shelby asked.

"About twenty-eight miles. Usually the driver would change teams halfway, but there aren't any relay stations on this route. That's why a team of six horses is used. They'll rest a full day before going back," Mr. Bovin said.

Even though the road from here north had not been graded yet, the driver did not slow up much. It was a bumpy ride. They pulled into the border cabin at noon. Shelby was asked by a French official if he was going to sell his furs at Pasquale's in Lac Megantic.

"Yes; can you tell me how far it is?"

"About twenty miles, Monsieur. Are you planning on walking?"

"Yes."

"You will come to an Abenaki village on this end of Lac Megantic. You might hire someone to take you in canoe to Megantic village."

"Thank you."

Shelby shouldered his bundle again and crossed into Canada.

He was feeling so much better today than he had two days ago, or even yesterday, and walking with a seventy-five pound load on his back—well, it was better than riding that stagecoach another mile.

Three miles beyond the border he came to a small village. There were only a few buildings and he didn't see anyone about. He kept moving on.

"Twenty miles, huh? If I don't stop anywhere I should be able to get there before dark."

Yes, Shelby Martin was feeling good. He had finally recovered from his ordeal last winter, something that he was not likely to ever forget.

He was walking through a nice spruce grove and up ahead there looked like a clearing near a stream crossing.

There was a noise and he stopped. Men were fighting and he heard a woman's voice. A panicking voice. As he came closer, he first saw a big burly guy beating a much smaller guy—an Indian. He could still hear the woman's voice.

Another big brute had the woman down on the ground and he was ripping every stitch of clothing off her. She was struggling, but he was so much bigger. The brute slapped her face and she was momentarily stunned. Then she screamed. The brute had his pants down and he lay on top of the struggling woman. She reached up with both hands and dug her fingernails into his face and clawed him severely, until the blood started to run.

He slapped her again. His pal was watching all this and enjoying it. The Indian he had been beating lay curled up on the ground. Shelby took his bundle of hides off and ran to the brute who still had his pants on. He grabbed his long hair in one powerful grip and the belt around his pants, and before this guy knew what was happening, Shelby ran him head-on into a large spruce tree, stunning him. But he was able to scream.

The other guy was so intent on raping the girl, he never paid any attention to his friend screaming. The girl was still fighting him. Shelby grabbed a handful of hair and literally lifted him off her and threw him. He screamed when he hit a rock. By now the first guy had gotten to his feet and was coming at Shelby with both of his arms outstretched in front of him. This guy probably was heavier than Shelby and a good six inches shorter. He was mostly fat and not muscle.

Shelby hit him on the end of his nose with the palm of his hand—not his fist. He staggered backward and then fell. By now the guy with no pants had picked himself up and was charging at Shelby. Shelby stepped to one side and put out his foot and tripped Mr. No Pants. He screamed again for obvious reasons. This guy was a little taller than his friend, but still mostly flab.

The girl stood up and rushed over to see how the boy was, and she watched as this stranger took on the two rapists. They both were coming at Shelby now. Shelby didn't wait for them. Instead, he charged at them and when he went between them, he put out both of his arms, taking each of them in the throat. They were both knocked over backwards. They both were bleeding. Mr. No Pants started to swing at Shelby. Shelby grabbed his arm and brought it down on his raised knee, snapping the bone. No Pants was really screaming now.

The other guy wasn't finished yet. Like a madman, he reached out with both arms again and charged Shelby. Shelby gave him a sideways blow to the ribs and he could hear bones breaking. He went down screaming again. Shelby walked over to him and grabbed his hair and pulled his head back and started to hit him in the face with his anvil-like clinched fist and the guy was able to say, "No more! No more!"

The other guy, No Pants, wasn't going to give up so easily. He staggered to his feet. He had a piece of wood in his left hand, his right arm being broken. Shelby didn't have any trouble feinting the attack, and he brought his fist down on the man's collar bone. He went down screaming and this time he stayed down.

Shelby stood up straight and stretched. He took his shirt off and walked over to the girl and said, "Here, you can put this on." She did and the shirt came down to her knees.

"Thank you, Monsieur. I believe these two would have killed my brother and me if you had not come."

"How is your brother?"

"He is hurt bad. Can you help him?"

The brother had bruises on his face, but the real trouble Shelby figured, he probably had a couple of broken ribs.

"Where do you live?"

"Not far," and she pointed towards the lake and not up the road.

"What you do with them?" and she pointed.

"We take them to your village and let your people take care of them."

"How are you called?" she asked.

"Shelby."

"S-h-e-l-b-y," she said slowly.

"Yes. How are you called?" he asked.

"I am called Apona. Means butterfly."

"Your brother?"

"He called Caponi."

"Caponi, can you stand?" He did, with great difficulty.

"I will carry you," Shelby said.

Shelby shouldered his bundle of fur again and said, "All right you two get up."

They did, also with great difficulty. "Where you taking us?" No Pants asked.

"To their village. If either of you give us any trouble or try to run off, I will break both of your legs. Both of you."

"No trouble, Mister."

"Apona, lead the way. You two follow Apona. Remember, no trouble." Shelby then picked Caponi up in his arms. "Is this okay, Caponi?"

"I will make it."

Apona watched as Shelby picked her brother up with that heavy bundle of fur pelts on his back.

It was a slow march.

After several minutes Apona asked, "Shelby, you wish to rest?"

"No, it'll be easier for your brother if we keep moving."

"Shelby," she asked again, "you know Man Who Was Not Afraid?"

"No."

"You like him."

Much to Shelby's surprise, Apona was in better spirits than he would have thought after experiencing what she had.

The distance was not far but it was slow going. Griswald and Gunther were having a difficult time.

"We close now," she said.

"Apona, can you run ahead and tell your people we are coming. I do not want any trouble."

"I go," and she ran off up ahead.

It wasn't long and a whole throng of people came running back. Two men took each brother and helped him, and Apona and an older man, perhaps her father. He said, "I take, you tired."

"I am all right."

Caponi said, "No, father, moving me around hurts too much."

Ranibir said, "Okay," and they continued on.

Ranibir said, "When daughter tell me what happen I sent four of my people in canoes to bring back white doctor and white man law."

"Good," Shelby said.

Apona came up behind Shelby and said, "Let me help you take this off."

She had the full weight of the hides when Shelby slipped his arms from the rope harness. She couldn't hold it off the ground, so she set it down. "This heavy. You carry this and Caponi. You like Man Who Was Not Afraid.

This was the second reference to this person and Shelby had no idea who she was talking about.

"Shelby, you come with me I give shirt back to you. Follow me."

He followed her into one of the lodges. "Ranibir my father, chief of the people. This is our lodge."

She took his shirt off and handed it to him. When he looked surprised she said, "Did not want to bare myself in front of village. You already see me naked. No surprise now. Okay?"

"Okay." But he couldn't help but look at her supple body.

She caught him looking at her and she said, "You like what you see?"

"Yes, I like."

"Good," and she dressed and Shelby put his shirt on. Then she wrapped her arms around him and began to cry. "I so afraid what the two were going to do to me. Both of them," and she cried some more. "I was scared. You came, stopped him before he was inside me. I fight him, but I think he would kill me and Caponi, too. I scratch his face good; wear scars all his life." She cried some more and Shelby held her, trying to offer some comfort.

He held her away from him and dried the tears on her face. "Come, we should join the others," he said.

"I feel good near you, Shelby, no longer afraid." They rejoined the others.

"Are you hungry?" Apona asked.

"Yes, and thirsty."

She went after some water for him.

Shelby walked over to see Caponi.

"How do you feel, Caponi?"

"Still hurt. Good to be in village. Two there would kill sister and me, not you come. Thank you. You strong man."

The four men who had gone after a doctor and a lawman could be seen canoeing to the village. Ranibir went down to meet them and Apona gave Shelby some water.

The doctor tended to Caponi first.

"Hello, Caponi. Can you show me where you hurt besides your face?"

"Here," and he put his hand on his side.

"What did they do to you?"

"Hit me, hit me many times."

"Yes, I would say. You have two broken ribs. I'll bandage your ribs. Your face will heal on its own." And he gave him some laudanum. "This will kill the pain, Caponi. I'll have to stay the night. I'll give you more in the morning."

Next, Dr. Trumble went to see the Macy brothers. "My, my, what do we have here?" He was well acquainted with the Macy brothers. "What did you do, attack the whole village?"

"No, Doctor," Ranibir said. "One man."

"One man did this to them?" and he began to laugh. "I want to meet this man," and he laughed some more.

While Dr. Trumble worked on the brothers Constable Elwyn Duguay talked with Shelby. "What is your name?"

"Shelby Martin."

"Where do you live?"

"Flagstaff."

"So you are from Maine. What brings you to Canada?"

"I'm a trapper and I brought my fur up to sell to Pasquale Furrier."

"Who else is with you?"

"Excuse me?"

"There's no way one person could beat the crap out of the Macy brothers."

"I am alone, Constable Duguay."

"Can you tell me what happened?"

Shelby told him every detail. "So you saw Griswold raping the girl?"

"I saw him hit her; he ripped her clothes off. I saw him take his pants off and I saw him lying on top of her making motions like he was raping her."

"We have been after these brothers for two years and it takes one man from away to put them down and bring them to justice. I will need you, along with Caponi and Apona, to testify at their trial a week from today."

Dr. Trumble had the brothers bandaged up and he had given them some laudanum also. "They won't be moving much. They are pretty beat up and sore. How did you ever get the best of those two young men?"

"Just lucky, I guess."

"Well, maybe, but it's my opinion, if not for you, the brothers would have killed both of them."

There was a feast that night, and as odd as it might be, the brothers were served first and allowed to eat as much as they wanted. When everyone had finished eating, they all gathered in what might be called an outdoor amphitheater. Shelby was asked to join Ranibir and his family. They were the entertainers.

Ranibir started off with, "Many years ago a man we call Man Who Was Not Afraid saved my life, my brother, Sahil, my sister, Helena and my mother, Advika and my father, Piopolis, chief." Ranibir retold the story of Marquis, Man Who Was Not Afraid, saving their lives and how he had killed the bear and how he had lost the memory of who he was.

"And now this man, Shelby Martin, so much like Marquis, saves the lives of my son and daughter. Shelby, all the people want to hear story. You tell."

"Chief Ranibir, I really think the story should be told by Caponi and Apona. They experienced everything."

Caponi spoke first, but he had to stop when he was in so much pain he had to curl up. Then Apona stood up and told everyone exactly what happened.

Dr. Trumble in a low voice said to Constable Duguay, "Shelby is some kind of man. A hero to these people."

"There are a lot of people, Dr. Trumble, that'll be glad to see these two in prison. Tomorrow I'll have no choice but to march them through town so everyone can see."

It was getting late and people were starting to break up. Apona was still by Shelby's side.

Chief Ranibir said, "Doctor, you and Constable Duguay sleep in our lodge tonight. The brothers have been moved to a lodge with men to guard them. Apona, you take Shelby to empty lodge behind."

Shelby heard this. Was he supposed to sleep with Apona? *She's so young,* he thought. But he didn't want to offend his hosts.

It was beginning to get cold outside, but someone had started a small fire in the lodge where Apona was taking Shelby. Inside the lodge, he saw two separate beds laid out. This was making him feel a little more at ease.

There were two sitting cushions near the fire and they sat down. "I do not want to sleep right now. I am some afraid to close my eyes. You understand?

"Yes, let us talk. How old are you, Apona?"

"Sixteen this spring."

"When in the spring?"

"I do not understand."

"What month and day were you born?"

"I know there are twelve months, from school, I not know which month or day. Only I was born in spring. Some days after I was born a butterfly landed on my nose. My father named me Apona—butterfly."

"How old are you, Shelby?"

"I turned twenty-one this spring, in April."

"I know April. You twenty-one, I sixteen. You have wife, Shelby?"

"No, I have no wife."

"You have—how do you say—special girl?"

"No."

"I glad. You live alone, with family?"

"I live alone. Last year I made me a log cabin in the woods by a river, and I am a trapper."

"You came here another time?"

"No, this is the first time I have ever been in Canada."

"You come back?"

"Yes, I will come back next year."

"Good. Sooner?"

He smiled before answering. "I don't know. Do you have someone special?"

"Yes." His heart sank. "You."

He began to smile again. And he was thinking, *If I had known you longer, Apona, I'd take you home with me.*

The flap on the opening was pushed aside and Ranibir and Apona's mother came in. "I worry about Apona. You okay?"

"Yes, mother, okay."

Shelby thought they were probably checking to see if they were sleeping together.

"See, I told you they okay. Come, woman, back to our lodge. Goodnight." And they left.

"Mother was seeing if we were in bed together."

The temperature was dropping and Apona put two more sticks of wood on the fire.

"At my log cabin, I made a lodge like this. I used dead trees and leaned them up to form the teepee. I used it to smoke-cure fish and then later to store my food. During the winter raccoons and some other animals broke in and ate all my food."

"You said teepee."

"Yes, another name for this type of lodge."

"We not call it teepee, we say wikitup."

"That even sounds better than teepee. It's getting late; I think we need to sleep.

"What were you and your brother doing where the brothers attacked you?"

"We go to pick fiddleheads."

Apona stood up and took her clothes off. When she saw Shelby looking at her she said, "You not take clothes off when you sleep?"

"Well, I take my shirt and pants off, but I sleep in long-johns."

"Who is this long-john?"

He took his shirt and pants off and showed her the long-johns. "See, these are long-johns. Keeps you warm when the air is cold."

She felt the long-johns and said, "Nice. I like long-john. We people take clothes off before get into blankets. Come take long-john off."

Might as well join the people, he was thinking.

They both crawled into their own bedding. "I like you, Shelby."

"Goodnight, Apona. I like you, too."

They lay in the beds in silence for a few minutes then Shelby asked, "Apona?"

"Yes."

"There is a name that keeps repeating in my head."

"What is this name?"

"Have you ever heard of anyone called Kalipona?"

She repeated it several times and then said, "No, I know no one called Kalipona. Where you hear this name?"

"I don't know, but it has been in my head all day."

"Kalipona," she said again. "Sounds to be a woman name."

"I don't know."

Apona fell asleep soon after and Shelby lay on his back thinking about the day's events and Apona's uniqueness, her forthrightness and honest curiosities. *She was a strong-willed girl, but would she ever be able to get over the attack on her?*

And for most of the night there was Kalipona still floating around in his head. *Who was this person?* If indeed Kalipona was a person. That was the rub. He didn't know. And the biggest question, why was the name in his head?

He did manage to get a couple of hours sleep.

There were voices outside as people were starting the day. Apona's mother Sopi opened the tent flap. She saw them in separate beds and she felt relieved. "Apona, come; we get food."

Apona stood up out of the blankets, still naked and Sopi didn't seem to be surprised. "Put clothes on, hurry." And she left.

"Constable Duguay, I send men and canoes to take you, doctor and prisoners to Megantic," Ranibir said.

"Thank you, Chief Ranibir. We should get started."

Dr. Trumble gave Caponi some more laudanum. "How do you feel this morning, Caponi?"

"Face do not hurt much. When take deep breath, hurts."

"That's because you have two broken ribs. You must not do any lifting for four weeks. Do you understand?"

Caponi nodded his head that he understood.

"Your body will tell what you can and cannot do. Listen to the pain, Caponi, and stop what causes the pain."

"Okay."

He gave the brothers more laudanum, also. They were in worse condition than Caponi. They were helped into the canoes then and taken to Megantic.

"Chief Ranibir, I need to leave also. I need to take my fur to Pasquale's."

"Take canoe."

"I go too," Apona said.

Shelby looked at Ranibir, and he smiled and nodded his head. Sopi stood beside him and they watched as they disappeared up the lake.

"Apona—she just like your sister, Helena. Always she tells you what she is going to do. Just like Helena."

"I like this man, Shelby. He would make good mate for Apona."

Sopi laughed and said, "She make him good mate. You see."

Apona did her share of paddling all the way to Pasquale's. Stroke for stroke, she matched Shelby's. They walked into Pasquale's. They were early and the only ones there. "Good morning," Henri said. "I hope you want to sell those furs. I'm Henri Pasquale."

"Good morning, Monsieur. I am Shelby Martin and I think you already know Apona."

"Oh yes, she makes fine baskets that I buy. Good morning, Apona."

"Monsieur Pasquale."

"Why don't we take these out back so we can have a good look at them?"

Pasquale undid the bundle and sorted the species on a long table.

"My, these are fine looking pelts. Especially the beaver."

"These five are over eighty inches and the rest are between seventy and eighty."

"Beaver prices went up a little after all the snow we had. Trappers were very limited. For the five over eighty, I'll give $30 each, and $25 for the others. Mink stayed at $40, martin went to $10, fox went to $25, otter went way up to $50, lynx up to $55 and fisher stayed the same. What about the castors, Monsieur Martin?"

"I use them for lure and had too few left to bother with."

"Okay, I bring the total to $1091.00."

"Make it $1100.00 even."

Pasquale paused only momentarily and then said, "I can do that."

"In US dollars."

"I can do that, also."

"Let us look around before you give me the money."

"Most certainly, Monsieur."

"Would you by any chance have any fresh meat?"

"Just by chance I purchased two pigs yesterday. They are hanging up in the basement where it is cool."

"Are they whole pigs or quartered?"

"Whole."

"I would like to look at them."

They followed Pasquale to the basement.

"How much for the biggest one?"

"Forty dollars."

"Thirty-five." Then, "US dollars. Can you wrap this?"

"I can with burlap." Shelby helped him wrap it and then he carried it down to the canoe. "Are you sure you don't want me to help you carry it to the canoe."

"No problem, Monsieur Pasquale."

Apona was smiling. Pasquale said to Apona, "He reminds me of Marquis. I was only a boy then. But I do remember him."

Shelby came back inside, "Is there anything you would like, Apona?"

"Yes, long-john."

"You heard her, Pasquale. Do you have any that will fit her?"

"I have several ladies long-johns. If you'd follow me."

"These are silk long-johns and they come all the way from India. These all have an elastic band around the waist so let me see," he picked out four. "These will fit Apona."

"Apona, take the two you want."

"Black and red."

"Do you have any that would fit me, Pasquale?"

"Yes, on the shelf behind you."

He picked out a black and a red pair also.

"Will there be anything else?"

"Yes, a money belt if you have one. I have a long ways to travel."

"Yes, I carry those. You would be surprised how popular these are with people who travel a lot.

"Anything else?"

"No."

"The long-johns are expensive, $5 each, that's $20, $35 for the pig and $3 for the money belt. That's $63. I owe you $1037.00."

Pasquale counted it out and handed the money to Shelby, who lifted his shirt. "Apona can you put this around me?" After she had fastened the two ends she hugged him and pressed her body up against his backside. Shelby didn't object. In fact it felt very good.

"I like your prices, Monsieur. Oh! Shoot, I forgot. Do you buy gold?"

"I do. Do you have some to sell?"

Shelby removed the pouch from his pocket and gave it to Pasquale.

He emptied the contents in his hand. "These are nice nuggets. I have a scale in my office. This way."

Shelby and Apona followed him.

"Hmm, you have eleven and a half ounces. Gold is selling for $20.76 per ounce now. I have to make a profit that comes to $238.74. I'll give you $220.00."

"Okay."

"Where did you find this?"

"On my own land."

Shelby put that in the money belt, too. Now he had $1257.00.

"Next year, Monsieur Pasquale, and thank you."

* * * *

People in the village saw Shelby carrying something and all had gathered at the cooking fire. "What you bring?" Ranibir asked.

"A pig to roast, and before the day gets any warmer, we should start roasting it now, so the meat doesn't spoil. The hide will have to come off first, though."

Ranibir directed three of the men to skin it and then to put it on a spit to roast. A pig that big would take the rest of the day and night to cook.

Apona took her package of long-johns to the lodge she had shared with Shelby.

"Shelby," Chief Ranibir said, "come with me. We talk. Let women cook pig."

Shelby followed Ranibir into his lodge. When Apona tried to follow, Ranibir said, "You stay. Me and Shelby talk."

Apona joined the other women at the fire. "Apona—I think you like this man," Sopi said.

"I do, Mother, like I already belong to him."

"He good man, daughter. You cannot have mate for another year. Maybe Shelby forget you, not come back."

"He come back, Mother. I know."

"You remind me so much of the man we call Marquis. That was not his name. When he fought with bear he lost his memory, who he was. My sister, Helena, nursed him back to health. Day and night. She in love with this man even though he still sleep.

"They mated and lived here with the people for fifteen seasons. He wanted to discover who he was before bear. They had daughter, Little Flower. In canoe they went back where he fight bear and his old camp. He made a wikitup before bear. Little Flower was bad sick. They canoed down river and found help for Little Flower, but had to travel to a place called Bethel, where Marquis lived before bear. He met wife he had then and all his memory returned.

"He, Helena and Little Flower stayed in Bethel. Have farm now. In warm time of summer each year they return to village."

"That answers many questions I had, Ranibir. What was his name before the bear?"

"Langdon, Langdon MacBayne."

"Not so many people here in the village now. White man is crowding us. Though we have friends in white man's Megantic. My people see pictures in newspapers and in Megantic of White Man's World, some want this life, too. They leave. My sister, Helena, left with Marquis. My daughter, Apona, will leave with you. Not now, too young. Next year know she go away with you. I know you give her good home and love her. Some of our people have gone to live in St. Francis. In few years no more people here on Lac Megantic. This is sad. My father, Piopolis, knew this. He and I talked many times of this. When all people gone, we be no more."

Shelby could tell the future was really bothering Ranibir. But there wasn't much he could do about it. "It is sad, Ranibir, and I think you are right, someday your people will be no more. Things change, Ranibir, and if we do not change with them we'll die away. Your people may all leave someday, Ranibir, but each one of them will have the memories of this village. You will always be remembered. So even when things do change, your people will still have their memories and stories to pass along."

"You are correct, of course. Enough of this talk. You and Apona go walk, be together."

As soon as Apona saw her father and Shelby leave the lodge she ran up to Shelby. He watched her running over to him and began smiling. She stopped in front of him. "What you so happy about?"

"I was happy seeing you run towards me. Come, your father said to go for a walk."

* * * *

While Shelby and Apona were walking, Sopi asked her husband, "Husband, what you and Shelby talk about? You talked long time."

"About what worries me so much. Our people leaving and

losing way of life."

"You worry too much about this, that you not going to change." Then on a different note she said, "You like Shelby."

"He is good man."

"Yes, he is. Apona now already in love. I think he always protect our daughter."

"Yes, you are right. This big comfort knowing Shelby is so good man. If she was year older I would let him have her now."

"I think good to wait year. Let hearts burn with fire for each other or cool like snow."

"You are always so wise, Sopi."

"Where did Apona and Shelby go?"

"I told him to take her for walk."

Apona took Shelby for a walk along a trail that the villagers used often that went to Lac des Jones. "Any fish in this lake?"

"Maybe sometimes. We don't net fish here. We hunt for frogs and turtles here. Do you like eat frogs?"

"Yes, I have a place where I live with many frogs. They are very good eating. I have never eaten turtle."

"Maybe sometime."

She led him down to a mossy sunny spot near the peninsula. He sat down and leaned back against a tree and Apona sat between his legs and leaned back against him. They remained like that for a long time without talking.

"Apona, I need to lay down. I didn't sleep much last night."

"Why?"

"There were many things going through my head last night."

"What things?"

"You, for one. I have never known anyone like you."

"How do you mean?

"It's like we have known each other for a long time. You are a beautiful woman and you have so much energy and you are always smiling and happy. You are like a breath of spring air, after a long cold winter. Do you understand this?"

"Yes."

"To me you are a combination of a delicate butterfly and a beautiful white water lily. Do you know what a water lily is?"

"Yes; they are very pretty."

"You do understand. This is you, and when I look at you I see a white water lily flower and a butterfly. This I was thinking about all night. That, and who or what is Kalipona."

Apona moved so Shelby could lie down. She lay beside him and rested her head on his chest. He put his arm around her. It wasn't long and they both were asleep.

They slept for two hours and were woken by loons calling back and forth on the lake. Apona woke first but she didn't move. She didn't want this moment to end. But he was also hearing the loons. When he did awaken she rolled over and lay on top of him. And she kissed him with real passion. He hugged her and kissed her with as much passion.

Eventually they had to get up and head back. When they were back in the village no one took any particular notice that they had been gone for so long.

"Apona, I need you help with cooking."

"Okay, Shelby I noticed when we woke up you need a bath. Go wash up in the lake while I help with food."

The water was even colder than he thought it would be. He managed to wash up and go under to rinse the soap off. He dressed then shaved. Many of the children were curious. They had only ever seen one other man shave—Marquis.

"I need to wash your clothes tomorrow," Apona said.

Caponi was feeling better. His face was not as swollen and he still had difficulty taking a deep breath. Dr. Trumble had left a little laudanum for him with Sopi. There was enough for tonight and in the morning. He hoped the two brothers were hurting worse. He knew, as did many of the people in the village, that if it had not been for Shelby, the brothers probably would have killed him and his sister after they were done with her.

"Ranibir."

"Yes."

"Ranibir, I feel I should help watch the pig roast tonight. I would like to help."

"Okay, Shelby. Good you have asked to help. Someone will watch the pig roast after you. So you can get some sleep."

Everyone had returned to their lodges for the night; Shelby sat alone watching the fire and occasionally turning the pig.

Apona picked up a blanket and started to leave her mother's lodge. "Where are you going, daughter?" Sopi asked.

"I will sit with Shelby and keep him company," she said and left.

"Does your daughter remind you of someone, husband?" Sopi asked.

"Yes, Helena. Same spirit. This is good, Sopi. She knows what she wants and not like a fish swimming in circles in a bowl. She has determination."

"I know, my husband. I sometimes wish we were young again like she is."

"Come here, wife, and for a few minutes, I'll make your dream come true."

"It has been too long, husband. Let me drink some white turtlehead tea first."

Apona sat down on a log with Shelby and wrapped the blanket around them both. "It is going to be cold tonight."

"Not now," he said. "I was hoping you would join me."

"The meat smells good. Making me hungry."

"Me, too. Have you ever had pork roasted like this?"

"What is pork?"

"The meat on the hog, or pig, is called pork. If you smoke it, it becomes ham and bacon."

"I have eaten ham and bacon before, but not pork."

"Then you are in for a real treat tomorrow. It is so good."

125

Every few minutes he would have to get up and turn the spit. He broke off a piece of crispy fat and gave half of it to Apona.

"Oh, wow, this is good. I now know I have never eaten pork."

"It is good," he said, as he finished chewing his piece.

Around midnight, Kuna and his wife, Lina, took Shelby and Apona's place and they went to Sopi's lodge.

We must be quiet, do not want to wake mother and father."

Sopi had arranged their beds on opposite sides of the lodge with the fire between them. Apona put the two beds side by each and put two sticks of dry wood on the fire and then undressed. "Take all of clothes off, Shelby." Sopi was awake now and watching.

"Put red long-john on, I wear my red long-john." Sopi had no idea what they were wearing, and she also noticed that they crawled into separate blankets.

Apona slid over so she could put her arm around Shelby and he put his arm around her. Sopi smiled to herself and went back to sleep. Oh, what she wouldn't give to be young again.

* * * *

Ranibir and Sopi were the first to awaken. Shelby still had his arm around her. They dressed and Sopi woke Apona. "Come, you need to get up," and she went outside.

When Shelby and Apona went outside almost everyone was gathered around the fire. The meat was cooked and Sopi and two other women were beginning to fill plates. "You go sit somewhere, Shelby, and I will bring our plates over."

A few minutes later she came over with two heaping plates of roast pork. Shelby took one bite and exclaimed, "This is even better than I remember."

"I have never tasted food so juicy and good," Apona said.

There was very little conversation as the whole village was

busy eating.

Afterwards the leftover meat went into large pans with covers and everything else, bones and all, went into another pot for a stew. Potatoes and mushrooms would be added.

While the women were doing this, Ranibir said, "Shelby, walk with me."

They strolled along the path that went out to the road where Apona and Caponi had been attacked. "Shelby, among our people, and I'm talking about other nations as well, we all have runners that go to another village with news of their area, and then bring news back that they were told. Some of these stories have had me suspicious of all white men. After knowing Marquis and you, and there are some others in Megantic who treat us with respect, I thought all white men were evil. I now must admit I have been wrong. Just as there are good and bad natives, there are good and bad white men.

"Someday I hope we can all live as brothers and not always be suspicious of each other."

"I couldn't agree with you more."

"Where you live, Shelby, are there many people?"

"No, I am a trapper, Ranibir, and I have a log cabin in the wilderness a day and a half from any people."

"You like living alone like this?"

"I like trapping and where I live—and maybe next year, if you'll allow Apona to marry me, we will live and work together."

There, it was out there. How he felt about Apona.

"I approve of you, Shelby, and next year if Apona still wants you, you can have her."

"My love for Apona will not change, Ranibir."

"I know."

Ranibir told Sopi about what he and Shelby talked about concerning their daughter. "You are not to say anything to Apona, woman. We will see if he is good to his word without building up hope in Apona and then he doesn't keep his word."

The days that followed, Shelby and Apona grew even closer together. You didn't see one without the other. The day before the brother's trial, Shelby talked with Caponi. "Are you going to be able to travel in the canoe to Megantic tomorrow, Caponi?" Shelby asked.

"Yes, but I will not be able to help you paddle."

"That is okay brother. I will paddle," Apona said.

* * * *

Caponi was able to walk on his own to the canoe, but Shelby had to lift him into it. He sat on a cushion of blankets and leaned back against the thwart.

It was a short walk from the wharfs in Megantic to the courthouse. The brothers were already there with their attorney. Constable Duguay and Dr. Trumble were there if needed.

Judge Norman Hardcore called open the session. He would also be the prosecutor in this case. "Griswald and Gunther Macy, you both have been charged with rape and assault and battery. These are serious charges. Are you ready for trial, Mr. Talford?"

"Yes, Your Honor."

"As the Province of Quebec's first witness, I call Caponi to the stand." He had to have help to stand. He was sworn in and was seated.

"Are you going to be okay, Caponi?"

"With help, yes, Your Honor."

"I understand you were with your sister, Apona, that morning. Is that so?"

"Yes."

"What were you doing?"

"We were picking fiddleheads for the village."

"What happened next?"

"We had only started to pick fiddleheads when those two," and he pointed to the two brothers, "came at us. The biggest of the two grabbed Apona and the other began beating me."

128

"What else?"

"I was beaten very bad and I hurt a lot. I could not see my sister, but I could hear her screaming."

"What happened next?"

"Someone grabbed the brother that was beating me and picked him up and threw him into a tree. Not the one with the scratches on both sides of his face—the other one, with broken nose and shoulder in cast."

Mr. Talford stood up and said, "Your Honor, I would like to ask Caponi some questions."

"Sit down, Mr. Talford. You'll have your chance to ask your questions, but not until I am through. Is that clear, Mr. Talford? If it isn't, you'll be defending those two through cell bars. Is that understood?"

Talford didn't answer, but he did sit down.

"Now I'll call Shelby Martin to the stand. Hmm, you're taller than either of the brothers but they are bigger than you. Did you have any help with them?"

"No, Your Honor."

"Hmm. You did all this damage to both of them? What did they do to you?"

"Nothing, Your Honor."

"Let me see your hands. Okay, turn them over. Hmm, no bruises or skun knuckles. Did you hit them with your closed fist?"

"Yes, when I hit Gunther in the ribs and his brother on the collar bone."

"What did you do to his arm?"

"I broke it over my knee."

"I surely wouldn't want you mad at me. What were you doing there that morning?"

"I was on my way to Pasquale's to sell my fur when I heard a woman screaming. I had a heavy bundle of fur pelts on my back and I took it off. Gunther was still beating on Caponi, so

I picked him up and threw him into a spruce tree. The woman was still screaming. I saw Griswald rip her clothes off and strike her in the face several times. He had taken his pants down and he was lying on top of Apona. She scratched his face and he slapped her again. In all appearances, it looked to me like he was raping her."

"What did you do then?"

"I grabbed him by the hair and lifted him off her and threw him."

"And then?"

"Gunther had gotten to his feet and was charging towards me."

"What did you do?"

"I used the palm of my hand and hit him on the end of his nose. He fell backwards. By now, Griswald was up and charging at me. I tripped him and he fell. Then both brothers came charging at me and I charged between them and put out both arms and caught them both in the throat. Griswald stood up first and came at me again. This is when I broke his arm over my knee. He went down screaming.

"By now Gunther was coming at me again and I hit him in the side and he went down screaming.

"Griswald stood up with a piece of wood in his good hand and he was coming at me. I side stepped and smashed my fist down on his collar bone. He went down screaming and this time they both stayed down.

"Apona was with her brother and I gave her my shirt to wear. I bandaged Caponi the best I could and I had to carry him back to the village."

"It's amazing that one man could do so much damage to two brothers that must outweigh you by fifty or sixty pounds.

"You're excused. Now I'd like to hear from Apona."

"Did you know these two brothers before this happened?"

"No."

"Had you ever seen them before?"

"No."

"Did Griswald hit you with his fist or open hand?"

"He slapped me several times."

"You understand I have to ask this next question."

She interrupted him and said, "You want to know if he was inside me?"

"Yes, you understand."

"I fight him pretty good. He didn't get in me. He tried. May I say something else?"

"Certainly."

"I heard them talking about they would take turns with me. Over and over and then kill my brother and me."

"Thank you, Apona. You are excused."

"I call now Dr. Trumble."

"Dr. Trumble, will you describe the injuries to all three."

"Caponi had been hit repeatedly in the face with fists and he was either hit in the ribs or kicked, and two ribs were broken.

"Gunther Macy had a broken nose and two broken ribs. Griswald Macy had a broken right arm and the right side of his collar bone."

"The injuries you have described on the brothers—could you say they were applied in anger?"

"In my professional opinion, no. If in anger, Mr. Shelby would have given them much worse. As it was, he stopped when the brothers quit fighting."

"Thank you, Dr. Trumble, that's all. Mr. Talford, after hearing the testimonies are you going to put forward a defense?"

"No, Your Honor."

"I didn't think so. The defendants will stand." They did. "The court finds you both guilty of rape and of assault and battery, and I believe what Ms. Apona said. There is no doubt in my mind you would have killed them both. I sentence you both to life in prison, and twenty of those years to hard labor. Case closed. Constable Duguay, you will escort these two out of here.

"Shelby Martin, please remain seated."

After everyone else had left Judge Hardcore said, "You did an excellent job testifying."

"Thank you, Your Honor."

"Have you ever thought about becoming a law enforcement officer?"

"No, sir, I haven't."

"You would make a good one. And thank you for what you did. I'm quite fond of Ranibir's people. Tell him I said hello."

"I will, Your Honor."

Shelby joined the others outside. He looked at Caponi and Apona and said, "Let's go home."

* * * *

Apona was real quiet the rest of the afternoon. She and Shelby went for a walk out to Lac des Jones and sat on the moss. "Why have you been so quiet, Apona?"

"It is finally over and behind me. And now you must leave," and she broke down and buried her face in his chest and cried.

"We knew this day was coming. I will be back next year. I promise."

Eventually they walked back to the village. While eating that evening, Apona was picking at her food, not really hungry, and her mother gave her some tea.

"Drink all tea, Apona. Good for you." She did and gave the cup back to her mother.

"What was that?" Shelby asked.

"Mother has been after me to drink this tea. When I asked why, she only said, it was good for me. It is very bitter."

Ranibir came over and sat down with them. "You will be leaving soon?" he asked.

"Yes. There is a stagecoach that arrives in Coburn Gore tomorrow and leaves at 7 o'clock the next morning. I must be on the stagecoach then. I hate to leave, but I have much work to do at my cabin this summer before it is too cold."

"What is this 7 o'clock, Shelby?" Ranibir asked.

Shelby pulled out his pocket watch and explained how the day was divided into twenty-four equal parts. And he showed him where the two hands would be at 7 o'clock.

"Here, Ranibir, I would like you to take this."

Ranibir didn't want to refuse. He really wanted the watch. He only nodded his head and walked off.

"That was a great gift, Shelby."

Not one person had mentioned anything about the trial once they were told the outcome. No one was dwelling on it any longer. Not even Apona.

When Apona and Shelby followed Ranibir and Sopi to their lodge, Sopi stopped them and said, "No, not tonight. You two take the other lodge. And Apona, you need to drink another cup of tea and another after you wake up in the morning."

When they entered the lodge, a fire was burning and the bed had been made. One bed not two separate beds. Without saying a word they both knew what this meant. They looked at each other in the fire light and they both were grinning.

She undid her clothes and let them fall. Then she undressed Shelby. Then they stood there hugging each other.

"Apona, I love you and I wish this was next year already."

"I love you, Shelby, and I, too, wish this was next year."

They lay down on the blankets. They did a lot of looking, exploring, touching and loving.

As the village was wakening and sunshine was trying to filter through the treetops, Shelby and Apona were still awake. They had no choice; they had to get up. Once outside, Apona went to help her mother prepare food.

"Daughter, you have a happy glow around you."

Chapter 8

Tomorrow came and Shelby had five miles he had to walk to the border. The stagecoach would leave at 7 o'clock, so he had to leave at 5 o'clock. He didn't want to miss the stage.

Apona wanted to walk with him as far as Woburn, but he said, "No, Apona. I want to remember you here safe in the village and not have to worry if you made it back. I promise, I will be here next year and then when I leave, you will be with me."

The sun was just bracing the spring time sounds of birds looking for a mate. As he walked he refused to think about leaving Apona behind, but instead every second that passed was bringing him closer to returning. This kept him from being sad.

At the border cabin, "Where have you been, Mr. Martin?"

"I had fur to sell at Pasquale's and I had to testify against the Macy brothers in court. That delayed my return."

He was allowed to pass and the stagecoach to Flagstaff was waiting. He was the only passenger and he was able to nap on the way.

He was missing Apona, but he would be glad to get home and start the root cellar and shed.

In the nine days that he had been away, most of the road had been graded and the coach pulled into the station in Flagstaff at noon. Before going to the farm, he stopped at Adalbert's store. "Mr. Adalbert, will you have my order ready by 2 o'clock?"

"Yes."

He had to get some boards at the mill too, so he only had time to say hello to his mother, brother and sister. He decided not to say anything about Apona and the village for now, nor anything about the brothers.

By 2:30 p.m. he had his canoe loaded with two wicker rocking chairs tied on top of his load. He was loaded heavy and he knew it probably would be dark by the time he was home.

He canoed downstream as if there was a real emergency. He tied up at his wharf a half hour before dark. None of the nail boards showed any signs that a bear or varmint had stepped on them. He unloaded the canoe. The food he had left for Mr. Mouse was gone. He wondered if he would show. For now he left the food stores inside. By the time he had the canoe pulled ashore and turned over he was tired and ready for bed.

* * * *

He was only a day digging a hole to build the root cellar in and he also had to dig a trench for the entry to the door. He was another day cutting and peeling enough cedar trees to build it. At the end of the week it was complete, with a vent in the top and two doors a foot apart. It was cool inside. He wished he had some ice to put in it. Oh well, next year before he traveled north. Yes, north to see his beloved.

He still needed to backfill it and he had a lot of sandy soil leftover. He needed a cart to haul the sand off and a cart would be handy for bringing firewood back to the cabin. So another trip to town was needed. While he was carrying the canoe over to the portage, he saw an idea in his head that made sense.

He first stopped at the blacksmith shop and told Carl what he wanted for a cart. "I want two wheels, Carl, to make it more stable."

"I have something new, Shelby, you might be interested in—a solid rubber tire."

"Okay, sounds good to me."

"What are you going to haul, Shelby, an elephant?"

"No, just firewood and sand. Can you have it ready by mid-afternoon?"

"Sure, this will be easy to build."

From there he went to the bank and deposited his money. He didn't have time when he was in town earlier.

"Mr. Martin you have $4795.10 in your account."

"Thank you."

He went to the mill and Charles Eustis already had an eighteen foot canoe just like the one Shelby had ordered earlier, with two more paddles. He was tired of carrying the canoe twice across the portage every time he came to town. He now could leave the second canoe at the portage and he would only have to carry his supplies across. That is, of course, after this trip.

He purchased almost a canoe full of food supplies, now that the root cellar was done. He also bought another pocket watch and a wind-up clock for the cabin. It was time to go home.

It wasn't an easy trip down river towing a canoe behind him.

He left the canoe turned over, back away from the river. Later he would chain it with a lock to a tree.

He was home a half hour before dark. He had time to put the food in the root cellar.

Between making shelves and two doors for the root cellar, he had used up his boards. Before he'd make another trip to town, he would do what he could on the shed. But first he had to catch some brook trout.

With these two projects he was as busy as he was last year building the cabin. But it would slow once he had the shed up.

When he had all the fish he wanted, he began cutting spruce and fir trees out back and peeling in the bark before he dragged them back. In two more weeks he was ready for another trip to town. He would use the window on that end of the cabin for the storage part of his shed and he would make a door entrance using the space where the window had been. He had enough boards left to box in the window frame. He wouldn't move it until he had the shed roof on and closed in. This time he didn't have to carry his canoe across the portage. "I should have thought of this before now. This is so much easier."

He bought sixteen more boards, two more kerosene lanterns, fuel and food supplies, and a short chain and padlock to secure his canoe at the portage.

He was back well before sunset because he had one less trip to make across the portage.

He wanted to leave one lantern in the root cellar so he wouldn't have to be carrying one back and forth all the time, and one in the storage part of the shed which would be closed in.

He didn't have quite enough boards to close in the shed roof. And he still had doors to make and a wall between the storage shed and woodshed. The woodshed floor was left dirt.

He picked up sixteen more boards, and at Adalbert's store he found something new to cover the roof. "This is rolled, asphalt-based roofing paper, Shelby. It is waterproof and would be ideal for what you need."

"I'll need four rolls and nails."

By the middle of July he had the shed done—both sides, window and doors.

Now he had to build a smoker. That evening he sat out on the porch in a wicker rocker. The loons came back, and for a while they stayed on the opposite side of the river watching and then they returned downstream.

As he rocked back and forth he began thinking of Apona—again. *How she has illuminated my life.* Every day that went by was one day closer to seeing her again.

When he awoke in the morning, he had his answer for a smokehouse. The old teepee smokehouse really worked good, but he was never able to get rid of the smell. He would build the new one from sawn boards and this would require another trip to town.

There was enough roofing leftover from the shed to cover the top of the smokehouse. Then he wrapped chicken wire two courses around it, just to make sure animals wouldn't be able to claw through.

There, his projects were done for this summer. Just then a buck deer stuck his head out of the bushes across the river. He got his rifle and leaned up against the door jamb.

Shelby whistled and the deer lifted his head and Shelby pulled the trigger and the deer went down. He dressed it off over there and washed it out in the river before bringing it across.

He hung it up in the woodshed and skun it while it was still warm.

It was early to be shooting a deer, he knew. In the morning he started a fire in the smokehouse. He would hang some in the root cellar where it was cool and he would smoke cure the rest.

Fresh liver with potatoes and onions was a nice treat. He wished he knew how to make biscuits.

His building done, he still had the sand to haul off and firewood. He was surprised how well the two wheeled cart worked and how much he was able to haul with it. He wasn't long cleaning up all of the sand.

The wooden poles that made up the teepee smoker, he blocked up for firewood and left it in a pile outside to get rid of the smell.

With the two wheels on the cart, he could pile the wood up just above the side boards. This was going to be so much easier and faster. In two weeks he had all of the wood he would need and he still had the pile from the teepee. That represented a lot of wood.

Even on the hottest days of August, it was too cool in the root cellar to stay for long without a jacket.

He had some time for himself now, and he walked out to Gold Brook, as he was calling the stream.

There were a few nuggets sitting on top of the sand and he

picked these up. Just for the heck of it, he reached down into the stream bottom and brought out a handful of sand. There were two nuggets. That was good for now. He put those few away inside.

He knew he was going to have to make two more trips to town, so he left the next morning. He wanted a few more boards, a copper canner and a wash tub. A couple more towels, wash clothes, soap and, of course, food and a calendar and newspapers.

He was intending to can the rest of the deer in the root cellar before it spoiled. The smoked meat was hanging inside the cellar.

It rained for the next two days, so he canned what meat he had. He got five quarts. He was hoping to get another deer during open season. And he planned on canning much of his beaver meat.

He made his second trip the following week and this time he visited his mother before returning home. Not much had changed at the farm.

He only had four more boards this trip and a canoe full of food, some winter clothing and reading material. He was all set for winter. "I'll be back in the spring, Mom," and he kissed her cheek.

"Be careful, son."

"I will."

* * * *

Two weeks before he started trapping, he filled his packbasket. He made covey sets and leaning tree sets, but only hung up traps in the trees. At the large marsh, the beaver dam at the outlet was even bigger now and he found another smaller flowage on the inlet stream. "This is really looking good." He had made nine sets plus what he would set on the dams.

One thing he had wanted to get this year was a bigger packbasket. Well, he forgot, and he wasn't going to make a special trip out.

He probably had enough fish heads for bait to get him started, but he caught a few more to smoke cure. He had to have something to do for two weeks.

When he had more than enough fish heads, he started dropping them in the water by his wharf. One evening a mink climbed upon the wharf carrying a fish head in its mouth. He sat on the wharf while he ate it and then dived into the water for another.

In all of his travels during the summer, he had been looking at mud flats for sign of wolves. He hadn't seen any. He hoped they had left the area.

He was better prepared this year going into winter with more food and a secure place to keep it. To be on the safe side, he had even nailed on some chicken wire to the outer root cellar door.

Most people finding gold as easily as he had would have gone crazy. For Shelby it was a secure feeling, but he was more interested in the trapping. He seldom thought about the gold.

One evening while sitting inside because of rain, he made an accounting of how much money he had spent that summer and how much was left in his bank account. Without adding in the interest earned he should have about $4580.00.

* * * *

The day finally came when he could start trapping. He crossed the river in his canoe at daylight. His first set was a dirt hole set for fox. Since he had seen several fox there while sitting on the porch.

Next was a brush thicket, like he had set in the blackberry bushes. There were deer tracks in his trapline trail.

The river made a bend and his trail was close. He made a water set for otter. The sky had cleared and even though the sun was out bright, the air was cool. That was alright with him.

His trail veered to the left and away from the river following the outlet stream from the beaver flowage; he made another water set for otter and fifty feet up the hill he made a stone covey set.

Then halfway from there to the flowage, he made a leaning tree set.

Then, the first beaver dam. The dam was long enough so he made three trough sets. And across the outlet about one hundred feet, he found an abandoned old fox den. While he was making this set, he heard two of the dam traps go off and the beaver splashing in the water. Then the third trap.

Back at the dam he pulled in three super large beaver. He was too excited to stop and take the time to cook some beaver meat. The pond had gone quiet and he moved on.

Halfway to the next flowage on the edge of the marsh, he made another leaning tree set. Then down to the dam. Here he made only two trough sets.

Everything was quiet so he moved on to where his trail turned sharply north and there he made another leaning tree set.

The next two along the side of Basin Ridge, he made one hollow log set and a covey in the roots of a large rock maple tree.

Then his trail turned west towards the river and he made one more land set in front of a large rock. Now home. He had thirteen land sets and five trough sets.

It was just getting dark. He started a fire in the cookstove only, and then put the three beaver on drying boards. He kept one hind leg of the beaver for supper and put the others in the root cellar.

Fresh beaver meat fried with onions and potatoes was a meal fit for a king. He cleaned up and went to bed.

The wind started to blow, but by morning it had blown itself out. The air was cooler, though.

As he left to tend his traps, he knew this would be an easier day. All of his traps were set. All he might have to do is reset some of the traps.

The first two traps were empty and the third one, a water set, held an angry large otter. He was a while getting into position to shoot it in the ear. The next set, also a water set, held another angry otter and about the size of the first one. Both otters were males.

There was nothing in the other traps until the first beaver dam. There he had two super large beaver.

And the trap between the flowages was empty and one super large beaver in the second flowage. And that's all there was for fur that day. With the absence of any land fur, he began to wonder if wolves had moved back into the area.

Three super large beaver and two otter represented a good day's work, but he was puzzled why there were no land animals.

He had finished putting those three beaver on drying boards and the two otters on stretchers. Then curiosity made him wander out to look at Gold Brook. There was only one visible nugget lying on top of the sandy bottom. He reached in to the sandy bottom where the water bubbled out from under a ledge rock. At first he brought nothing back. Then after a few handfuls of sand, he brought up half of a handful of nuggets. This spot seemed to be the repository for the nuggets.

He reached down again trying to get up and under the ledge rock and he again brought out an almost handful of nuggets, after letting the sand wash between his fingers. He now had a little more than last year and that was enough. Too much at any one time might alert too many people.

He canned what beaver he had and filled five canning jars.

The next day was almost a repeat of the previous day except he only caught beaver. Two super large and an extra-large from the second pond. He did find a second beaver house at the first pond and it was much larger than the other one. He knew now that this one pond probably held a dozen beaver or more. But he would not take them all.

The next day he had nothing at all and no traps had been sprung. The next day he changed positions of the troughs and filled in the old ones and used more castor scent on all five sets.

The following day he had five beaver, two super large and three extra-large, but no land animals.

It went like this for a week. Then one morning there was an inch of new snow on the ground and it seemed the fur bearers literally came out of the woodwork. By the end of that day, he had picked up three martin, one fox, two mink, a bobcat in one of the trough sets on the second dam and two fisher cats. But no beaver. Still, all in all, a good day.

He was also encouraged by the amount of deer coming and going from the marsh.

Another week passed and he had six more beaver. One super large and five extra-large. Nineteen beaver from the two flowages and no small ones yet.

He also caught another fox, across from the cabin, one more mink, two more bobcats and two martin.

He caught two more extra-large beaver and one small one. He pulled all of his beaver traps.

By the end of trapping that season he had picked up seven more martin, two more fisher and one lynx. He was satisfied with his catch. He had no doubt but what he could certainly catch more, but he saw no point in being greedy. That made him fifty pieces for the season. But he wasn't sure if he'd sell the small beaver, or it might reduce the price on beaver. He also now had ten pounds of castor he would also sell along with his fur.

After checking his calendar, he saw there were only two days left to get a deer. He would put a concentrated effort to get one.

He canned more of the beaver meat and also what deer meat was still hanging in the root cellar.

This year all of his fur was safely hanging in the enclosed shed and his food stores were well protected in the root cellar.

* * * *

After a big breakfast, he crossed to the other side of the river with his .30-30 rifle. There were fresh deer tracks in the snow in his trapline trail. There was only one big track, which was probably a buck following a bunch of does. He was also seeing many martin and fisher cat tracks. He was happy to see he had not over-trapped.

Up near Long Falls where his trail turned some to the left the deer tracks left his trail and headed for the marsh. He continued following his trail. The wind, what little there was, was coming from the north and now the deer had turned into the wind. He followed his trail around to the other side of the marsh where he had seen the deer tracks coming and going from the marsh. This would be a good place to stand and watch.

While he was standing he happened to remember the canoe at the portage needed to be put on a rack. He would do that soon.

After standing—sitting—there for two hours, the wind shifted directions and was now coming out of the east. This usually meant a storm was coming.

Down the trail he saw two martins chasing each other from the hardwoods down into the marsh. Just then, he could see a set of antlers sticking above a clump of short fir trees. The deer's head was tilted back and the buck was sniffing the air. He probably had caught a little of his scent.

Shelby waited for him to come into the open. And he did, looking downhill and away from him. He hit the deer behind the right ear and he went down.

He left the heart and liver inside the twelve point buck and began dragging in a straight course across the marsh towards the river. The deer was heavy, well over two hundred pounds, he figured, and he had to stop occasionally and rest. *I must be getting weak.* It was almost a mile drag back to the canoe.

After hanging the deer up in the woodshed, he nailed on some chicken wire in front to keep out the scavengers. Satisfied, he took the heart and liver inside and washed them out good with water.

An hour later the storm hit, first as rain and then it changed to snow. He now was glad the deer came along when he did.

Come morning there was a foot of new snow. The sun was out and the sky was blue and the temperature stayed below freezing all day.

After breakfast he put his canoe in the water, and with just his ax he canoed up to the portage. The snow was dry and fluffy and easy to walk through.

He was surprised that up here there was ice forming along the riverbank, but not below the falls. He made quick work of making a rack for the canoe under a green stand of spruce trees and he locked it with the chain wrapped around the tree.

Back at home he put the canoe back on the rack and the paddle in the shed and he turned the pelts on the stretchers; some of the beaver pelts were dry and he took them off the boards. Then, he laid them flat on the work table so they wouldn't curl like some of them had last year.

Then he fixed himself a cup of coffee, sat in one of the rocking chairs staring out the window at winter's cold, feeling warm and comfortable. The only thing that would be better was if Apona was there with him. Next year. Oh, how he was missing her. And then—then, for no reason he could later think of, the name KALIPONA floated through his head. No image, no memory, only the name. *Why?*

That night the temperature dropped to -20⁰ by daylight. All night the sap in the fir trees was freezing and as it expanded, the bark would suddenly splinter and it would sound like a .22 gun being fired.

The river was now iced over, but probably not strong enough to stand on. He banked around the cabin and immediately he could feel the difference. For lunch that day, he fried up thick slices of bacon for a sandwich and washed it down with coffee.

* * * *

January thaw arrived on the 10th and lasted for a week. The snow settled and it was now good snowshoeing, so he took a trek out to the marsh where he had shot his deer.

He brought his summer deer hide inside to warm the hide so he could rub hemlock bark into the fleshy side to preserve it and soften the hide.

He'd let his legal deer dry a couple of more days before bringing it inside.

He cut the ragged edges off the summer hide and then spent most of that day rubbing bark on the fleshy side. When he was satisfied, he put the hide on the floor for a rug.

Two days later he did the same with his legal deer. When he put that on the floor next to the summer deer hide there was a strong difference in the color of the hair. The summer deer was more red or rust color than his legal deer. He now had three deer hide rugs covering almost half of his floor space.

Every time the wind blew that winter, it would drift the snow filling the walkway into the root cellar. His food stayed fresh inside the cellar for a long time without freezing.

The snow settled during a warm spell in the middle of March and animals began to move around. One morning he saw tracks, or better yet, a trail from the woods to his new smokehouse. Some animal had tried to claw through the door again. The smokehouse was empty, but any animal would be able to smell the lingering smell of meat. There were claw marks in the wooden door, but because of the chicken wire fencing, the door was intact.

He checked the root cellar door and the same animal had tried to claw through that door and failed. There were tracks in the snow this time and he wasn't really sure what animal it was. The tracks looked somewhat like a big cat, but still different.

This seemed like a reoccurring event each winter, and next year he would put out traps and nail boards.

Spring was coming and in another six weeks he would see Apona. His feelings for her had not changed.

* * * *

Shelby went to bed feeling good about his life on the river and thinking about how happy his life would be when Apona was here to share his life. He fell asleep in comfort, excited about seeing her again.

Before he awoke the next morning, while it was still dark, he suddenly opened his eyes to a brightly lit cabin interior, to find Kalipona standing at the foot of his bed, smiling at him, "Kalipona, you have come back."

"You remember my name," she said. "I see life here is good for you."

"Yes, I enjoy living here. Who, or what, are you?" he asked.

"There will come a day, Shelby, when you won't have to ask. You will know. Now I must leave you. You will not see me again for a while."

"Don't leave, Kalipona."

"Apona will be a good wife for you, Shelby. I will return some day. Do not forget my name," and she was gone.

When Shelby awoke later he only had a fading memory of his visit from Kalipona. He repeated her name, "Kalipona."

* * * *

Between the cabin and the river were some bare spots now, the snow on the river had melted and the snow on the cabin roof was melting fast.

"ICE! Holy cow, I almost forgot." He took his ax and started cutting out blocks close to shore where the ice was thicker. He carried six blocks of ice up. He needed sawdust to cover the ice but he didn't have any. So he cut fir boughs to cover the ice. Before the summer was over he would have to get a couple of grain bags full of sawdust from the mill.

On April 28th the river opened up with only a channel in the middle. Two days later the river was wide open. He prepared his fur pelts, shaved his beard and waited two more days to make sure there wouldn't be any ice jams on the river.

He nailed on window boards and got the nail boards from the shed. He made another nail board to put down in front of the door going from the woodshed to the enclosed shed. He also nailed boards across the root cellar door and locked the padlock. The sun was just beginning to filter through the tree tops.

He knew he would have to spend the night in the hotel, but he continued to paddle, putting his shoulder into every stroke.

He pulled his canoe ashore in the field and walked across to have breakfast with his mother.

Rebecca fried up some potatoes and ham and scrambled three eggs. "What is Raul going to do after he finishes school this year?"

"He has really changed, Shelby. He doesn't take any crap from his father. He's not as strong as you, but he is a lot like you. He made it clear to his father this spring that he was going to stay on the farm and clear more ground for cows and he was going to get paid for his work."

"That's good to hear. I'm proud of him for standing up for himself."

"Sis wants to be a nurse."

"That's grand. I think she would be a good nurse."

"Things aren't bad here now, son."

"That's good. I have to leave now, Mom. I'm going to Lac Megantic again with my fur. I'll stop when I come back."

After visiting with his mother, he stopped at Adalbert's store and gave him a list. "I'll pick these up when I come back from Megantic."

From there he went to the bank. "Mr. Edwards, do you have any idea how I would go about filing for a homestead?"

"I could help you some, Shelby, but there's a new lawyer

four doors down that could help you."

"Thank you."

Shelby found the office and entered. "Good morning, can I help you?"

"Are you Mr. Sinclare?"

"Yes."

"I'm interested in filing for a homestead. Can you help me?"

"Yes, won't you have a seat? When do you plan to settle?"

"I did, two years ago."

"Can you show me on a map?"

"Right here on the river."

"Within five years of the filing date you must show improvements. What have you there now?"

"I have a log home, shed, woodshed and a root cellar."

"Is it year round occupancy?"

"Yes."

"How in the world do you support yourself way out there?"

"I trap and I make a good living."

"The grant will be for forty-two acres."

"Can a husband and wife both file for adjoining parcels?"

"Only if she is the head of her household."

"Okay."

"There's a five dollar filing fee which has to accompany the application. Plus there'll be my fee of fifty dollars."

"When do I pay you?"

"When the homestead deed comes back."

"One more point, I'd like to have my wife's name on the application also."

"And her name?"

"Apona. We'll be back in a week to ten days, and when we are we'll stop in."

"I probably won't know anything that soon. But do stop in."

149

Next Shelby got a haircut and a shave and then went back to Adalbert's. He bought casual clothes to wear on this trip.

* * * *

The stagecoach left promptly at 7 o'clock and again this year, the road crews were grading the road. There were two passengers besides himself this year.

Near two in the afternoon, he could see the people in the village. Apona saw him and came running while shouting, "Shelby here! Shelby here!"

He stopped and took the bundle of fur off his back and Apona ran right up to him and jumped up and wrapped her legs around his waist, all the while kissing him. "I knew you would come back! I knew you would."

"There never was any question that I would. I've been dreaming about this ever since last spring. I love you, Apona."

"Did you have a good winter?" Apona asked.

"Yes, better than last year."

"Oh, what was the trouble last winter?"

"Animals got into my food and I almost starved."

"You never said anything last year, why?"

"I didn't want you to worry about me this year."

"Trapping looks good by looking at the bundle."

"Yes, it was very good."

There was a feast that night to celebrate Shelby's return. Caponi had finally healed and was laughing along with everyone without his ribs hurting.

As they were sitting together, Apona said, "You cannot sleep with me tonight. Have to wait until we are mated."

Shelby smiled and looked at her and said, "Okay."

"We sleep in lodge with my family. Our lodge to be kept special until we are together."

"When are we to be married?"

"In two days."

"That'll give us time to go to Pasquale's and sell the fur pelts, and maybe buy a pig like last year."

"That would be good.

"Oh, Shelby, I can't wait to be your wife and go home with you."

He only smiled at her and hugged her.

Before retiring for the night, Ranibir pulled Shelby aside to speak with him. "I knew you would return this year, Shelby. My daughter never doubted your love. And now I know you are sincere and I happy to give you my daughter. You will be mated after the pig celebration. Now it is time for sleep. We will speak again tomorrow."

Shelby was tired after traveling all day, so he and Apona went in the lodge to sleep. Sopi noticed that both Shelby and Apona were wearing the red long-johns. "Husband, I would like the long-john too." Shelby heard, but didn't say anything.

Shelby and Apona, in their separate beds, faced each other and fell asleep.

* * * *

"Ranibir, I will try to bring back a pig to roast like last year."

"This is good. Last year you called pig, hog."

"It means the same thing, Ranibir. Usually, Ranibir, if the pig is over one hundred twenty pounds it is called a hog. It is a play of words. They virtually mean the same."

Pasquale was pleased to see Monsieur again with so much fur. Shelby put his bundle on the table and undid the ropes. The castors were in the center of the pile. "Good, you bring de castor this year. Worth $1.50 a pound.

"European market is very good now and prices have gone up a little. The super large three dollars to thirty-three, extra-large three dollars to twenty-eight. Otter is fifty-five. Martin only a dollar to nine dollars. Fox two dollars to twenty-two.

Mink five dollars to forty-five dollars. Bobcat took big jump to fifty dollars, fisher is now twenty-five. Lynx is fifty-five and ten pounds of castor worth eleven dollars and fifty cents.

"You fur come to $1406.50. Do you have the gold this year?"

"Yes," and Shelby handed him the same small pouch, except it was heavier this year.

"This feels more gold. Let's see. Same price as last time, but now you have twenty-one ounces. This is good. I give you four hundred dollars for gold. Total fur and gold comes to $1806.50."

"Make it an even $1810.00 and we do some shopping."

"Okay, US dollars."

"Yes."

"Now what you want?"

Apona was off in another section looking at long-johns. "Monsieur, do you have gold wedding rings?"

"I have a few."

"I need one for Apona and one for me." While Shelby was looking at the rings two men came into the store. They were about Shelby's height.

"Monsieur Shelby, those two men who just came in, they are no good. They always bother women. You might want to watch Apona."

"Thank you, I will. I will be right back."

The two spotted Apona and walked over to her.

"Hey, Ralphie, ain't this some perddy squaw."

"My mouth is watering already, Percy. I sure could use a little of her."

Apona heard what they had said and she turned to look at them. She also saw Shelby standing behind them and when she started smiling, Percy said, "What's so funny squaw?"

"You turn around—you see."

Before they could turn Shelby knocked their heads together

and they both fell to the floor, still conscious.

"Now, before I let you stand up you are going to apologize to my wife for being so offensive." When they just sat there Shelby said, "Now."

"Who ta hell are you?" Ralphie asked.

"I'm the one who is going to beat both of you within an inch of your life if you do not."

"You think you can take on both of us?" Percy asked.

"That wouldn't be a problem. Men who pick on women are no better than garbage rats."

Ralphie said, "Go to hell, mister."

Shelby slapped Ralphie's face knocking him sideways. "How about you, Percy?"

"Okay, okay, mister, Ma'am, I'm sorry for offending you."

"It's your turn now, Ralphie."

When Ralphie hesitated Shelby drew back to slap him again. Ralphie put up his arms to shield his face. "Okay, okay, I'll apologize. I'm sorry."

"Oh, Ralphie, you can do better than that. Make it sound like you mean it," and he drew back to slap him.

"No, no, don't, I will. I'm sorry, Ma'am, for offending you."

"Now you two stand up and leave."

Shelby followed them outside. "You two got off easy. If I ever hear that you have insulted another woman, Indian or white, or have been mean to any of the tribal members, I will hunt you down and break both of your arms and walk you through town naked. And before you two go anywhere, take a bath. The smell of you is offensive. You two smell worse than a pig pen. Now go and remember what I said. Go!"

They did and never looked back.

Pasquale had been standing on the porch watching and now he was laughing at the two.

"Shelby, I'll never be afraid with you."

Back in the trading post, Pasquale said, "When I was only

153

a small boy a man came in here and did the same thing you just did. Marquis was his name."

"I've heard of him."

Apona went back to look at the long-johns and Shelby bought the rings and put them in his pocket. "Would you by any chance happen to have another pig?"

"Yes, one left. You want?"

"Yes, and would you wrap it for me?"

Shelby helped him to wrap it in paper. "I'll help you with this, Monsieur."

"No need. But you might steady the canoe for me."

With the pig in the canoe they went back inside.

Apona had two pairs of red long-johns. "Anything else, Monsieur?"

"Yes, how about some candy for the children. How many children, Apona?"

"Sixteen, I think."

"Give us thirty-two peppermint sticks please. Now, that's all."

"That comes to ninety-two dollars. I give you $1718.00, okay?"

"Okay." Shelby put it and the rings in his money belt.

"Will you folks be back next year?"

"Yes."

"Good, I like your fur, your gold and both are good customers."

* * * *

Men started skinning the pig as soon as they had it hanging and then it was put on the spit to roast.

When the others were taking care of the pig, Apona and Shelby were handing out peppermint sticks to the children. When they saw the peppermint their eyes were like full moons. "This was the best gift you could have given them."

"No, Apona, we. You and I, we, do things together, not just me."

"Okay, we. Now we give long-john to Ranibir and Sopi."

Sopi was ecstatic. Ever since she had seen Apona in long-johns she had wanted a pair. And now hers and Ranibir's were also red.

Ranibir put his long-johns on his bed and went outside. "Shelby, you and I talk," and he led the way down to the lakeshore.

At first neither one spoke, then Ranibir said, "Long-john will be good when in the cold. Thank you. Shelby, I still worry about my people. I know we can never go back to life before white man. I have come to accept this, but how do we fit into the white man's world?"

"I do understand your concern, Ranibir. Your people all speak French and English, plus Abenaki. That is remarkable, Ranibir. I can only speak English. Apona can read and write. Are there other people who can read and write?"

"Some. I and Sopi cannot."

"Your young people need to go to school like the white man's children do. Either that, or a teacher comes here to teach your children.

"I think what you really need, Ranibir, is a lawyer to help you."

"What is this lawyer?"

"It is a person who studies law. You know what law is right?"

"I know what law is, I do not understand all law."

"A lawyer would be like an advisor for you. You would still be chief to make the decisions for your people, but a lawyer would help you understand and could probably open a lot of doors for you and your people."

"How do I find this lawyer?"

"I have a lawyer back home. When Apona and I leave here

we have to stop and talk with this lawyer, Ron Sinclare. I will ask if he can send someone to help you."

"You will do this for my people?"

"Tomorrow, Ranibir, do I become a member of your people? Even though we may live far from here?"

"This is true. Tomorrow, we have mating before pig. Now come we talk long enough."

Ranibir stopped walking part way back to the others, turned and looked at Shelby directly in the eyes. "You come to Ranibir's people no accident. You guided here."

Shelby heard from somewhere, maybe in his head, the name KALIPONA.

Apona saw them coming back and she ran down to meet them. She took Shelby's arm and said, "Many people want to talk with you."

Apona's brother Caponi had heard his sister telling their mother about the two roughnecks at Pasquale's, and he wanted to hear all about it.

All while he was talking, Apona noticed he was not quite himself. She pulled him aside when she could and asked, "You have such a long face, Shelby. What is troubling you?"

"Remember last year I asked you if you knew someone or ever heard the name Kalipona?"

"I remember."

"When I was walking back with your father, I heard this name again."

"Did someone speak this name?"

"I don't know. It may have been in my head. But it happened, I heard it spoken."

"I don't know what to tell you, Shelby. Maybe someday you will discover and then you can tell me.

"Come, it is time to eat."

* * * *

After everybody had eaten and the food and dishes had been cleaned up, it was now time for storytelling. And the story everyone wanted to hear was Shelby's encounter with Percy and Ralphie. He asked Apona to help tell the story. She was excited. She had never been a storyteller before, only one who listened. She told her story with enthusiasm.

Because Shelby and Apona would be married the next day, they were not asked to watch over the roasting pig. The aroma of the cooking pork was wafting into every lodge.

Come morning, the pork was so near done, breakfast would be pork, but not until Shelby and Apona were mated.

Apona handed Shelby a package. "Here I would wish you to wear these clothes today. I made them for you during the winter."

He unwrapped them and held them up. Matching shirt and pants made of deer buckskin. A light tan color and not brown. "These are beautiful, Apona. Thank you."

"I made some for me too."

When the people saw Apona and Shelby emerge from the lodge they gathered and everyone was instantly quiet. Ranibir and Sopi stepped up. Ranibir said, "This man, Shelby Martin, came to our village after protecting our son and daughter. He has done much to help us. He once again saved our daughter's life yesterday.

"Apona will be protected and he will not ever travel alone again. Apona has strong spirit inside her which will light and guide the way for you both. The great goddess KALIPONA has made it so. She had guided you, Shelby, to our village and to our daughter. You being here was no accident."

Apona squeezed his hand. All the memories of Kalipona were now awakened in his mind. Everything she had said to him. Even how beautiful she was.

"Later," she whispered.

Ranibir continued. "She has opened the door for both of

you. She will not let any harm come to either of you. This is a great honor for you, my daughter and my son.

"Is there anyone here who thinks these two people should not to be joined?" Everyone was silent.

"Good, Shelby Martin you are now one of the people and husband to Apona." Shelby placed Apona's gold ring on her finger and she put his ring on his finger.

That's all there was and Ranibir had said everything that needed to be said.

Shelby and Apona were given the first bowl of roast pork. Then everyone else was served.

"You must eat fast, my husband. We need to go to our lodge. There we will remain uninterrupted all day while the people feast and celebrate."

Sopi watched as they walked hand in hand to their lodge. There was a glow surrounding them. She smiled.

They were not long taking their clothes off. "Mrs. Shelby Martin. I like how that sounds."

"So do I, my husband. Sit and I will tell you about Kalipona." They sat cross legged facing each other on their bedding.

"Kalipona is not the Great Creator, but a Goddess. She has watched over our people for a long, long time. When you first asked about her last year, I could not tell you. No one outside our village is ever told about her. Even after you first asked and knew the name I—no one could tell you. When you said her name I knew you had been visited by her and she had paved the way here for you. And when I knew you were here because of Kalipona and not an accident, I knew you and I were to mate and marry, and I fell in love with you. Not because of Kalipona, but because of who you are. Can you understand all this?"

"It seems so simple now. Yes."

"Good, because I have waited a year to feel you inside me again. We have all day and no one will come to bother us."

* * * *

The next morning everyone had pork stew with potatoes and onions. Shelby and Apona were starving. Sopi could see a glow around them, especially when they were standing close.

"When will you be leaving?" Ranibir asked.

"In four days, on Tuesday."

Shelby noticed that Ranibir didn't seem to be as worried now. He was relaxed.

Some of the men were fishing, some looking to shoot a bear and Apona and some women went to pick fiddleheads. Shelby helped a group of men with firewood.

One night while waiting for sleep Shelby said, "When we get to Flagstaff, we'll have a magistrate marry us again."

"Why again?"

"Marriage in my country is a legal contract. The magistrate will give us a paper document that he will sign and we will sign. Then we'll deposit this money in my bank account and I'll have your name added to the account also.

"Are you afraid of leaving the village?"

"No, because I will be with you, and Kalipona will watch over us."

"We will have a long walk to the border, I think we should get some better shoes for you, so you don't hurt your feet."

So they made another trip back to Pasquale's. Pasquale had exactly what she would need. A light leather shoe that was only ankle high. She tried them on and they were comfortable. "Do you have much you want to bring with you?"

"No, some clothes, quite a bit of tea that we use to keep from having babies."

"I'll have some, too; maybe we should buy a packbasket."

"No need, all these baskets you see here we make at the village. We have a packbasket to use."

* * * *

While Shelby and Ranibir talked Monday evening, Apona

packed what she would be taking with her. The tea she and her mother had been preparing for a year for her to take took up the most room. "I will miss you, Apona," Sopi said, "but you go with a good man. Kalipona brought you two together, so I know this is a good thing. I know you will always be safe."

They hugged and Apona said, "Next spring, Mother."

Ranibir was more concerned that Shelby not forget to talk with his lawyer friend, Sinclare. He had had a year to prepare for his daughter leaving.

That was their goodbyes. Early the next morning they started walking for the border, wearing their new buckskin clothes. They were quite a matching pair.

There was no problem crossing the border. The officer remembered Shelby from the previous year. The stagecoach wouldn't leave for another half hour, so they went inside and had a coffee and fresh donuts.

"These are good, Shelby. How are they called?"

"Donuts."

"Good. Do you know to make?"

"No."

"I will have to learn."

"You folks heading for Flagstaff?" a burly man asked. "Oh, is that you, Mr. Shelby? I didn't recognize you."

"Yes, Rex, it's me, and this is my wife, Apona."

"How-do, Ma'am. If you're going to Flagstaff you'd better get aboard, I'm leaving as soon as I get atop of the rig. Must leave at 7 o'clock."

They climbed aboard and no more than closed the door and the stage started.

"How long will this ride take?"

"The road is good all the way to Flagstaff; it shouldn't take maybe four hours. We'll be there before noon."

"You have never told me much about your family."

"My mother, Rebecca, one brother, Raul, who is four years

younger, and there's my sister, Sis, she is five years younger."

"Same age as me."

"Yes. I think the world of Mom and my brother and sister. When I left home two years ago there were some harsh words between me and my father. So I only visit my family when I know he won't be there."

Rex was making good time. Every half hour he would slow the teams to walk for a few minutes before resuming the pace. They arrived in Flagstaff a little after 11 o'clock.

"Thanks for the ride, Rex."

"You bet."

Rex took the mail into the station before taking care of the team. Shelby and Apona got a room at the hotel.

"Good morning, Mr. Martin," Sue Blight said. "Will you be needing a room?"

"Yes, and this is my wife, Apona."

"Pleased to meet you, Mrs. Martin."

Apona enjoyed being called Mrs. Martin.

Still dressed in their buckskins they left the hotel for the magistrate's office.

"Hello, Helen. Is the magistrate busy?"

"Yes, can I help you?"

"Yes, Apona and I married according to her customs, now we would like to be married with a license."

"Wait here I'll go ask if he can perform the ceremony."

Helen came back in five minutes and said, "You can go right in, Shelby."

Before 12 o'clock they were married with a legal marriage license.

"How about some of my mother's home cooking?"

"I'm starved."

"Me, too."

Still in their buckskins, they proudly walked, holding hands, to the farm.

"Hey, Mom!" Sis hollered.

"What?"

"You'd better come here."

"What is it, Sis?" Rebecca asked.

"I think it is Shelby, but he has a pretty woman with him."

Raul was just coming from the barn and he recognized his brother instantly. "Hello, Shelby."

"Raul, I want you to meet my wife, Apona."

"Holy-cow! Hello, Apona. Gee, Shelby, she is pretty."

Apona blushed and smiled.

"Apona, this is my mother, Rebecca, and my little sister, Sis. This is my wife, Apona."

Rebecca and Sis hugged Apona. "It is so nice to meet you, Apona. Come in. Are you hungry?"

"Starved," Apona said.

"Well, come in, come in and tell me all about your wife, Shelby, while I warm up some beef stew and biscuits."

Both Shelby and Apona told them everything about their time and life together, except for Kalipona.

"How old are you, Apona?" Sis asked.

"Seventeen."

"I'm seventeen, too," Sis said.

"Here you go, beef stew and biscuits."

"Umm, I like these biscuits." They both had two bowls of stew and two biscuits.

"When are you going back home, Shelby?" Rebecca asked.

"Tomorrow at noon. We still have many things to get at Adalbert's and some more lumber and two bags of sawdust."

"What on earth do you need the sawdust for?"

"I built a root cellar last summer and I cut ice this winter for it and the sawdust is to cover the ice.

"Raul, would you have two grain bags you'd let us have?"

"Sure."

"You're a grown man now, Raul. And, Sis, it won't be

long and you'll be quite a lady. I imagine you already turn a few heads."

When Rebecca started to pick up the used dishes and put the food away, Apona helped her.

"Maybe you two can come for breakfast in the morning. Armand will be gone by then."

"Apona is a princess." Sudden silence. "Her father, Ranibir, is chief of the Abenaki tribe in Lac Megantic. Her mother is called Sopi and I like them both very much. I have stayed at the village both years I have gone north to sell my fur and the first time I was there for two weeks. This year, ten days, and I have never seen any bickering or fighting among any of them. They live a very peaceful life. A good life.

"We'll talk more at breakfast. We must be going now. We still have business in town."

"I'll make you two apple pies and biscuits. I'm so happy to meet you, Apona, and I have never seen Shelby so happy. You are good for him."

"He is good for me, too, Rebecca."

"Please, you are my daughter-in-law now, call me Mom."

"Mom."

"Do you have a sister?" Raul asked.

"No. A brother though, and she looked at Sis. "He will be chief someday."

She hugged Apona for a long moment. "Maybe I can go back with you to your home for a few days some time," Sis said.

"We would be glad to have you," Apona said.

* * * *

They stopped first at the bank. "Mr. Edwards, we have a deposit to make."

Of the $1718.00 for fur and gold he deposited $1600.00. "And, Mr. Edwards, I would like my wife's name added to the account."

"And your name is?"

"Apona," she said.

"You now have $6215.00 in the account."

"Thank you, Mr. Edwards."

From there they went to the lawyer's office.

"Mr. Sinclare, my wife, Apona."

"How do you do, Mrs. Martin?"

"Very well, thank you."

Shelby told Sinclare about Ranibir's problem and asked if he knew of an attorney near Lac Megantic that could help.

"I do know one attorney, Henri Pardis; he already helps some Indian tribes. He lives in Saint-Cecile-de-Whitton, which is not far from Megantic. I will send a letter this afternoon and ask him to go see Chief Ranibir."

"Thank you, Mr. Sinclare," Apona said. "Chief Ranibir is my father."

"I haven't heard anything yet about your application for homestead."

"As I said, every time we are in town we will check with you."

They had one last stop, at Adalbert's. "Mrs. Adalbert, we will be needing some clothes for my wife, Apona. Two casual dresses, three pairs of pants and shirts and all the undergarments, Mrs. Adalbert. Oh, and a pair of leather boots, rubber boots and a light jacket for now. We'll get a winter coat before winter, and gloves and a lady's watch.

"Apona, while you're shopping I'm going to the mill for boards and sawdust. I'll meet you back here."

"Okay, I like this shopping."

"Good afternoon, Mr. Eustis."

"Hello, Shelby, more boards?"

"Yes, six and could I get some sawdust? I have two grain bags."

"Surely, but why?"

"To cover the ice in my root cellar."

"Good idea. Hey, it's all over town you have a beautiful wife."

"Yes, Apona."

"Where is she?"

"Mrs. Adalbert is helping with a wardrobe."

"I'd like to meet her, Shelby."

"Certainly. Next time we are in town."

"Ah, close the door would you, Shelby. No need of anyone hearing what I'm going to say. A few days ago, Shelby, there was someone here asking me if I knew an Armand Martin. I told him the only Armand I knew was Martinique. You changed your name to Martin?"

"That's what is on my birth certificate. Did this man say what he wanted?"

"He wouldn't say."

"Was he the law or something?"

"I couldn't tell you that either. He would have been between fifty-five and sixty. Well-dressed, full head of gray hair."

"What was his name?"

"Winslow."

"Where was he from?"

"He wouldn't tell me that either."

"I wonder if the law is after him for something he did before we moved here. I was only four then.

"Thank you for telling me, Mr. Eustis, I'll keep it to myself."

Shelby carried the six boards on his shoulder and grabbed the two sawdust bags in his huge left hand and walked down to the public wharf and put everything under the canoe. Then he went back to Adalbert's. Apona was all done shopping and everything was wrapped together.

"When do you need the list of things, Shelby?"

"Before noon tomorrow. I'll pay for everything then, if that's okay."

"Certainly; you are a good customer."

"I liked the clothes Mrs. Adalbert helped me to pick out."

"I'm glad."

* * * *

At breakfast the next morning, Rebecca asked, "Apona, would you rather have tea or coffee?"

"Tea."

She took a sip and said, "This is not as bitter as my tea."

"What kind of tea do you have?"

"It is made from the white turtlehead flower. We pick the blossoms and dry them and crush them into a powder."

"I have never heard of it," Rebecca said.

"Probably not," Apona said, "We drink so baby will not grow in our belly."

"Birth control, how about that, Mom. Will you show me this flower sometime?" Sis asked.

"Yes, but not until late in summer."

"Sis," her mother said.

"The flower grows in wet areas. I'm sure there must be some near the river," Apona added.

While Raul was doing chores and Apona and Sis were chatting, Shelby steered his mother into another room. "Mom, did you know there was a man inquiring about Armand Martin?"

"No, I didn't."

"Why would someone be looking for him?"

"I don't know unless it has something to do why we left Rockford in a hurry. Maybe he was in some kind of trouble and it is now catching up to him."

"Don't say anything to Raul or Sis or anyone. I wasn't supposed to say anything. But I had to know if you knew anything."

"No, I don't, and I won't."

Rebecca packed the two pies and biscuits in a box for them to take back and they said goodbye.

"I like your family, Shelby."

What Shelby had said to her about a man asking questions about Armand—Rebecca began to look back on their life before leaving Rockford. And for the first time she began to wonder if this had everything to do with them leaving Rockford in such a hurry and changing their name. *Maybe your past will catch up to you, Armand.*

* * * *

The canoe in the water and loaded they set off downstream for home. "Now we're going home, sweetheart."

"How long will it take?"

"There is one portage. With you paddling and helping to carry the portage—maybe three hours."

"Good, I can't wait. How do you say when I tingle and really want to make love with you? How do you call this?"

"It means you are horny."

"Hmm, horny. I am horny."

With Apona helping to paddle and carry over the portage, the portage took more time than canoeing. When she saw the second canoe she said, "You have second canoe, so you don't have to carry it back and forth. You think like an Indian."

Below Long Falls, "This is so beautiful through here, Shelby."

When she saw the cabin she asked, "Why boards over window and doors?"

He explained so to keep the bear from getting in. "Good idea. We had bear problem once. Then Ranibir killed it with a spear."

"I'm not so horny now. I want you to show me everything."

They unloaded the canoe first and Apona helped him to put it up on the racks. Then they carried the bags of sawdust to the root cellar. "You keep food in that?"

"Yes, wait until you feel how cool it is inside."

He opened both doors and lit the kerosene lantern so Apona

could see. "Brrr, it is cold in here. I understand why food does not spoil." She helped to empty the sawdust and spread it over the ice blocks.

"The sawdust will keep the ice from melting all summer."

"Ice will not melt?"

"Very slowly."

"You have some food in here now."

They carried everything else into the cabin for now. "This is nice, husband. And this is as much mine as it is for you?"

"Yes. Everything I have is also yours."

"This will take some time to get used to. Indian girl owning something. What behind that door?"

"Come, I'll show you. I skin my fur here and put it on stretchers."

"And that door?"

"It goes out to the woodshed. Open it."

"Nice, so you don't have to wade snow for wood."

They walked through the woodshed. "What is that little building?"

"Come, I'll show you," and he opened the door.

"Pew, I get idea. And that roll of paper?"

"Toilet paper, to wipe you clean after you go to the bathroom."

"Hmm, nice. So much here to get used to."

They unpacked and set aside some potato, carrots and onions for a venison stew. What needed to go to the root cellar they took out and brought back a quart jar of deer meat. Some things were put in the shed.

Apona's new clothes were put in the drawer under the bed. "Will you show me how to use the stove?"

He explained everything and showed her how to start a fire. He helped her to peel the potatoes, carrots and onions.

"What is this door?" she asked, pointing to the door in the stove.

"Open it."

"It's hot in here."

"Yes, you can bake or roast food in there. It's called an oven."

"Will biscuits warm up in there?"

"Yes, don't put them in until the stew is almost done."

"Where is water?"

"Come, I'll show you, and he took a bucket with them.

"It is so nice and peaceful here."

"It is."

"What's this?"

"Before I made the root cellar, I would keep some food in this to keep it cool."

"Good idea. But I like the root cellar."

"So do I," and he laughed.

Shelby scooped up a bucket full of water and they walked back inside.

Shelby set the water down and turned to look at Apona. She was crying.

"So much has happened since we married and here I am now standing in my own home. Everything is catching up with me and I love our home so much. This is like a castle."

"A castle for a princess."

She started crying again and he held her and hugged her. "I love you Princess."

She began to laugh then and said, "Come, we eat. I am getting horny again."

Later as they lay exhausted in the soft glow of the lantern listening to the wind blow, "This is my heaven, my husband, and the wind is the Great Creator's music. I am feeling so good and so happy. I love you, husband."

Chapter 9

Two days after Shelby and Apona visited home, a strange man knocked on the Martiniques' door one evening.

Sis answered the door. "Yes."

"Is Mr. Armand Martinique home?"

"Yes, one minute please.

"Dad, there is a man asking for you at the door."

"Who is it?"

"I don't know."

Armand went to check who was asking for him. "What can I do for you?"

"Are you Armand Martinique?"

"Yes, who are you?"

"I am Marvin Hillary, special investigator for the Attorney General's office in Augusta."

"What do you want with me?"

"Only to ask you some questions."

"Well, you might as well come in. We'll sit in the kitchen."

"That'll be fine."

"Now, what do you want?"

"You left Rockford eighteen years ago and you changed your name from Martin to Martinique. Why?"

"Being this close to the Canadian border, I thought we might be more readily accepted with a more French name."

"For years, Mr. Martin, before you left Rockford, there had been a series of midnight assaults and robberies."

"I remember something about those."

"After you and your family left Rockford the assaults and robberies stopped."

Armand was thinking that this all happened so many years ago that the statute of limitations must apply.

"The perps last victim was in a state of unconsciousness for almost a year before he died. Now that makes it a case of murder and there is no statute of limitations.

"You, Mr. Martin, were high on the Waldo County Sheriff's list of suspects. Because you had changed your name after you left Rockford, the sheriff was unable to find you—until a recent article appeared about a Shelby Martin from Flagstaff, who had testified in a Quebec court on a case against two men charged with rape, assault and battery with the intent of murder.

"Sheriff Winslow is retired now, but when he read that article he went to the AG's office in Augusta. And that, Mr. Martin, is why I am here.

"I cannot arrest you tonight, Mr. Martin, but the attorney general is going to present this case to the grand jury and if the jury finds there is probable cause there will be a warrant of arrest issued.

"I'll be staying in Flagstaff waiting for a message from Augusta. Goodnight, Mr. Martin. I'll show myself out."

Armand still sat in the kitchen, in a panic and his world was slowly collapsing on him.

"What did he want, Armand?" Rebecca asked.

"Nothing. Go to bed, woman, and leave me alone."

He got up and fixed himself a pot of coffee. He drank the whole pot and then went outside. He had no idea what to do now. Where could he run? The gig was up. Could he make it across the border to Canada? He paced back and forth all night and no sleep.

Without breakfast, he harnessed the team like he would every morning, then he left. His only resolution was Canada. He only had the money in his pocket. He didn't dare take the time to withdraw his savings from the bank.

He pushed the team beyond their limits and they started to slow. He whipped them and began hollering at them. He made it as far as Sarampus Falls when he fell to the side and hit the road, already dead. The team was about worn out and they stopped.

Rex was southbound from Coburn Gore in the stagecoach and spotted the team tangled in some bushes and Armand lying in the road.

Armand was a big man and it took Rex quite a while to get him into his own wagon and hook the team to the back of the stagecoach.

* * * *

The AG's special investigator saw the stagecoach towing a team and wagon and followed it to the coach line office. "Well, I'll be damned, if it ain't Armand Martin."

"Where did you find him, Rex?" Hillary asked.

"Sarampus Falls, right in the middle of the road. Who are you, anyhow?"

"Special investigator for the Attorney General, Marvin Hillary.

"Anyone else around?"

"Not a soul. The body was still warm too. Looks like he fell off the wagon. But I don't understand why he was up there. He hauls freight to and from the Green Farm in Coplin Plt. Besides he had an empty wagon. Looks to me he was running from something or someone."

"You might be right, Rex. Looks like my case is closed, though."

* * * *

Rebecca was not informed about her husband's death until the following day when the team and wagon were returned. Raul

172

wasn't long taking up the slack in his father's absence. Now he was hauling freight and taking care of the farm.

"Mom, I'm making good money hauling freight, the same as Dad. What did he do with all of his money?"

Rebecca talked to attorney Sinclare and he discovered an account at the bank, and now that was Rebecca's property as well as the farm. That night at home at the supper table she told Raul and Sis about the bank account. "We have money in the bank, Raul and Sis. Thirty-two hundred and fifteen dollars. We don't have to live like paupers any longer."

* * * *

There was no period of adjusting to living in the deep wilderness for Apona. She felt very much at home. And with each passing day she was becoming happier and happier. She had never known so much love and happiness. There was no one telling her what to do. Her husband had so accepted her into his life. She was included in every decision and everything they did; they did everything together.

Because of his wife's serene happiness, Shelby was in heaven every day. How could life be any better?

"Apona, I saw an idea in my head the other day."

"What did you see?"

"How would you like to have water inside the cabin?"

"We have water. The buckets are all full."

"What if you didn't have to go to the spring every day for water? Especially in the winter."

"How can this be?"

"Have you ever seen a hand pump?"

"Yes, I think, at your mother's home. I have no idea how the water comes from it."

"We can have a pump right here," and he put his hand down on the end of the sink.

"I can dig a trench from the cabin to the spring and hook a

pipe from the spring to the pump."

"It would be nice."

"We'll have to make a trip to town."

"We need to finish canning these fiddleheads first."

"Okay, we can do that today and tomorrow we can go to town. If we leave here early, we'll have time to visit the family."

"We'd better get busy," she said with a smile.

During the three weeks they had been at home, they had built more shelves, canned a dozen quarts of fiddleheads, some mushrooms, brook trout and worked up a little firewood.

"We going to eat breakfast before we leave in the morning?"

"I have always left as the sun was beginning to shine through the tree tops. We will be early enough to have breakfast at the farm."

"Okay. Maybe Sis can come back with us for a few days to teach me how to use the oven and make pies, biscuits."

Apona was excited about going to town. She was awake and up long before daylight.

"Come on, husband, get up," she prodded.

The sky was clear and they could still see a few late morning stars as they pushed off. When they reached the top of Long Falls, they now could see sun through the trees.

Sis saw them walking towards the house and ran out to meet them. She hugged Apona first and then her brother. "Have things changed around here, Shelby," she said excitedly.

"How so, Sis?"

"You haven't heard, have you?"

"Heard what, Sis?"

"Dad died last week. I'll let Mom tell you all about it."

Shelby wasn't glad that his father was dead, but he was happy that the family would no longer have to live under his shadow.

"Where is Raul?"

"Come in the house, son."

While Rebecca fixed them breakfast, Apona asked, "Sis, would you like to come back with us and teach me how to use the oven and make biscuits?"

"Is it okay, Mom?"

"Yes, you can go for three days."

As they ate breakfast, Rebecca told them everything that had happened. "And Raul now has his father's job hauling freight and making good wages. I never knew how much Armand was making. I learned you didn't ask." Then she told them about all the money he had in the bank.

"We need to leave and go see Mr. Sinclare and stop at Adalbert's store. Why don't the two of you meet us for lunch at the restaurant at noon?"

"We'd like to, son. I must say how happy you two are. I'm so happy for you."

"What should I bring with me?"

"Just some clothes," Apona said.

They left the farm and stopped first at Attorney Sinclare's. "Good morning, Mr. and Mrs. Martin. I have good news. Your homestead request has been granted. And I'll need you both to sign this deed." They did. "Now I'll file it at the county seat. You will need to mark off forty-two acres and when that is done come in and show me on the map."

"I can do that now Mr. Sinclare."

"Two thousand feet north from this little feeder stream, and west nine hundred and fifteen feet."

"You'll have to set iron posts at each corner.

"There is one stipulation, which I don't think will apply to you two, but you must remain on the land for five more years."

"That won't be a problem, Mr. Sinclare. Now how much do we owe you?"

"Five dollars for filing fee and fifty dollars for my services.

"Before I forget it, I have heard from Attorney Henri Pardis in Saint-Cecile-de-Whitton, and he did talk with Chief Ranibir and said he could give his people a lot of help, and his services would be paid for by the Bureau of Canadian Indian Affairs. So it is a win-win situation."

"Oh I am so happy there will be someone to help my people," Apona said.

They left and went to Adalbert's. "What can I do for you today?"

"A hand pump and some pipe."

"Is this inside or outside pump?"

"Inside."

"Here is what you need. How far to the water source?"

"Thirty feet to the spring and a five foot piece threaded on both ends and an elbow."

"May I make a suggestion?"

"Sure."

"Put this well point in the spring. There is a check valve already on the point."

"Okay."

"You're going to need couplings, and do you have wrenches?"

"No."

"That'll do it for plumbing, anything else?"

"Yes a roll-away bed or cot."

"I have a wood and canvas army cot."

"That'll be fine, Mr. Adalbert."

"Apona?"

"Eggs and bread, just in case."

Mrs. Adalbert put four dozen eggs in another wooden keg. "Next time, Shelby, would you bring the keg with you."

"How much for everything, Mr. Adalbert?"

"Fifty-five for the pump and plumbing and ten dollars for the cot. Sixty-five total."

They carried everything down to the canoe in two trips and then waited in the restaurant for Rebecca and Sis.

They didn't have long to wait. They had an enjoyable time eating out. "You know, it seems so nice to be able to meet you here for lunch. If Armand was still alive, we wouldn't be able to. We're happy at home now—not that we are glad that he is dead, but we no longer have to live in a suppressed existence. But from what I overheard Mr. Hillary say, Armand would be convicted of murder and he'd be gone by now, regardless.

"And I am so happy for Raul. When you left, Shelby, he came out of his shell, but he is the man of the house now and he has taken on more responsibility.

"I think what upset Armand most was the fear of that article written about you testifying in court against the brothers that attacked you, Apona, and your brother. The article apparently used your name, Shelby Martin, and you were from Flagstaff. This made a retired sheriff curious and he started looking and asking questions.

"I think Armand wanted to blame you, son, for bringing his past down around him.

"And one good thing about all this, I now have money to send Sis to a nursing school.

"What about you two? Will you stay on the river?"

"Yes, Mom, we make a good living by trapping and it'll give us a trip each year back to visit Apona's people."

"Mom, there is not any place I would wish to be except at home with my husband. We both love our home so much," Apona said.

"What more could a mother ask, than to have her children doing what they enjoy."

Everyone had a slice of apple pie. "Sis, can you teach me to make this apple pie?"

"I sure can, if you have apples and a rolling pin."

"What is this rolling pin?"

"We'll need it to roll the dough out flat. We'll need a baking dish also."

"Perhaps you and Apona should go to Adalbert's and pick up what you'll need. I'll talk with Mom a little longer."

"I like Apona so much, son. I feel I have known her for a long time. And she obviously makes you so happy."

"We are good for each other, Mom."

"I'm glad."

They talked for a few minutes more then met Apona and Sis. "We bought two glass pie plates, a rolling pin, apples and— what was the other thing, Sis?"

"Cinnamon and sugar."

Rebecca stood on the wharf and watched until they disappeared around the bend. She was so happy she began to cry.

"How long will it take us?"

"Little more than two hours," Apona said.

It didn't take long to canoe to the portage. Shelby put the canoe on the racks and locked it. "Do we walk to the cabin from here?" Sis asked.

Apona said, "No, canoe at other end of portage."

Shelby was so proud and happy to see Apona step up like that. He carried the steel pipes on his shoulders and the pump on his other arm and he tied a rope on the cot and carried that on his back, and Apona carried the food supplies while Sis got everything else.

"You mean, Shelby, you had to carry everything across this portage?" Sis asked bewildered.

"It wasn't too bad."

At the end of the portage, Sis asked, "What is that noise?"

"That's Long Falls," Apona said.

In only a few minutes they were home. "Oh my, you two, this is beautiful."

"Apona, show Sis around. I'll unload this."

He put the plumbing in the woodshed, the apples in the root cellar and the rest inside.

"This is much nicer than I thought it would be. Shelby, if

you get the fire going I'll give Apona her first lesson in baking biscuits."

While the cooking lesson was going on, Shelby started digging a trench to the spring. First he had to get in underneath the cabin. This took a while as he was on his knees a lot of the time. Once that was done he began the trench. The soil was sandy and it was easy digging. When Apona called him in for supper, he had dug ten feet, plus under the cabin.

"What's for supper?"

"Beaver stew and biscuits," Apona said excitedly. "Look how these turned out."

"Golden brown."

Sis said. "This beaver stew is better than beef stew."

"Very good for you," Apona said.

"These biscuits are as good as they look," Shelby said.

"Did a good job," Apona smiled.

After eating Shelby went back to digging. He had another six feet dug when Apona and Sis came out to see how he was doing. "How long will it take, Shelby?" Apona asked.

"I should have the trench dug tomorrow, if I don't come to a large rock."

"You stop for now, husband. We need to bathe in river."

"Okay, I'm tired and sweaty."

"Take off clothes out here so not to bring dirt inside. I have towels and soap. You bathe too, Sis." To Sis that didn't sound like a question.

"Okay."

They all undressed and tiptoed into the rather cool water. Apona didn't hesitate. She went out into deep water and submerged. Shelby and Sis worked their way slowly.

"This water isn't as cold as when you told me to take a bath at the village. That water was freezing."

Sis noticed how being naked was so natural for Shelby and Apona and she soon lost her shyness.

Eventually Shelby and Sis joined Apona and they splashed around in the water playing for a while before soaping up. Then they had to submerge again to rinse the soap off.

Sis said, "Okay, I'm done."

They all waded back to shore and dried off with towels before going back inside to dress.

"That was fun and refreshing. We'll have to bathe again before I leave."

Sis went back to teaching Apona about cooking with the stove and writing down recipes she could follow, and the temperature of the oven for different foods, while Shelby sat in a rocker on the porch.

When the lessons were done for the evening the girls joined Shelby on the porch. He got up and brought out the other chair and the cedar block of wood for himself. "I think we need another chair, my husband."

"It's a nice night, isn't it," Shelby said.

"I think I can understand now why both of you are so happy here." Then she asked, "Who owns this land, Shelby?"

"We now own forty-two acres of it. We filed for a homestead deed to forty-two acres and it was approved."

"Apona, tell me more about this tea."

"Go ahead Apona," Shelby encouraged.

"With our people a girl not allowed sex until she mates, usually."

"There's a but in there, isn't there, Apona?" Sis said.

"Yes, first year husband come to village after some days, my mother began giving me this tea—for three days before Shelby and I enjoyed each other, and then another tea morning after.

"Girls are not told about this tea until they are to mate. Now, I have one cup of tea each day and the morning after we have each other. In the morning I give you this tea instead of coffee."

"Will you show me this flower?"

"Yes, but no flower until later. I think you probably have some on farm. It grows in wet areas."

"When I go to nursing school I would like to take some with me."

The sun was gone and the temperature was now cool. They went back in and Shelby set up the cot. "You sleep with Apona, Sis, and I'll take the cot." Just so Sis would feel more comfortable, he left one lantern on and the wick turned down so there was only a small flame. It made the cabin feel even cozier.

* * * *

Shelby was up first the next morning. The army cot was not as comfortable as his bed. He dressed, being quiet, and started the fire in the cook stove and put water on for coffee.

He looked out the front windows and there was a large loon by the wharf and it looked as if he had just swallowed a fish. For his breakfast. Then he called. Probably to his mate.

Apona and Sis heard the loon and began to stir. Apona climbed out of bed and joined Shelby at the window watching the loon. Sis was so comfortable she hated to get up.

With some prodding from Apona she finally got up. "Ummm, that coffee smells good."

Apona gave her a cup of her tea. "Try this, Sis."

She took a sip and said, "It is a little bitter, but not bad."

"I'll go out and get the bacon," Shelby said.

The sky was promising to be a nice day. Everything was so peaceful.

"Will you slice the bacon, sweetheart, while I help Sis?"

After the bacon was sliced, he poured himself another cup of coffee and went out on the porch and sat in the rocking chair.

Mayflies were beginning to gather on the water surface and a huge brook trout jumped free of the water after one. He smiled, thinking he could never live anywhere else.

"While you're watching the bacon and pancakes, Apona, I'll set the table," Sis said.

"Everything is very good, girls."

"She did a very good job. Today we will make a pie, Apona."

"Next trip to town, we'll have to get more syrup," Shelby said.

"We can make our own syrup," Apona said. "My people have been making maple syrup for a long time."

"You know, we can. There are several rock maple trees out back. We'll have to get some equipment, but it'll be fun."

After he had his fill, he said, "I need to get to work."

Refreshed and full of energy, he was almost at the spring by noon. Before going any closer he would have to study on it.

He sat down under a tree and closed his eyes, not thinking about anything in particular. Then suddenly he had his answer. He got up and went back to the cabin.

"I was just going to call you; lunch is ready," Apona said.

"That pie sure smells good."

"It'll have to cool before we can eat it. We'll save it for dessert tonight.

"How are you coming?"

"I think I might have it done today."

They ate last night's leftovers. Shelby ate fast. "I want to get started on an idea I saw in my head."

He cut a hole for the pipe in the sink counter and the floor, then he screwed the short length of pipe into the pump and slid it through both holes and let the pump rest for now on the counter while he crawled under the cabin to check on it. It was looking good.

Then he began attaching the other lengths of pipe and tightening them with the wrenches. He had one length to go. Before going any further, he checked everything so far.

Near the end of the last pipe he had connected, he filled

in the ditch two feet, to stop a flush of water if things should go wrong.

The sandy soil up against the bank at the end of the trench was damp. He laid the next length down to see how much further the ditch had to go. Only a few inches and he'd be at the end of the pipe. He dug a little concave space and the sand was still damp. He drove his spade down into the bottom of the trench and removed the spade full of sand. An inch below the bottom of the trench the sand was even wetter. He could see water beginning to seep in.

He buried the shallow hole and removed enough of the sand at the end so he'd have room to work. He laid the last length down, and taking into consideration the threads, set the point in and drove it down with a block of wood, so not to damage the point. It went into the ground so easy he could almost push it with his hands. He could see water now in the point.

He connected the length of pipe making sure everything was tight and pushed the point down enough so the pipe now laid flat in the trench.

Before filling in the trench, he took a bucket of water inside to prime the pump. To his surprise water was already down to the end of the five foot nipple. A few strokes of the handle and he had water. A bit sandy at first, but it soon cleared.

"Wow, this will be good," Apona said.

"It sure will, especially when the snow is deep and when it gets real cold. Now I have to insulate the nipple somehow."

He went outside walking around and thinking, while Apona and Sis sat on the porch talking. He was looking at an old fir tree that was on the ground and the center was hollow rotten. "I could split something like that and put it on the pipe nipple like a sleeve."

This tree was too far gone to be of any use, but it had given him the idea. He began looking for a live standing tree that would have a lot of green moss or mold all the way around the base. He didn't have far to go. He located a six inch tree and cut it down. It wasn't hollow, but the center was red heart, which he was able to cut out after splitting a five foot piece.

He wired this together around the pipe nipple. It fit snuggly. He wasn't long back filling the trench. "I'll wait to smooth it over after supper."

"Are you done?"

"Yes, after supper I'll smooth out the ground. What have you two been cooking?"

"Sis calls it boiled dinner. Ham, potatoes, cabbage and carrots."

"It sure smells good."

"Here, you didn't drink your tea this morning."

"You mean, Apona, the man has to drink the tea too?"

"Yes, but not as often as we do. But remember it is very important that you have a cup the morning after."

"I'll remember."

"How long before supper is ready?"

Apona looked at Sis, "Half hour to an hour."

"Then I will have time for a bath. I'm filthy. I'll smooth over the ground tomorrow."

They undressed in the cabin and took towels and soap to the river. Again, Apona was the first to get completely wet.

This was feeling so natural for Sis now. She didn't even give it a second thought. "Dark clouds are coming," she said.

They all soaped up quick, rinsed off and ran for the cabin. It was already raining, and thunder was in the distance.

"Wow, that was close. I don't like thunder and lightning," Sis said.

They dried off near the heat of the stove and then dressed in clean clothes.

"I think everything is ready," Sis said.

"I hope everyone is hungry. We made a big kettle full," Apona said.

"Oh, wow, this is so good."

"Save room for pie, sweetheart," Apona said.

Just then there was a close lightning strike and thunder was almost immediate. It was deafeningly loud. "Holy shit!" Sis exclaimed, "That was too close."

"Sis, I have never heard you use language like that before," Shelby said.

"That scared me."

There were more strikes and thunder, but the storm was moving east. The rain on the roof was loud.

Shelby finished his boiled dinner and said, "I think I'll wait until later for a slice of pie. I'd explode if I eat anything else."

They all agreed. The thunder and lightning had moved off, but the rain was still coming strong. Just before dark they all had a slice of apple pie.

Apona waited before she sampled her piece. She wanted to see their reactions first. The two said at the same time how good it was. This brought a smile to Apona and she tried her slice. "It is good."

"Are you surprised, Apona?" Sis asked.

"A little; this is my first pie. Sweetheart, we need apple trees, so we can have our own apples."

"I'll have to paw through the apple peelings for the seeds."

"I saved the seeds," Apona said and when she looked at Shelby he was smiling.

They went to bed soon after the pie and all three lay on their back listening to the music of rain falling on the roof. By midnight a light wind blew the storm out and the sky cleared.

Shelby was awake before the sun in the morning and very quietly he started a fire in the cook stove. It had cooled during the night. He put the water on for coffee and went out on the porch to watch the sun rays filter through the trees. Old Mr. Loon was by the wharf again. He had submerged and come back up with a nice brook trout. This morning, instead of calling, it swam off with the trout between its bill. He probably had young to feed.

Apona soon joined him still wearing her red long-johns. "Brrr, the air is cool this morning."

Soon Sis came out wearing Apona's black long-johns. "The air smells so fresh and clean this morning," she said.

"I think it is going to be a nice day," Shelby said.

"What are you going to do today, my husband?"

"The rain last night smoothed out the ground, so I don't have to do that. I was thinking about the three of us canoeing down to the other end of this dead water."

"That sounds like fun."

Apona and Sis went back inside, dressed and started breakfast. "I'll have to go out to the root cellar, Sis, for the bacon and eggs."

"I'll come too."

"It's actually cold in here," Sis said. "I'll take the eggs, Apona, if you want to take the bacon."

While the bacon was frying, Apona made some fry-pan bread.

While the two were fixing breakfast Shelby walked the pipe line and he checked the spring. He was thinking that he should probably build a box over the spring and the point head and insulate with sawdust to keep it from freezing in the winter.

"Shelby! Shelby, breakfast is ready!" Sis hollered.

* * * *

After breakfast, Shelby put the canoe back in the water while the girls were cleaning up. He took his ax, in case, and some fishline and hook.

Sis brought down two pillows to sit on and to lean against the thwart. "Everybody ready?" Apona pushed off and then jumped in.

"How far is it to the end?" Apona asked.

"About two miles."

"What is at the end?" Sis asked.

"Well, I have never seen it, only heard it—Grand Falls."

There was a huge bull moose in the marsh on the right and as soon as he had seen the canoe he took off running. "Boy, he was big," Sis said.

Not far from there, Shelby saw fresh peeled beaver wood in the mouth of a small feeder stream. "There must be a new beaver flowage up this stream. We'll have to remember this when we start trapping this fall."

They leisurely canoed the river enjoying the scenery and the wildlife. Two bald eagles circled overhead and he stopped paddling and remembered when Kalipona had sent the eagles to his cabin and dropped fish at his doorstep. *If not for the eagles I would have died.*

"Thank you, eagles!" he hollered.

This got both Apona and Sis' attention.

"What was that all about, Shelby?" Sis asked.

Apona asked, "Kalipona?"

"Yes," he said.

"Okay, you two, what's going on?"

Shelby knew he had to tell Sis something and he had to be careful too. "I went through a bad time the first winter I was out here. I was starving and those two eagles brought me food to eat and saved me from dying."

"Wow," is all Sis could say.

"Not a word to Mom, Sis, I don't want her to worry about us."

"Okay."

"You promise?"

"I promise."

The eagles circled again and they both shrieked a call back and circled one more time and flew off.

When they came to some small islands in the river Apona said, "I can hear the water."

"Can we put ashore, Shelby, and walk down to the falls?"

"Sure we can."

He saw a sandy shoreline and turned the canoe towards it.

Apona jumped out and pulled the canoe onto the sand and steadied it while they climbed out, then Shelby pulled it ashore. He took his ax, in case. They stayed with the shoreline so they wouldn't miss anything. When they were at the last pitch they all were disappointed. "I thought for sure it would be more of a falls than this. The roar of the water sure sounded like it."

"It is a pretty spot though."

They circled back through the trees to the canoe. "Anyone hungry besides me?"

They both said, "Yes."

Shelby rigged up an alder branch with fish line and then the three started looking for white grubs for bait. They had broken apart several rotten logs and Sis hollered. "I have a whole bunch here." Shelby scooped up five. "This should be enough."

He put one on the hook and gave the pole to Apona. "You two fish and I'll get a fire going."

It wasn't difficult to find dry dead wood in amongst the softwood trees. He soon had a fire going on the sandy shore. Then he cut two crotch sticks to support the fish with a stick through it for a spit.

As soon as the grub hit the water a brook trout took it. Apona backed up and pulled it on shore. "That's a nice one."

Shelby cleaned it and put it over the fire to cook. Then he went for four more crotched sticks and two to go through the fish.

Apona handed the pole to Sis and she put another grub on the hook. "Your turn to catch one, Sis."

Sis screamed, "Ahhhh! I've got one," and she pulled in one like Apona's.

Apona baited the hook and said, "Go for it, Sis."

Shelby was happy watching his wife and sister having a

good time. He was glad Sis could come out for a visit.

"That should be enough Sis, unless you have a hollow leg," Apona said while laughing.

Shelby had to make another spit and he added some more wood to the fire.

When the fish were done they all sat on the shore to eat fish like corn on the cob.

"I have never eaten fish like this. It is very good," Sis said.

After they each had had their fill of brook trout they boarded the canoe and headed for home.

* * * *

Back at the cabin, Shelby and Apona sat in the rocking chairs on the porch and Sis said, "I think I'll walk around out back for a while."

"Don't go far, Sis. I don't want you to get lost."

"I won't be going that far."

"Shelby," Apona said, "If you would get me some ash logs I could make some baskets. I have heard you say you need a bigger one for trapping and I'd like to make a clothes basket for your mother."

Shelby and Apona went out beyond the spring with the crosscut saw. There were several ash trees there. "Brown ash is best if there are any."

"There's an eight inch brown ash, is that okay?"

"That'll do."

Apona got on the other end of the saw with Shelby and they weren't long felling the tree. It came crashing down. "Six-foot lengths."

They cut out five six -oot lengths before they reached any branches.

"Can you carry this small one, sweetheart?"

"Yes."

Shelby put the butt-end log on his shoulder and picked up

the saw and they headed back to the cabin.

Sis had found a mossy spot to lay down, watching the fluffy clouds overhead. And she began thinking about her visit here and Shelby and Apona. *They had to work at surviving this kind of lifestyle.* What she would call work. *But for Shelby and Apona this was more like a vacation.* She had had fun while here but in all honesty, she knew she could never live permanently like this. *And Apona, she is the epitome of pure innocence. After all you are a princess, Apona. And your innocence has changed my brother. At home he was always deep within himself, like almost afraid to come out of his shell. Now look at him, Apona. He is not the same man now. There is a peaceful knowingness about him. And he is a protector for you, Apona. And in a way, Apona, you have changed me by your innocence. Before two days ago I would never have taken my clothes off to join him and you bathing. It seemed so natural for me with no inhibitions or lured guilt. Being able to do that, I think, has changed me forever. But I don't think I'll tell Mom. She wouldn't understand. Or Raul.*

She began laughing out loud then. And she said aloud, "I bet I could take my clothes off and walk back to the cabin without either of them making any snide remarks." She began laughing harder and she said, "I'll do it," and she took her clothes off, even her shoes and walked barefoot and naked back to camp. The cool air on her skin felt good.

Shelby and Apona were busy peeling bark from the ash logs. She walked over to them and asked, "What are you doing?"

"Apona is going to make some baskets after she makes narrow strips from the wood."

"I'll put my clothes back on and I'll help you. Aren't either one of you going to ask why?"

"I figured you'd say something when you got around to it," Shelby said.

"I know, it feels good doesn't it, Sis," Apona said and then, "I have done the same thing when I was off by myself. The cool air feels good against the skin."

Inside Sis was rolling with laughter. *I was right.*

With all three working, it didn't take long to strip all the logs.

"How do you cut out the strips, Apona?" Shelby asked.

"I'll need an ax and I'll show you."

Shelby came back with the ax and gave it to Apona. She took it and began pounding the wood in a straight line down the length of the log and then with a sharp knife she made two parallel cut lines about three quarters of an inch wide the length of the log, and then she loosened one end and began lifting. The strip came off with ease.

Shelby got his hammer and started doing the same thing with another one.

When there were several strips Sis took Apona's place stripping and Apona began weaving the strips into a basket.

"Sis, would you put the kettle on the stove? We'll have leftover boiled dinner."

After supper, Apona said, "We should bathe now. Then I can finish the basket."

"Is it my imagination or is this water warmer today?" Sis asked.

"I think it is warmer," Shelby said. He and Sis didn't hesitate about getting wet. They soaped up and rinsed a couple of times each and played in the warmer water.

Instead of toweling off they air dried while sitting in the breeze. Once dry, they dressed and Apona continued with the basket. The sunset was a bright reddish orange. "It'll be a nice day tomorrow; look at that sunset."

Apona finished the basket before the sun had totally set. "This is beautiful, Apona. Will you make one for me to take with me to nursing school?"

"We'll bring it out the next time we come, okay."

"I'm tired," she stood up and stretched.

* * * *

Again the next morning Shelby had the fire going in the stove and water on for coffee before Apona and Sis were awake.

Sis woke up first to the smell of fresh coffee. "It's still dark outside."

"I couldn't sleep any longer so I got up."

There was no real hurry and they ate a hearty breakfast and enjoyed each other's company over a cup of coffee and Apona's tea. "I really hate to leave. I have enjoyed myself so much. I have felt at ease here with you two, felt at home. Maybe I can come back again before I leave?" she asked.

"We would love to have you, Sis."

"It's time to go," Shelby said.

"Apona, would it be okay if I helped to paddle today?"

"Sure you can."

"Shelby, don't forget the wooden keg for Mrs. Adalbert."

"I'm glad you reminded me."

Apona put Sis's few things in the basket along with two pillows for her.

At the portage, it was Sis who jumped out and pulled the canoe up so Apona and Shelby could step out. Then he dragged it up on higher ground.

It was 8 o'clock when they pulled up to the public wharf behind Adalbert's. With basket in hand they walked to the farm. "You know after spending time with you, this doesn't even feel like home now."

"You ready to become a wilderness wife, Sis?" Shelby asked jokingly.

"No—I don't think I'm ready for that just yet."

Apona proudly carried her basket to the house. Rebecca saw them coming in the driveway and went out to meet them.

"Well you look happy, Sis."

"I am, Mom."

Apona held out the basket. "For you, Mom."

"Oh my, this is so nice. Did you make it?"

"Most of it. Shelby and Sis did help."

"Well come in, are you hungry?"

"Not this time, Mom. We had a big breakfast before we left."

"I suppose Raul is working."

"Yes, and I have a surprise also. He heard the stage line was up for sale and he has made arrangements to buy it and still haul freight."

"Hmm, my little brother is becoming a business tycoon. I'm glad and proud for him."

While Rebecca and Shelby talked, Sis and Apona made sandwiches for lunch. While they were alone, Sis wanted to talk with Apona. "Apona, you are truly the essence of pure innocence. My brother is not the same person that he was before you. He no longer hides inside his shell. You are good for him. And I think there is more to you, Apona, than anyone knows. I wish we had grown up together. You are my friend, my sister. I like you Apona and—you truly are a princess." Sis hugged her then.

"Thank you, Sis, and I think you are wonderful, too. And this I know, no matter where you go or what you do, you will never be alone. You will be watched over."

They ate a quick lunch. "Next time we come out, Mom, we'll stay over. Sis wants to come back before her nursing training begins—maybe in three weeks, the middle of July."

They said goodbye in the yard. Sis hugged and kissed Shelby and said, "You take care of her, brother. She *is* a princess." Sis and Apona hugged again and then Apona hugged Rebecca.

* * * *

They took the empty keg into the store and bought syrup, molasses, apples, brown sugar, potatoes and bread.

"More eggs?" Mrs. Adalbert asked.

"Not this trip. The next time we come out. Mr. Adalbert,

do you have, or can you order, equipment for making maple syrup?"

"I have it in stock. Put away out back now."

"Maybe next trip."

"Sweetheart, what about straight back chairs?"

"Yes, do you have any?"

Mrs. Adalbert showed them what they had and they bought two for now.

"I think we bought more than you were thinking of."

It was still one trip across the portage and they were home early this trip. After everything was put away and the new chairs brought inside, "Sweetheart, I have had an itch all day."

"Me, too."

Chapter 10

"What are we going to do today, sweetheart?" Apona asked.

"I think we should run the property lines in case someone comes to inspect the homestead."

For the southeastern corner he chose Halfway Brook, then he and Apona, using his hundred-foot tape and compass, laid out the east line along the river. The north line was not far beyond Gold Brook. They scarfed trees with the ax along the line.

Using his compass he sighted in a 90° turn to the west, and they measured down 915 feet, and like the northeast corner, he made a corner post from a cedar tree and drove it into the ground as far as he could and then they piled up rocks around it.

Joking, he asked, "Are you hungry, Apona, or do you have an itch?"

She laughed and said, "Right now, I'm hungry. Maybe we'll scratch the itch later."

"That didn't take as long as I thought it would," Apona said.

"The next line, the south line going west, will take us longer. We'll have two brooks to cross."

As they were eating lunch on the porch, Apona said, "Sweetheart, I noticed on our trip to town, flowers growing at people's houses. Do they grow by themselves?"

"Some may, but most of them are planted."

"I would like to have some flowers here in front."

"Okay, next time we go out. Why don't you start making a list of things we need."

Because of the two brooks and alder bush patches, they were all afternoon running the south line back 915 feet. "We have the four corner posts in; tomorrow we will check the distance between the two posts on this west line. I'm tired, and I know you are."

Let's bathe before we eat. I'm filthy."

"Me, too. I think I'll take my clothes and boots off out here. I'm so covered with mud."

They didn't bathe with towels or soap. They ran into the river and splashed around having fun. "You know, husband, I miss Sis."

"I think she actually liked being out here much better than I thought she would have.

"Hey, I just had an idea; follow me." As he started swimming downstream, Apona beside him, not following.

He stopped, "You see that little brook?"

"Yes."

"About fifty feet from the river, the water comes out from under a ledge rock. And that brook is where I have been finding the gold. With the water level down some, I wanted to check the sand at the mouth of the brook."

"There, do you see those yellow rocks?"

"Yes, is that gold?"

"Yes." He picked that one up and they began finding more. Before long they had their hands full.

"Let's take these back to the cabin."

They put the gold in a bowl. "Are these rocks really worth money?"

"Yes, men will kill for these. We must keep this quiet. That's why I sell to Pasquale, not in Flagstaff. If only one person learned of this, everybody and their brother would be out here. We must keep this to ourselves. You are the only person besides me that knows."

"I won't say a word. How much is this worth?"

"It's a little more than I sold to Pasquale last month, so I'm guessing maybe five hundred dollars."

The gold filled the pouch he had been using.

"Can you keep this in the bottom of your sugar box?"

"I'll have to empty the sugar first, then pour it back in. I'll do it tomorrow."

"If the fur market ever goes to hell, we'll still have an income with the gold."

"Did you know the gold was here when you decided on this sight?"

"No, I only found it after the cabin was built.

"My family doesn't even know."

"Okay."

* * * *

The next morning they finished running the back line, the west boundary line. The northwest corner post was about twenty inches to the north from where it should have been. He called it close enough.

The following days they worked on firewood in the morning before it became too warm. Apona was there helping on each tree. She helped on the two-man crosscut saw, limbing with the ax and she would help Shelby cutting the long length wood to stove length firewood. "I always wanted to help with firewood in the village, but my father said that firewood was not women's work."

Each morning they would work up, split and pile in the woods between two trees, a half cord. "I'm not sure if we can put all this wood in the shed or not."

"Then we'll have a good start on the firewood for next year," she replied.

The day came when they headed for town. Since they were staying over at the house they did not leave home until noon.

"The river is really low, isn't it," Apona said.

"It's lower than last year at this time."

They stopped first at Adalbert's and Apona gave them her list. "We'll be here in the morning." Their biggest pick up was the maple syrup equipment, and that really didn't take much room in the canoe. There were a few food stores and Apona's flower plants and two rose bushes.

Adalbert helped Shelby with the equipment he would need. Six buckets with covers to keep the rain out and a dozen metal tipped wooden spirals.

Apona picked out eight plants.

"Mr. Adalbert, what are these lights?"

"Propane gas lights, much brighter than kerosene lanterns."

"Where does this gas come from?"

"It is a by-product of petroleum refining."

"Is it new?"

"Around here, yes. But the big cities have had it for ten years now. It comes in hundred pound bottles. Come, I'll show you."

They went outside and Adalbert showed him the bottle he had connected to his lighting system.

"There are cook stoves now that use propane gas instead of wood."

"How expensive is the gas?"

"A bottle like this one will cost you five dollars, and if you are only using it for lights it should last a year."

"Here's what I want to do, Mr. Adalbert. I can't take it this trip, but the next trip I'll take it."

"How many light fixtures will you need?"

"Four."

"I have that many. I'll give you a roll of copper tubing and if you bring back what you don't use I'll only charge you for what you did use. You'd have to have a few special tools also. You can pay me when you bring what copper you didn't use back. When will you be back?"

"In a few days. Sis is going with us for a visit and we'll have to bring her back."

"I'll have everything ready for you."

"What we bought today, we'll pick up tomorrow morning."

As they were walking towards the house, Shelby saw six horses in the field. "Raul's freight business must be doing good."

Sis saw them coming and ran to meet them. "Oh, it's so good to see you two again," and she hugged and kissed each.

"Whose horses, Sis?"

"Raul's; he has expanded."

"And who is that boy coming out of the barn?"

"Freddie, Raul's hired help."

"Wow, he must be doing good."

Rebecca met them at the front door. "Wow, Mom, you look so different."

"A new dress and hairstyle can do that for a woman. Plus I'm happy."

"That'll do it also, Mom. And you do look happy and not so rundown," Apona said and then she hugged her.

"You're just in time for supper. We'll eat as soon as Raul gets home."

"What about your nursing training, Sis?" Apona asked.

"There's a program in Waterville that begins on September 5th to May 15th next year. A year from now, I'll be a nurse."

"Where will you go then?"

"I haven't thought that far ahead."

The front door opened and Raul walked in. Shelby walked over to greet him with a hug. "Wow, brother, you have never hugged me before."

"I'm proud of you, little brother."

"Hello, Apona," and she hugged him.

"Those aren't exactly freight driver's clothes," Shelby said.

"I don't drive anymore, brother. I hire drivers. I also bought up the franchise for the Bigelow line. I work in the office now. And I hired a boy, Freddie, to take care of the horses here."

"You must be doing well."

"Let's say right now a lot of money passes through me."

After supper, Apona and Sis went for a walk in search of the white turtlehead flower and Rebecca stayed back to talk with Shelby and Raul.

"Sis, over here behind the barn. Does this look familiar to you now?"

"Yes, this grows everywhere down by the river. How do you prepare it?"

"You pick the flowers only and only when the flowers are mature. Then dry them out of the sun. They become dry and crumble easy when you rub them between your hands."

"I wonder why we never knew about this?"

Jokingly, Apona said, "You have to be an Indian to know this," and they both laughed.

"Shelby, I don't know what it is about Apona, but since Sis came back from her last visit with you two, she is not the same dull, lifeless girl. Now she is so full of energy—and happy."

"All I can say, Mom, is that Apona is special. She affects people like that. I have never seen her cross or moody."

Down near the river, they found more of the flowers growing. "I do not know if these will mature before you leave or not, Sis."

"Apona, can I ask you a personal question?"

"Okay."

"Are you and Shelby going to have children?"

"Maybe sometime. But not in the near future. You see, we want to play and have fun, and I want to go with him when he traps and I can't do these things with babies to look after. We talked about this and Shelby agrees."

* * * *

After breakfast Rebecca watched her family walk to town. Freddie was just coming up the driveway. Raul went to work and Shelby, Apona and Sis loaded the canoe.

Before they got across the portage it started to rain. Light at first, but by the time they reached home it was coming down in sheets. They were all soaking wet, so they took care of the canoe and the flowers were left on the porch. The syrup equipment was put in the woodshed.

"We'd better get out of these wet clothes," Apona said.

"The clothes I brought with me are wet also."

"You can put on some of my clothes, Sis."

Shelby started the fire in the cook stove and went out back for rope to make a clothes line to dry their clothes.

"Apona, will you help me make a clothes basket like the one you made for Mom? Maybe not so big."

"Yes, and I need to make a bigger packbasket for Shelby."

"As wet as we are, I guess we won't have to bathe later."

"Not unless you want to cool off," Shelby said. "When the rain stops I'm thinking it'll get humid."

It was later afternoon before the rain stopped and Shelby was correct, the humid air followed.

During the rain, Apona and Sis were able to pound out enough ash strips to make her basket.

Shelby gathered rocks with the two wheel cart for a fire place to boil down maple sap. When he finished he went for a swim to wash the dirt and sweat off and to cool off. The girls were still busy inside and didn't join him.

Sis was not as fast as Apona making the basket and she had to wait until morning to finish.

It was too hot in the cabin to use the blankets; they were folded up on the end of the bed. And it wasn't long before all three shed what clothes they did have on.

Around midnight Shelby sat on the edge of the bed and said, "I have me an idea." Now Apona and Sis were both sitting up. "When I was talking with Adalbert about the gas lights he was telling me about a propane gas stove. This wouldn't heat the cabin like the wood stove does."

"That would be nice," Apona said.

"I can't ever remember a night as hot as it is right now," Sis said. "It makes you want to get up and sit in the river." But no one went outside.

They lay back down and eventually they were able to sleep. They were still sleeping after sunrise and a noisy loon out front woke them.

"At least it has cooled off," Apona said. There was a breeze blowing through the open window. "That feels good."

For breakfast they ate cold sandwiches and water, to save from heating the cabin up with the wood stove.

Sis finished her clothes basket and she and Apona pounded out more strips for a pack basket. As soon as Apona had enough strips to get started, Sis took over pounding out more strips.

Shelby kindled a fire in the new fireplace outside and roasted fresh brook trout.

They ate outside and washed it down with spring water. Shelby had taken his shirt off while he was working to stay cool.

"Have you ever had any alcohol, Shelby?" Sis asked.

"I had some ginger brandy once. It was good. And you?"

"I had some wine last winter. I liked it," Sis said.

"How about you, Apona?" Sis asked.

"There's something that the people in my village make every summer from berries, that bubbles after it sits for days in large jugs."

"That sounds like wine or home brew," Shelby said.

"We should have brought some out with us. Too bad the store is so far away," Sis said.

"Maybe it is good it is so far," Apona said.

After eating, Shelby went back to his lights and the girls to basket weaving. Apona let Sis do some of the weaving now.

When they finished the packbasket they started cooking supper on the outdoor fire. Shelby was almost finished with the lights. He only had to connect the copper tubing to the propane tank. "I'll do that after supper. Anybody tired but me?" Shelby asked.

"Yes," they both answered.

After eating, Shelby finished the lights and he showed the other two how to turn the gas on and lit the burners in the light fixtures. "They all work. We'll try it again when it gets dark," Shelby said. "Right now I'm going to take a bath and sit in the cool water."

They left their clothes in the cabin and were so intent on the cool water they forgot the towels.

"This is almost like bath water," Sis said.

"It's cooler out here where it's deeper." Compared to the water in the shallows it was like ice water.

They stayed in the water until the skin on their hands started wrinkling like prunes. It was almost sunset when they finally had cooled enough. Then they sat on the porch drying themselves off.

They were all quiet and suddenly a pine martin chased a red squirrel across in front of the cabin. "What was that?" Sis asked.

"A pine martin."

"Isn't it dark enough, sweetheart, to try the new lights?"

"Okay." They went inside and he lit the first one.

"That illuminates the whole cabin," Sis said in surprise.

"Isn't that nice," Apona said, "Something as simple as that."

"I like it," Sis said.

"It is nice. But for a night light we'll still have to use the lantern. These lights only have one position."

"That's okay, sweetheart. I like the lantern."

* * * *

There was a breeze all night through the open windows and they slept well, until the loon showed up at sunrise. Shelby dressed and started a fire in the cook stove and set water on for coffee. Apona and Sis were still snoring, so Shelby went outside to let them sleep.

He walked out to the root cellar to get some bacon and eggs. Some animal had tried to claw at the outer door, but couldn't get past the double layer of chicken wire. He checked for tracks, but in the soft sand there were no clear prints. *I bet it was the same animal as before.* He had stopped him this time.

The animal obviously could smell the food inside, so at night he would have to start putting down the nail boards.

He went back inside and the girls were up and dressed. "Where have you been?" Apona asked.

"Well, I went out to get us some bacon and eggs and was sidetracked." Apona was waiting for a better explanation. "Remember I told you about the animal that clawed through my first smokehouse, the teepee smokehouse?"

"Yes."

"Well, it was back last night and tried to get into the root cellar. The chicken wire on the door stopped it."

"What kind of animal, Shelby?" Sis asked.

"I don't know. It never leaves any clear tracks."

"So where are the bacon and eggs?" Apona asked.

"I forgot. I'll go back out."

After breakfast, Apona said, "Sis and I are going to take the canoe and look for white turtlehead flowers."

"Okay, I'm going to work on firewood until it warms up too much."

They went up Halfway Brook first. At the end of the marsh Apona spotted several. "There, Sis, on the right. And the flowers are all out. Let's pick as many as we can."

They had to go on foot to get to them. Sis jumped out to pull the canoe in on dry shore. She landed knee deep in mud. She was able to pull and push the canoe up on dry land for Apona. Then she had to wiggle her way out of the mud. Apona reached out with the paddle. "Take the paddle, Sis, and I'll pull you in."

Things were going fine until Apona slipped on some rotting wood and she sat down in the wet dirt. By then the girls began laughing.

Eventually they were able to get Sis out and they started picking flowers. "Pick only the blossoms, Sis, so the plant will grow next year."

"We didn't bring anything to put them in," Sis said.

"Take your shirt off and use that."

Shelby had worked up two trees and needed a drink and a break. He walked down to the spring. After quenching his thirst, he stood up and stretched. He could hear Apona and Sis laughing, giggling and talking. "I wonder if they are picking any flowers."

He went back to work. There were a few nice big rock maple trees near where he was working and he was taking care not to fall another tree against the maples, damaging them.

After two more trees, he filled the cart and started back. After he had piled the wood in the shed, he went out front to wash up in the river. He could hear the girls coming back. The sun was in his eyes, but he could swear neither one of them were wearing a shirt. When they paddled closer it became obvious.

When he saw how muddy they were even with dirt in their hair, he began to laugh. Sis passed him her shirt full of flower blossoms and then Apona did.

"You two better take your clothes off out here and jump in the river. I think there's a story here."

"You look pretty hot and sweaty and dirty, sweetheart," Apona said.

"Okay, I'll join you."

After washing up, Apona and Sis spread the flower blossoms on the work table in the back room to dry.

"How long does it take to dry?"

"Until the pedals are brown and crunchy, about two weeks."

"Before I leave for school, I'll make me some tea."

* * * *

It rained again during the night and stopped around midnight. And about that time there was an animal that had been drawn back to the root cellar because of the smells of the food within. He could smell human scent near the door, but there was human scent everywhere so he didn't pay any attention to it.

He wasn't being cautious and he bounded at the door barrier with both front feet and his rear feet came down on the nails and then the front feet. He screamed a blood curdling scream and ran off limping.

Sis sat up in bed and said, "Holy shit, what in the fuck was that?"

Apona said, "Shelby, what the hell was it?"

"I'm guessing we have an unhappy predator that stepped on that nail board. We'll find out in the morning."

"I don't think I can go back to sleep now. I need to pee, but I'm not going outdoors."

"I have to, also, and I'm not going out, either," Apona said.

"Okay, hold on, I'll get a bucket from the shed."

"That was the scariest sound I have ever heard," Apona said.

"I sure haven't heard anything like it either," Shelby said.

"I'm glad we aren't sleeping in a tent," Sis said.

"Do you think it was a bear?" Apona asked.

"Maybe, I'm not sure. Let's go back to bed." The cot was anything except comfortable.

None of them slept much for the rest of the night.

In the morning Shelby waited until it was daylight before venturing out to see if he could tell what the animal was. He carried his .44 revolver, too. Apona and Sis were close behind him.

"Holy cow, look at all that blood covering the board and in the sand. Still, there are no identifiable tracks."

Apona picked up a clump of hair from the nail board. "Look at this."

"Keep that, Apona. Look at the bent nails, I'm wondering if the animal might have gotten all four feet punctured by the nails.

"I bet he or whatever it is, will never bother you again," Sis said.

"I hope not," Apona said and then she took Shelby's hand.

"After we eat breakfast, I think I'll try to follow the blood trail."

"Any idea—guess—what it might be?" Sis asked.

"I really don't know. I have never heard anything like it," Shelby said.

He ate fast, loaded the .30-30, laid the .44 revolver on the table and said, "If you go outside, take this and stay together."

"How long will you be?" Apona asked.

"I'm not sure. I'll follow its trail until I lose it."

He kissed Apona and went out to the root cellar. There was a clear blood trail heading west away from the cabin. At the edge of the property, he found where the animal had laid down in some pine needles for a while. There was only a little blood there. But when it started moving again there was more blood.

He didn't dare try to imagine what he was following. If he did, he might lose his concentration and miss the blood trail or worse yet, not see an attack from the animal. So far the animal had not veered from its westerly route. Was it going back to a den? Or simply trying to leave the area?

He was more than a mile from home now and there was still a visible blood trail. But not so much.

He stopped to wipe the sweat from his forehead and no more than a hundred feet in front he heard a rabbit's death scream. Whatever he was following had just killed a rabbit, *Maybe it will take the time to eat it before continuing on.*

Placing one foot ahead of the other as silently as he could, he kept moving forward. He stopped; there was a deep throated growl coming from behind a rock.

Not wanting to accidently stumble onto it by sneaking across the rock, he moved off to the left. The underfoot was fir and spruce needles and quiet walking. When he had gone about thirty feet south, he started advancing west again, so he could see the other side of the rock. The animal was still growling.

One more step and he saw a ball of black, brown and gray fur. It was too small to be a bear and it certainly wasn't a cat.

When he turned to look at it the animal sensed something was wrong and lifted its head. Looking at Shelby, the animal stood his ground, protecting his kill and growling more vocally and baring his teeth. Instinct made Shelby raise his rifle to his shoulder and take a quick bead on the throat. He pulled the trigger. The animal dropped on top of the dead rabbit.

When he was certain the animal was dead he cautiously moved in.

He still wasn't sure he knew what it was. It actually looked much like a fisher cat, only much bigger. He had heard of wolverines, but he had never seen any pictures of one and he never heard of a trapper catching one. He picked it up and carried it under his right arm, upside down so the blood from the wound would not get on him.

Three hours after leaving home he hollered to let them know he was back. He laid it on a rock out front. "What is it?" Sis asked.

"Apona?"

"I think this same kind of animal that came into our village. I was only a little girl then. The men surrounded it and after a while they were able to kill it. It looks much the same. I only know the French name, carcajou; my people feared this animal more than any other animal."

"But it isn't very big," Sis noted.

"No, but is most fierce; my people tell stories of carcajou attacking wolves and bear."

Shelby rolled it onto his back. "It's a male and I'd guess about sixty pounds. Look at his paws. Each one has more than one puncture wound. Yet when I found him, he had just killed a rabbit."

"Do you think this is the animal that broke into your smokehouse your first winter here?" Apona asked.

"Yes."

He skun it, being careful not to make any slip cuts. He did around the head and ears and each paw and toe. Then he nailed it to the inside side of the woodshed. His drying boards were too small. "When this is dry, I'll make it into a rug," Apona said.

After lunch, Apona and Sis helped Shelby with firewood. The first tree was a white maple about fourteen inches on the butt. Sis watched as Apona helped on the other end of the saw. It came crashing down.

Shelby saw his sister's interest and said, "Here you and Apona saw the wood into stovewood lengths. Apona knows how long to make them."

He straddled the tree and picked the butt end up so they wouldn't have to bend over. Sis always knew her brother was strong, but this exhibition was more than she was expecting. Apona set the saw where she wanted it and said, "Don't push the saw, Sis, only pull it back to you. Ready?"

The first few strokes were awkward, but then Sis got the hang of it and it wasn't long before the whole trunk of the tree was blocked up. "The limbs we'll drag back to the woodshed and lay across the saw horses."

"I enjoyed that," Sis said.

"Well, let's do another," and he felled another white maple. They worked up four trees like that and then started splitting the blocks. The girls piled it into the cart as Shelby split the blocks.

By the time they finished what wood they had worked up,

it was time for a dip in the river.

"This water is so different than the first time I bathed in it. It was so cold then. I wish I didn't have to leave tomorrow," Sis said.

"We would like you to stay longer, Sis, but Mom may need your help."

"I know, she'll be busy soon, canning the vegetables from the garden."

"Maybe when you finish nursing training, you can come and stay with us again," Apona said.

"I would like to."

That night no one wanted to go to bed, knowing this would be Sis' last night. They stayed up until after midnight talking.

* * * *

Morning *did* come and they ate a hearty breakfast. Then they were on their way. "Can I paddle, Apona?"

They all were talkative until they pushed off in the second canoe. Then it was a subdued hush.

"We'd better say goodbye here, Sis, we have a long day ahead of us with this stove. Explain to Mom."

"I will, and goodbye," and she hugged and kissed them both. "Try to come out again before I have to leave—okay?"

Apona hugged and kissed her and said, "We will."

Adalbert explained to Shelby how to hook the stove up to the propane tank. "This stove has a wood fire box also, but I'm not sure if you'd be able to cook on it or not. Maybe keep food warm."

He helped Shelby dismantle it enough so it would go into the canoe. Shelby had to buy a few tools he didn't have in order to put it back together again.

"If I were you I'd get a second bottle of gas before winter too."

"Mr. Adalbert, do you have any brandy?"

"I only have a fifth of ginger brandy. Good for colds, it is. Mrs. Adalbert uses it to baste roast chicken."

They had to make two trips across the portage because of the hundred pound gas tank. There was one heavy piece to the stove and several smaller pieces. They were home about 2 o'clock.

That afternoon he ran the copper tubing from the tank. He'd wait until tomorrow to install the new stove.

"You look tired, my husband."

"I am. We were all up late last night and up early this morning. And carrying that hundred pound tank didn't help any."

"I think we both would feel better if we took a cool bath and then fix supper."

After supper they sat on the porch in the rocking chairs. "I do feel better, sweetheart."

"I know what we're missing," he said and stood up. "You wait right here. I'll be right back."

He poured some ginger brandy in two glasses and returned to the porch. "Here, don't drink it. Only sip it."

"It smells good," and she tasted it. "It tastes good too, but tickles my throat going down."

Shelby sipped his. "It is good." Instead of sitting in the other rocking chair she sat across his lap and kissed him with passion. He responded, almost spilling his drink on her.

They talked and laughed for a long time, sipping brandy. "I wonder if I put a little of this in an apple pie ..."

"Try it. It sounds good."

She unbuttoned her shirt and then his and said, "Let's go to bed. I want to make love with you until we fall asleep."

* * * *

The next day he had the new gas stove installed in time for Apona to use it for making coffee at lunch.

"Wow! This is so much easier, sweetheart, than building

a fire and waiting for the stove to get hot enough, and heating the cabin up. When you first decided on a propane stove I didn't know what to expect. Gas lights, gas stove, we're really modern, aren't we."

He picked her up in his arms and twirled her around.

"I have an idea, my husband. I love having Sis here with us, but I need you beside me in bed. Can we build another bed over ours?"

"I have a better idea. That wall is empty. What about a bed there?"

"Okay."

That evening as they were sitting on the porch, "Sweetheart, there is something that has really been bothering me."

"What?"

"I don't know exactly how to say what I want to say. I love our home. We have a beautiful cabin, gas lights, gas cook stove, water at our hand and a root cellar to keep our food from spoiling. I could never return to living like you found me. My people have been here—I don't know—from the beginning? We have so much more than my people. There are more people who I'm sure have so much more than we. Why have my people never—how do you say moved beyond living in hide lodges. It makes me want to cry. Are we less of a people, husband?"

She did start to cry and he picked her up and sat her in his lap. "You know, sweetheart, there are people living across the Atlantic Ocean in Europe who are more advanced than we are. Many of the improvements we have—the ideas came from Europe.

"Sweetheart, I don't think you should look down on your people; try looking at it this way. Who did the Great Creator choose to people this country? From the Atlantic to the Pacific Ocean. It wasn't the white race. It was the natives. Your people, sweetheart, tamed a fierce, hostile land ruled by vicious animals. The mountain lion, wolverines, giant bear, buffalo and poisonous snakes. The whites came only after your people had tamed this country. Your people, I think, know more about the spiritual works than the white man and the people were very comfortable living as they did and didn't want things to change. But when this land was tame enough for the white man, he brought new ideas. Does this help you?"

"Yes, now more than before, I can be proud of my people."

"Our attorney, Mr. Sinclare, has talked with another attorney, Mr. Pardis, who will help Ranibir and the village to adjust to these new ways and more. When we visit next spring, I wouldn't be surprised to find some changes."

"I love you so much, Shelby Martin. You never look down on me or my people. Kalipona not only bring you to me, she brought you to help my people, and you have, with this Attorney Pardis. She know what she do. I feel better.

"You pretty smart man. I think I'll keep you and not throw you back."

Chapter 11

Apona made her apple pie with ginger brandy. "This is so delicious, Apona. It is the best apple pie I have ever had."

"You think so? It doesn't bite you like sipping brandy. I wonder why?"

"I don't know."

"We don't have much left for meat, Shelby."

"I think it is time for you to learn how to shoot. When we go to town I want to get a .30-30 rifle for you. And you'll be shooting animals, when we start trapping."

They went out back and Shelby nailed up a board between two trees with a piece of white paper stuck to the board. Before any shooting, he went over with her how to use the rifle safely and how to aim and how to pull the trigger.

"You ready?"

"Yes."

"Load one shell and you're on your own." The target was fifty long paces away.

Her first shot was a 6 o'clock just below the paper. "That is good for your first shot."

The next four shots were all in the paper. "Wow, you're an expert. That's enough with the rifle, now the .22 revolver." Her first cylinder full of bullets were all over the board. "That's not bad, sweetheart, considering you were shooting at fifty yards. We'll move halfway up."

This time three shots hit the paper and the other three were close to the paper.

"Do I shoot another cylinder?"

This time four hit the paper and two were close. "That is real good shooting."

He showed her how to clean both and then he put them away.

"How are you doing with firewood?"

"The shed is full. There is still some that I want to pile up outside the shed and then find a dead cedar tree for kindling."

The next day though they went frogging. "I like frog legs," Apona said.

"What we don't eat tonight, we can can."

Apona thought this was more fun than fishing for brook trout. They ate their fill that night and canned two quarts.

The wolverine hide had dried and everyday Apona would rub hemlock bark on the flesh side until it had turned a rich brown color. It was soft now too.

"You know husband, if we sell this with our fur pelts next spring, I think we might get a lot of money for it."

"We'll try then."

Apona started making the rectangle hand baskets for Rebecca and Sis while he was out looking for dead cedar.

He heard one rifle shot coming from the cabin. "Uh oh, I wonder what she shot?"

He walked back and when he came around the corner of the cabin she was grinning. For a few moments they just stood there grinning at each other. "Okay, what did you shoot?"

"A deer."

"Did it have antlers?"

"Yes but not big."

"Good, let's go get it."

It was a nice spikehorn. After pulling out the innards Apona helped him to wash the inside of the deer in the river before putting it in the canoe.

215

For now they hung it in the woodshed and Apona took the heart inside to fry up with onions and potatoes.

Shelby nailed the hide up on the back of the wood shed. The deer was quartered and then hung up in the root cellar.

The next day Shelby helped Apona can much of the meat. Since the root cellar was cool they left one hind quarter hanging, so they would have some fresh venison.

"You know, wife, you shot an illegal deer?"

"What do you mean?"

"There is a season when you can shoot a deer which doesn't begin until October 15th. But I shot a summer deer last year, too. I just wanted you to know."

"At the village we could kill deer, moose and caribou anytime because we're natives. Maybe that goes here, too."

"I don't know. Anyhow good shooting."

* * * *

When the deer was all canned, Apona went mushroom hunting, while Shelby caught brook trout to smoke cure for the winter.

She returned with a basket full of mushrooms. "These would be better eaten instead of canning."

"Your flowers are growing good."

"Pretty, aren't they?"

"Looking at the cabin from the river, they make the cabin and setting."

The end of August was coming and their last trip to town until next spring. They had firewood, a new propane gas stove and gas lighting. They had some food stores, but this next trip would fill that need. They did catch a few more brook trout to smoke cure and the heads were put in a bucket and on ice in the root cellar. There was still more than half of the ice that he had initially put in.

"We must leave tomorrow, sweetheart."

"I'll be ready. The only thing I want to take are the baskets for Mom and Sis. Plus, I made a ginger brandy apple pie to give to Mom. It'll fit in the basket. This will be another large load coming back."

"The canoe will handle it okay. We'll just have to make a couple of trips across the portage."

That night he put out the nail boards, but left the windows. In the morning he did nail a board across the front door plus the nail board. "You ready?"

"Let's go."

As usual they left home before the sun was fully up. The water level in the river was up and they made good time. They had business in town before going to the farm. They gave Adalbert's their list for supplies and then Shelby wanted to walk over to the school house. And by chance Mrs. White was there, getting things ready for classes in two weeks.

"Hello, Shelby, what are you doing here?"

"Mrs. White, I want you to meet my wife, Apona."

"Hello, Apona."

"Mrs. White, by any chance would you have any geography books or history books we could have for the winter? We wouldn't be able to bring them back until spring."

"I have some old ones you can have."

"That would be nice, Mrs. White."

From there they walked to the farm. The farm boy was just putting the horses out to pasture.

Both Rebecca and Sis came running out to meet them.

"This is a special pie. I won't tell what went in it, until you have a slice. And here are hand baskets for both of you."

"Are you all ready for your school, Sis?" Shelby asked.

"Yes, and I'm excited."

Rebecca stood up and motioned with her head for Apona to follow her. Shelby and Sis were talking. Once outside, "Walk with me, Apona. Since Sis's two visits with you and Shelby, she is a changed person. She has come out of her shell and I think you had a lot to do with that, Apona. Just being who you are. She's now ready to face the world. Before the change, I was doubtful about letting her go to the nursing school. After all, she would be on her own. I'm no longer concerned, Apona. This summer she has gone from being a little girl to a young woman who knows what she wants."

Rebecca hugged her then and said, "Thank you, Apona. I love you as much as I do my daughter."

"Thank you, Mom, that is the nicest thing anyone has ever said to me."

Shelby and Sis came out then, "What's going on out here with you two?" Shelby asked.

Rebecca said, "Just a little girl talk."

When Raul came home, after supper, he and Shelby were talking business and the three women went for a walk looking for that special flower.

"How is your business going, Raul?"

"It has really picked up. So much so, I have had to hire two more wagons and drivers."

"I'm proud of you, Raul."

"What about you, Shelby? Are you and Apona going to stay in the woods forever?"

"Until we get tired of it, Raul. You see, we make a good living from trapping and we now own forty-two acres that the cabin sits on. Life is rough sometimes, but I imagine the freight business doesn't always run smooth."

"You know, brother, more and more people are reading about you in the newspaper. In a way you have become a legend around here. And people know I'm your brother and those that would normally like to cause me trouble, don't. I've heard it's because the troublemakers are afraid of you. Those two that you man handled, behind Adalbert's store, Louis and Edsel, are a good example. Now, they don't drink anymore and they have spread the word about you.

"When you and Apona walk down Main Street, I have heard people say, "There they go.""

Everyone ate so much for supper they all agreed to wait for dessert until later. "This pie looks delicious, Apona," Rebecca said.

She served the pie and everybody raved about it. "There's something different. What is it, Apona?"

"A little ginger brandy."

"Hmm, I've never heard of using brandy, but this sure is good."

* * * *

"We won't be back out, Mom, until spring," Shelby said.

"You two be careful and take care of each other." Rebecca hugged them, and then Sis. When Shelby hugged his sister he slipped a hundred dollars in her hand and said, "If you should ever need anything. And not a word, Sis."

"We'll see you, Sis, next spring," Apona said.

They walked with Raul to town and said their goodbyes there. Adalbert had all of their supplies put together and helped to carry them down to the canoe. The new mattress was laid on bottom and everything else on top of it. They had to make two trips across the portage again. The canoe was put on the rack and secured with a chain and locked.

The first thing they did was to check the nail boards. There was no evidence that an animal had been there. He removed those and the boards nailed across the doors.

That evening while sitting on the porch, Shelby said, "I gave Sis a hundred dollars and I told her ... if she ever needed it."

"I think that was a good idea. After all we have spent this summer, how much do we have left?"

"$5858.00, and yes we did spend a lot, nearly a year's income.

"I saw an idea in my head that I liked."

"And what did you see, husband?"

"Do you know what a honeymoon is?"

"No."

"When two people get married, if they can afford it, they'll take a trip, just the two of them, to celebrate, and they do a lot of love making."

"I think I like this honeymoon."

"Where we go, I'll keep it a surprise until we are on our way. And to pay for it, I think we should see if we can get some more gold nuggets to sell to Pasquale."

"Okay, let's go."

They took their shoes and pants off and waded out into the river in front of the Gold Brook inlet. There were a few lying on top of the sand and they found more by reaching down into the sand. By dark they had more than enough to fill another small pouch.

"We have so much food the root cellar is almost full."

Apona's flower blossoms were finally dry and she crushed them into a powder. She needed more. She and Shelby went by canoe looking for another patch and found them downstream, almost at the top of Grand Falls. She had brought a packbasket this time and they almost filled it.

There were so many they completely covered the work table in the shed.

Shelby caught some more brook trout, as much for trapping bait as food for them.

"Husband, I like cooking on this new gas stove very much. And it doesn't heat the cabin up like the wood stove did."

"It is getting close to trapping and tomorrow we need to walk out the traplines and clear the bushes and the dead falls from the trail, and leave a trap at each set so we will have less weight to carry when we do set up."

"What about lunch? Will we be back in time?"

"Probably not."

"Then I'll bring some smoked fish with us."

They sat out on the porch and Apona was in his lap. She kissed him with a real hunger and unbuttoned her shirt and whispered in his ear. And they went in and on the bed.

The air was getting cold anyway.

* * * *

The sunset the night before was promising a nice day. Shelby strapped on his holster and .44 revolver and filled his packbasket with traps. "You ready?"

"Let's go."

They started up along the river on the number one line first. There were a few dead branches in the trail but no blow downs.

The trail was clear after he made the turn to the left on higher ground.

Beaver were busy on the outlet stream from Lower Shaw Pond. The dam was two feet higher and much longer. "I trapped this two years ago but not last year. It looks like there are even more beaver here now."

At the next flowage they found more activity, also. "I think we should follow the inlet stream to this pond and see what there is."

They had traveled some distance before they found any sign. Then, the bottom of the little stream was littered with peeled beaver wood. "I never came up this stream this far two years ago."

A little further and they came to a large marsh and a large flowage. The dam had a lot of new wood and mud on top of an old dam. The house was huge. "Boy, is this going to be good trapping."

They hiked back to the number two trapline and back up along the river to home. It was time for supper. "Are you tired, sweetheart?"

221

"Some, my butt hurts when I slipped and sat down."

"I'll massage it later."

The water in the river was cold, but Apona insisted they bathe. But it was a short bath.

That night as they were lying in bed, Shelby said, "I liked what I saw today. It'll keep us busy for a few weeks. And there'll be a lot of beaver meat to can, too."

The next day while Apona was baking biscuits, Shelby worked on the additional bed. He had made it with two drawers like the other bed.

While the biscuits were baking Apona crushed the white turtlehead flowers into a fine powder and filled another quart Mason jar. She had almost three quarts of the tea now.

The nights were getting colder and there would be evidence of frost some mornings. Apona's flowers were gone and flocks of geese and ducks were flying overhead, going south every day. "Tomorrow we set traps, sweetheart."

"What about another deer? There isn't enough meat left to last us through the winter."

"There is a special place where we can shoot a deer across the river. But we'll wait until we are finished trapping. We should go to bed early, so we'll be well rested. The first day may be a long one."

"Should I put up a lunch for us?"

"No, we'll eat beaver."

But we haven't caught any yet, she thought to herself.

As they were lying in bed, Apona said, "If tomorrow be a long day and we tired, I want to make love now."

He rolled over and cupped her face in his hands and said, "I love you, Princess. You have an insatiable appetite for sex," he said jokingly.

"I can't help it. I'm horny all the time. Do you mind?"

"Heck no. I'm glad. I love you just like you are."

* * * *

The daylight hours were shorter and they left the cabin at first light. They both shouldered their packbaskets.

Apona watched Shelby make the first set, a water set for mink. The next one she did by herself while he went ahead and made a dirt hole set. The next set was a covey in tree roots and she watched him smear something on the tree. "What's that cream?"

"It is beaver castor ... smell," and he held out the jar.

"Ooh," was all she said.

"The smell drives meat eaters insatiable. They can't seem to stay away from it."

The next set was another covey and Apona made the set just like Shelby had and she smeared on a little castor.

Shelby went high to the woodchuck hole. The next two were more covies and they each made a set.

When they came to the leaning tree set, Apona had to watch him set this one. Then they came to the first beaver flowage. "How do we set traps here?"

"Take your basket off and bring the wire and cutters. I have the traps." He showed her how to make the trough and then she was on her own. After he had his set he watched and helped her.

"Why so much wire?"

"When the beaver is caught in the trap, it will naturally swim for deep water and there it'll drown. We need to secure the trap, so it won't swim off with it, and so we can pull it in."

They went ashore and stood behind a fat little fir tree. Shelby pointed to a swimming beaver. "Sssh."

The beaver swam straight for Apona's trough and snap. He was caught.

"Now we wait for him to drown."

"Here comes another one," Apona whispered.

This went to inspect Apona's trough first and then Shelby's and he was caught. "This is much easier than I thought it would be."

"Okay, your beaver has stopped struggling, you can pull him in. Be careful you don't slip and fall in." He stood beside her to help if she couldn't get it in.

"Wow, he feels heavy. Here it comes I can see it." She pulled it onto the dam and he showed her how to release the tension on the trap jaws.

She had all she could do to lift it. "You'd better let me carry it ashore. You can bring the other one in."

She pulled in another, as big as the first one. And Shelby went out to carry that one back. "I'll reset these," Apona said.

"I'll start skinning." He took them back away from the flowage before he started skinning.

When she had finished both traps, she joined Shelby and said, "Lunch."

"Are you hungry yet?"

"No."

She watched with real interest as he fleshed the hide as he was skinning.

"You know, with my people, women do not trap animals or hunt. I already have done both. What stories I'll have to tell the people come spring."

Shelby was smiling. She was really having fun. And he was enjoying watching her unfold like a beautiful water lily as her consciousness and discoveries were expanding.

Just then another trap snapped closed and for a brief moment the beaver was splashing in the water before it swam off.

When the water went calm, she didn't have to have Shelby tell her to pull the beaver in. Excitedly she hollered, "It's another really big one!"

"Do you need help?"

"I'll drag it across the dam." And she did and then she went back to reset the trap.

The pond went calm then. As he was skinning, Apona was

cutting off the legs, "Where are the castors?"

He showed her. She also cut the tails off. "These tails are good to eat."

The meat, castors and tails were wrapped in hides and put in his bigger packbasket. The traps were moved to Apona's.

He threw the carcasses into the pond and carried the other one to the ground set on the side hill. He let Apona make the water set in the inlet.

The next two sets, a ground set in fir tree roots which Apona set, and he set the other one, a ground set, and he dug a bigger hole for the carcass.

When they came to the next beaver flowage, Shelby didn't have to tell her what to do. When those two were set; they no more than made it ashore and two beaver came down and both were caught. "If you want, sweetheart, you can do the knoll set up the side hill."

He pulled in two more super large beaver, reset the traps and began skinning. The pond went quiet. "I figure we can eat at the next beaver pond."

They picked up and started following the little stream. This dam was so big they made three troughs. Then they went ashore and built a fire.

"I'll make a land set while you're making a fire," Shelby said.

They were roasting beaver meat before a beaver came to inspect the dam and see why water was leaking. While Apona cooked lunch, Shelby pulled that beaver in, another super large beaver, and reset the trap.

He had the beaver half skun when Apona said, "Meat is done."

They ate their fill of beaver, then another trap went off. "I'll get that," Apona said.

And the pond went quiet.

Apona was now carrying a beaver hide and meat in her

packbasket. And they continued on the trapline.

They made three leaning tree sets and a dirt hole set on high ground and he used a carcass for bait.

From Halfway Brook they were in the dark. "I'll start supper and I'm afraid all we have out is beaver."

"That's okay. I'll set these baskets in the shed. On second thought, I might as well start putting them on boards."

"How about a fire in the big stove. It's cold in here."

"Okay." Then he started working with the beaver. He even had one on the board before Apona said, "Supper is ready." He turned the gas light off, so not to waste the gas.

As they were eating, he said, "We made twenty-four sets today and caught seven super large beaver. That's a pretty good day's work."

"How much are those seven worth?"

"More than two hundred."

* * * *

After she had the kitchen cleaned and beaver meat in the root cellar, she helped Shelby with the last two beaver.

"Before we go to bed, we both need to wash up good. We smell."

They took their clothes off and hung 'em up in the shed. No sense getting more clothes smelling like beaver. "We might as well wear these tomorrow."

It was 10 o'clock when they turned the gas light off and crawled into bed. "It was a long, busy day, sweetheart. Are you tired?"

"Yes."

"Do you want me to scratch your itch?"

"No."

* * * *

"Are you going with me or can beaver?"

"I feel better now. I want to go with you."

He had only built a fire in the wood stove portion of the new gas stove. He'd let it go out now.

The first two sets were water sets and they had one mink. The martin set was empty and the next two were covey sets and there was one martin and one fisher cat.

"Holy cow! Shelby what is that? It is too big for a bobcat."

"Lynx, and he is angry. You take the .22. I'm going to get his attention." He came in front of the lynx, downhill. He now had the cat's undivided attention. "Okay, come in from behind close enough so you can shoot him in the ear."

The cat was now crouching down as if it was going to leap, except he was being held securely. He was unaware of Apona's approach and she placed her shot in his left ear; the cat dropped. "Good shooting, Apona."

"He is so big."

"Yeah, the biggest lynx I have ever seen."

He put it in his packbasket and said, "I'll skin this when I start skinning beaver."

In the next two covey sets they held a fox each. He put these two in Apona's basket. At the first beaver flowage both traps were empty. "It happens," and they moved on.

There was an otter in the inlet set and Shelby put that in his basket.

In the ground set in the fir tree, there was a vocal martin. The ground set where he had used a beaver carcass was empty. On the hillside he had another lynx. A much smaller one and a female. He put this in his basket, also.

In number two pond, both traps had been pulled into the water and they each held a super large beaver. "Now it's time to do some skinning." He did beaver first and two hours later he had all of them skun and packed away in his packbasket.

At the number three beaver pond, all three traps were pulled into the water and they pulled out two super large beaver and an otter.

Apona started a fire and started roasting lunch.

They caught one more super large beaver there before the pond went quiet. When he had that one skun, he ate more roasted meat.

"This is fun, sweetheart."

That beaver hide and meat was put in her packbasket. By the time they had tended the last trap they picked up three more martin. That was a pretty good catch for the first tend. "Let's go home."

"I think I should stay home and can all this beaver meat tomorrow."

* * * *

The temperature dropped during the night and there was a thin film of ice on the river next to shore. "Winter is coming, sweetheart."

"You go and have fun. I'll can all of the beaver meat. Be careful."

Apona had meat from thirteen beaver to clean, cut up and can. When she had filled the last jar, it filled the canner and she turned the gas on to bring it to a boil. She also kept the wood stove going. Maybe once the water started to boil she could move over on top of the wood stove and save the gas.

All of the traps up to the first beaver pond were empty and one extra-large beaver in the first pond. He reset and skun the beaver. The pond was still quiet, so he moved on.

All of the traps up to the next pond were also empty and one extra-large beaver. He skun that and moved on. And the third beaver pond, he had two super large beaver and all of the traps back to the river were empty.

"You are home early; how'd it go?" Apona asked.

"Three beaver and no land animals."

"How come?"

"I don't know, but it has happened before. How was your day?"

"I canned twelve quart jars and they are in the root cellar already.

"Why no animals?"

"The first year there were wolves. After I trapped three, the other wolves moved on and the fur animals became active. We'll just have to wait and see."

"I'm glad you're home early."

"What do you have for supper?"

"Venison stew with biscuits."

"Have I time to do some stretching?"

"Maybe one hide. Then wash up."

* * * *

There was two inches of new snow in the morning and there was a chill in the air. "We have stew and biscuits for supper, so I go with you today."

During the night the fur bearing animals were on the move. There were fresh tracks in the snow the whole length of the trapline.

They picked up one extra-large beaver at the first beaver pond and the decision was made to pull those traps before they started catching small beaver.

At the number two pond, one super large beaver and one small one. They pulled those traps too.

At the number three pond all three traps were in the water and the troughs had been filled in. "There's obviously more beaver in here," Shelby said.

They pulled in two more super large beaver and an otter. While Shelby was busy skinning, Apona reset the traps and then started a fire to roast lunch.

Before Shelby had finished skinning, Apona ran out to the dam and pulled in an extra-large beaver and reset the trap.

"We're doing good today. Five beaver and an otter, four martin and a mink," Apona said.

While the meat was cooking and Shelby was still skinning the otter, she checked the hillside trap. There was a very upset fisher cat caught by both front feet. She shot it in the ear and brought it back to the fire. Since Shelby was still busy skinning, she started skinning the fisher cat.

By the time all the animals had been skun, lunch was ready. They were ahead of schedule today, so they didn't hurry. But as they were picking up to leave another trap snapped and went back in the water. They waited five minutes, before pulling in another otter.

He hung the otter up and began skinning. The pond went quiet. "Shall we move on?"

"Lead the way."

Just the beaver alone represented a good day's work and pay. Before reaching home, they picked up another fox, another fisher cat and a martin.

During the night the weather changed. It was warm and raining. "This will be a good day to stay home," Shelby said.

He was running out of stretchers and drying boards, so he had to take some of the hides off that were ready. And Apona canned another five quarts of meat.

Two days later they tended traps again and had another super large beaver in the number 3 pond. "We have many beaver from this flowage and I think we should pull the traps."

When they stopped trapping for the season they picked up another seven more martin, two bobcat, two more mink and two fox. "I know we could catch more, but I think we should leave the rest for seed for two years from now."

"That's okay with me," Apona said, "We have done very well. I've kept count what we have and there are fifty-four pelts total. It's amazing, husband."

"What is?"

"In four weeks we earn a yearly income."

"I think I know what you mean. But it takes work every day to live out here like we do."

"I think you would have made a good Indian." They both laughed.

"When are we going deer hunting?"

"We'll have to go tomorrow. The day after is the last day. You'll want to wear an extra pair of socks, a warm coat, a hat and gloves. We'll be standing a lot, waiting."

"Do we really need two deer?" Apona asked.

"To see us through the winter, no. But if we can as much as we can, then it should see us through next summer and maybe we won't have to shoot an illegal deer."

"What is the fine for shooting a summer deer?"

"Probably about fifty dollars."

"Would they put you in jail?"

"I don't know—maybe, if you couldn't pay the fine." Shelby knew what she was thinking.

The temperature that night didn't drop below freezing and the snow was not crunchy. And the shell ice along the shore of the river had disappeared.

There were fresh deer tracks in his trapline trail heading south for a ways and then the deer had turned east towards the big marsh. Shelby followed his trail to the same spot where he had shot deer his last year.

The air was cool, but not cold and so far, no wind. A half hour into standing, Apona whispered, "I need to pee."

"Okay, give me your rifle and pee right here. I don't want you moving around."

As she was pulling her pants up a red squirrel overhead started scolding them. Apona made a snowball and threw it at the little bugger. She hit him on the end of the nose toppling him off the branch into the snow. He quickly picked himself up and ran off, not to be heard from again, "That was a good shot," he said.

They waited some more. *A summer deer was much easier,* Apona was thinking.

There was a lot of noise to their right just out of sight on the hardwood ridge. "What was that?" Apona asked.

"I'm not sure, maybe a moose."

Then they could hear it again and this time it sounded closer. They waited, not knowing what to expect. Then he saw movement and then it ran across the trail in full view and maybe ten seconds behind that bull moose was a bigger one chasing it. "They're heading for the deer yard. Maybe they'll chase the deer up this way."

And ten minutes later that is just what happened. First, two does with young fawns came running up the trail and beyond them. Then a minute later a spikehorn and a much larger buck came walking up the trail.

They both pulled their rifle up to their shoulder. Shelby said, "You take the one in front when I tell you. I'll take the one in the rear." He was about thirty feet back from the spikehorn.

Apona wanted to shoot. She had to pee again. The spikehorn was only thirty feet away. "Okay now," he whispered. The spikehorn heard Shelby and stopped and lifted his head high. She fired and then Shelby. Both deer went down.

"I thought you were never going to let me shoot. I have to pee again." Both deer had been hit in the throat and they were both dead. When Apona was ready, she held both deer on their backs as Shelby dressed them.

"That didn't take long. Now what?"

"Can you drag your deer by yourself?"

"I think so."

Shelby took the lead with the bigger deer and headed cross country through the marsh to the river. He had to stop often so Apona could rest. The deer obviously was heavier than her. But she never whined or complained.

When they had both deer at the canoe Shelby stood up

straight sniffing the air. "Do you smell that?"

"Smell what?"

"Liver and onions."

"You're hungry aren't you?"

"Just a little."

"Me too."

* * * *

They did have their liver and onions, and boiled potato and mushrooms. "A meal fit for a king," Shelby said.

They canned all of Shelby's deer and the spikehorn was left hanging in the root cellar for fresh steaks and roasts.

"I used the last of our Mason jars."

"Hmm, maybe next year we should get another box just to be on the safe side."

Their work for preparations for winter was done and now Apona used the time to study, not just read, the world geography book and the world history book. She was now being introduced to the rest of the world. Shelby also enjoyed reading them. All of the fur was now dry and stretched and one by one, he primped and combed each one until they shone like shellac. One day he strapped on his snowshoes and went for a hike around his traplines. "I want to see what there is for animals left after we pulled the traps. Do you want to go?"

"No, you go. I'm going to do some more studying."

He wasn't sure about the river ice yet, whether it would be solid enough or not. So he snowshoed backwards, this time starting with the number two trapline trail. Even after all the fur they had taken that year, he was impressed and excited about the sign he was seeing. But then, of course, one martin, for an example, in a day can leave a lot of tracks. But he was also finding fisher cat tracks and bobcat's. And at the number three beaver pond he saw a red wolf trying to dig down through the smaller of the two beaver houses. The wolf was so intent in his digging Shelby was able to sneak up within thirty feet of the house, before the wolf sensed something. When he spotted Shelby he bolted and never looked back.

He walked around the pond just looking at things and found the beaver were still coming ashore for fresh wood to chew on, by swimming up a spring freshlet. In really cold temperatures even this freshlet would freeze over and then the beaver's only food would be from their feed bed.

He snowshoed cross country through a beautiful stand of hardwoods to the number one beaver pond. There he found a lynx trying to dig down through the beaver house. The lynx was more alert than the wolf had been and as soon as Shelby was on the ice the lynx bolted.

Before returning home, Shelby took a few minutes to reflect on his life. All he had ever wanted from his father was his love. As much as he had always wanted to hate him for all of the fault finding and domineering towards his entire family, he now understood that if his father had not been exactly as he had been, he might still be on the farm and would never have his home on the Dead River or have ever met Apona. His eyes watered and he had to move on before he started crying. *Thanks Dad, you were what you were and that made me what I am.*

Chapter 12

After that revelation about his father, when he was back home he hugged Apona and said, "You are the best thing that has ever happened to me."

"What brought this on?"

"While snowshoeing, I began to understand how lucky I am. That's all."

"These books Mrs. White gave me to study have surely opened a new world for me. A world I think I would be afraid to face without you. You opened a door for me, husband, but I would like you to walk through it with me."

He wanted to tell her that that door was the real reason he wanted to take her on a honeymoon, after they returned from Lac Megantic in the spring. But he didn't, he wanted it to be a surprise, so he only smiled.

Knowing it would soon be time to tap the maple trees, he began making snowshoe trails in and around each tree to freeze down a solid walking path.

One night while lying in bed talking and listening to logs in the cabin snapping, and to the bark of the fir trees explode like a .22 rifle shot, as the sap froze from the -40° cold, the river was making ice and cracked so violently that the cabin shook and a crack opened up in the middle of the river all the way up to Long Falls. And the snowshoe trail was now as hard as concrete.

Warmer weather arrived and the sweet tasting sap began to leak from the maple branches, freezing at night into maple flavored icicles. It was time to tap trees.

Shelby bored the holes with a bit-brace. Apona would drive the spirals in and hang the buckets and covers. There was one beautiful rock maple that was about three feet on the butt and it went straight up without a branch for thirty feet.

He drilled three holes and as soon as Apona had inserted the spirals sap began to run in a small steady stream from all three. He had only bought six buckets, so they only hung three more. "This doesn't seem like enough buckets, but we should be able to collect enough sap to boil down enough syrup for us."

"As fast as this is running maybe we should get everything ready," Apona said. While she was bringing out the evaporator pan, Shelby was collecting dead limbs from the many trees behind the cabin. "I hope we don't use up all of our wood," he said.

"Remember, husband, we didn't use as much wood in the kitchen stove this winter. It might be a good trade off."

After lunch, while he was gathering more dry wood, Apona checked the buckets. The three on the big maple trees were almost full and the others were about half full. She went after two buckets and emptied all of the sap in the evaporator pan and started the fire. Shelby came back carrying an armload of wood.

She anticipated his question and said, "I had no choice. The buckets were almost full."

Once the sap came to a boil, they didn't need such a hot fire. While Shelby tended the fire, Apona went inside and washed out several Mason jars. They had emptied more than enough jars of food, so there were now enough for syrup.

Before dark he emptied the six buckets and went in for supper. He ate fast and went back out.

When Apona had taken care of the food and cleared the table and dishes, she went out to see how he was doing. "Shelby, you go lay down and sleep until midnight, then you come out and I'll sleep."

He kissed her and went in. He took his boots off and lay down with his clothes on. He left the gas lights on, as this gave Apona some light through the windows.

Sometime later he awoke to find the inside of the cabin was in darkness, except for a brilliantly illuminated woman standing at the foot of the bed. He instantly knew who she was. "Kalipona."

"Good, you do remember who I am.

"You had a bridge to cross."

"What bridge?" he asked.

"The bridge between hate and love."

"I don't understand."

"Until you came here and built this cabin, your feet were stuck in the muck on the hate side of the bridge. You were living in your father's shadow in hate. You killed the raccoon and let the pretty pelt go to waste because of the anger that had built up inside you. You needed to pay for that, so the wolverine clawed through the door, so the raccoon could enter your food storage building and ate everything left by the wolverine. The debt had been paid. When you were starving, you caught the mouse and you were willing to sacrifice your own life for the mouse. You could have easily squeezed the life out of the mouse and ate it. That is why the eagles brought you food.

"You saved Apona from being raped, and her brother and herself would have been murdered. You didn't hesitate. You put their well-being ahead of you.

"Am I making any sense?"

"I understand what you are saying."

"All this time you were crossing this bridge. You made it to the other side when you realized that nothing of this life here, Apona, the cabin, the gold, would have happened, if your father had not treated you so badly. You forgave him and thanked him. That was the final step across the bridge. This bridge is not one way. You can walk back across anytime. That decision will be yours alone. Am I making it clear?"

"Yes."

"I chose you, because of your fortitude and love that you carry with you every day. You see this isn't only about you. You opened a door for Apona's people and you also have opened a door for Apona. A door which she is about to step through. She will, but the time is not yet to come. It will, though.

"I will not be back anytime soon. But be assured I am always watching over you.

"Apona is coming to wake you now and I must leave. When you awake, me and what I have spoken will only be fading images."

"Why? Why will I not remember?" he was almost pleading.

"You have yet another bridge to cross. When the time is right, the door will be opened.

"Until next time, Shelby Martin, may you and Apona live well and enjoy each other."

* * * *

Apona shook Shelby awake. "It's midnight, sweetheart."

"Oh, okay. Wow, did I just have a terrific dream."

"What was it about? Not another woman I hope."

"I'm not sure now. The images faded so fast. How is the syrup doing?"

"I ran off enough to fill a quart jar, and I had to collect the sap again. It was filling the buckets so fast."

"Before going to bed, I'm going to have to wash up. I smell like smoke. Even my hair."

Before daylight, he had to run off another quart of syrup. After breakfast while Apona was watching the sap boil, he tried to lie down for a while. That lasted about five minutes and he remembered he had to cut ice for the root cellar.

The ice was thick this year, but once he had the first block out, the rest went more easily. The old ice had finally melted by the end of November. He carried the blocks into the root cellar and buried them with sawdust.

By the end of their syrup making days, they cooked the syrup a little longer until the foam had the right color and they poured it over snow and it cooled into a chewy candy. "We used to do this in the village each year and the last of the syrup was poured over snow for the children. Actually, everybody had some."

They had boiled down enough sap to fill six jars with syrup. "I was going to suggest we take some for the village when we go, but I guess they have their own."

"We could give some to your family. I'm sure they would appreciate it."

"Okay."

Warm weather arrived early in April and the river ice soon turned to yellow slush. One day the temperature rose to 75° and it rained the next day, washing the ice downstream. Apona's flowers were beginning to poke through the ground. The daffodils were the first to show and blossom.

The water level in the river had dropped and the ground was beginning to dry. One day Shelby checked to see if any more nuggets had been washed out into the river. He was surprised at what he saw.

"Apona, do you want to get wet?"

"What are you talking about?"

"There are gold nuggets that have washed out into the river. Someday someone is going to come through here in a canoe, and I don't want those nuggets to be seen. It would only cause a lot of trouble."

"I agree with you."

They each had an empty can and they took their clothes off and waded out in the cold water. "I'm glad the air is so warm," Apona said.

They collected only the nuggets they could see on top of

the sandy bottom without digging for them. Twice they had to come ashore and warm up in the sun. They had filled one can with nuggets. "How much is there, sweetheart?"

"I'd guess two—three pounds." They picked their clothes up and went back to the cabin.

"We should be making a list of things we need. It won't be long and we'll leave."

"I want a braided rug for the cabin and not those deer hides."

"Okay. It would look good wouldn't it?"

"I think so."

He had their fur bundled and the gold was put into two wool socks, the ends tied off, and put in the middle of the bundle.

"We'll leave tomorrow after breakfast and probably stay over at the farm."

He had to make another nail board to place in front of the door between the firewood shed and the enclosed shed or workshop. He had to get another board to nail across that door also. He checked the chicken wire wrappings to make sure they were okay. The last thing he did Sunday evening was to secure all the doors and windows. There would be no food at all left inside the cabin or the shed for animals to smell.

"Do you suppose we could get two apple trees from Mr. Adalbert? It would be so much easier if we grew our own apples."

"We can ask."

While Apona made breakfast Monday morning, Shelby put an empty propane tank in the canoe to take back to Adalbert's with the bundle of fur. They left the doors open while they ate, so to air out the inside of any food smells.

He locked the front door and they stood for a moment on the porch holding each other and looking at each other. "I love you, Apona—wife."

"And I love you, my husband. Let's go."

There was no hurry this trip and they canoed at a leisurely pace.

At the portage, Apona helped Shelby get into the rope harness that supported the fur bundle on his back and shoulders. "Can you carry the tank, sweetheart?"

She tried to lift it. "No." She already had a packbasket on filled with their clothes and such.

"It probably weighs more than you. Can you stand it up on end so I don't have to bend over?"

"What are you going to do?"

"Lift it on my shoulder if I can."

She helped to lift the tank up. "There, as long as I don't stub my toe."

She walked beside him just in case. At the upper end he said, "That wasn't as bad as I thought it would be."

It was mid-morning when they pulled the canoe ashore behind Adalbert's. He carried the fur up and left it on the stoop in front of the store. "Mr. Adalbert, we brought back an empty propane tank, and here is a list of supplies we will be needing."

"Do you have any apple trees?" Apona asked.

"I do."

"Would you set two aside for us?"

"Surely, anything else?"

"Yes, a braided rug," Apona said.

"I'll have to order that."

"Let me show you a catalogue, Mrs. Martin," Mrs. Adalbert offered.

A half hour later they were walking towards the farm with the bundle of fur and Apona's packbasket. "I ordered three rugs sweetheart. I hope that's okay."

"Of course it is."

"Two smaller ones between our bed and the heater and another, same size between the other bed and the heater and one in front of the front door."

"When will they be in?"

"She said at least a month."

From Adalbert's they went to the school house and gave the two books to Mrs. White. "Would you have any more I could read, Mrs. White?"

"Oh yes. When would you like them?"

"Not until the end of summer."

Sis was hanging out clothes when she saw them walking in the driveway and she ran out to meet them.

Sis helped Apona with her packbasket. "Don't drop that, Sis, we brought two quarts of maple syrup out for the family," and she took the Mason jars out.

"Hello, Mom, you're looking good."

"How was your winter?"

"It was good, Mom. We are both very happy living where we do."

"Well, come in, come in. I have been making donuts. Sis, will you make some coffee? The water is hot."

They drank coffee and ate donuts, all while talking.

"Have you bathed in the river yet, Apona?"

"Yes, but it was quick."

"I still want to go back with you when you come back from Lac Megantic. By then maybe the water will be warmer. I cannot wait to go bathing in the nude. It's much more fun to bathe in the river than a tub. A tub wouldn't quite fit the three of us."

"Sis, tell us about nursing," to change the subject.

"I am a registered nurse now and I have a job in the Farmington Hospital, but I don't start until August first."

"We built another bed for you, Sis."

"So you won't have to sleep on the cot anymore."

They were so full of coffee and donuts that no one wanted lunch.

When Raul got home from the office the five of them stayed up late talking.

In the morning, Shelby and Apona put on their buckskin clothes and packed the others in her packbasket. After breakfast they walked with Raul to the stage terminal. "I'll see you on your return, brother. Apona, always a pleasure to see you again," Raul said.

There were two men who boarded the stagecoach that were going to a lumber camp near Bugeye Pond south of Chain of Ponds. The road crews were late grading the road this year and it was a rough ride all the way to Coburn Gore.

Rex handed down the bundle of fur and the packbasket. At the border all the officer asked was, "Where are you going?"

Apona answered, "To see my father, Chief Ranibir."

He wished them well and let them pass.

When they could hear children playing they knew they were close. The first thing they saw was a new building. "There are changes here," Apona said.

Ranibir and Sopi came down to meet them. Caponi wasn't far behind them.

Because the road was rough, the stage was a little late arriving at Coburn Gore and now Shelby and Apona were too late for the noon meal.

"You like new school?" Ranibir asked. "School here because of you, Shelby and Apona. Pardis attorney, he good man. He says same as Marquis and Shelby, our people must be educated. Says best thing we can do for our people. We now have help from Canada's government. They pay for new school and teacher. Pardis, he find work for some of the men. They buy things at Pasquale's that we need. Since Kalipona brought you here, life is now better."

"I am so happy for you, Father," Apona said.

They talked all afternoon and when the women started preparing the evening meal, Apona wanted to help. "No," Sopi said, "You guest. Not have to work."

That night they had the same lodge to themselves. "You know, my husband, I am so glad to see my people again, but I would rather you and me were at our own home."

In the morning they borrowed a canoe and took their fur to Pasquale's. Ranibir and Sopi watched them go. Sopi said, "Apona, she no longer my daughter, Ranibir. She belongs to Shelby now. She will have good life with this man."

"Yes, Sopi, I think you are right. I like Shelby. He is so good for Apona."

Before letting Pasquale see all of the pieces, Apona pulled the wolverine pelt out of the bundle first. "How much for this, Monsieur Pasquale?"

"Wow, you nice job finishing this. I'll pay you two hundred dollars."

"Okay," Apona said.

And Shelby gave him the gold next. "You have more than last year." And he weighed it. "You have seventy-four ounces. Gold same price as last year. Gold comes to $1536.27. I give $1490.00."

"Okay," Shelby said.

"There is a high demand for fur in Europe right now and the prices have gone up some."

Pasquale was busy pricing each specie and he was taking longer than usual. "For the fur and castors I give you $1940.00."

"Okay."

"With gold and wolverine hide that comes to $3630.00."

Shelby tried to keep a straight face. Apona didn't have any trouble. "Do you have pigs again this year, Pasquale?"

"Yes, you want one? I have two hanging up downstairs."

"Yes, one. And we will look around. Apona, is there anything we can get for the village?"

"Maybe more candy for the children. The pig is enough."

"Okay. A big bag of different candies."

"Okay, pig and candy is $55.00. I now owe you $3575.00."

"US dollars."

"Yes, yes of course."

Pasquale helped with the pig and said, "You come back

next year."

"We will," Apona said.

"This pig is heavier than last year."

The heavy spit was already set up when they returned to the village. After the skin was removed it took four men to secure it to the spit. Everyone was excited about the feast the next day.

When Shelby wanted to help tend the fire and pig during the night, Apona pulled him aside and said, "I know you mean well, my husband. These people are proud. You can't do everything for them. You brought the pig, let them cook it okay,"

"Okay, and I understand."

* * * *

Because the pig was bigger this year, it was not ready to eat until Thursday at noon. Even after everyone had eaten as much as they could there was plenty of leftovers for another meal plus a huge stew for everyone.

That evening as everyone was gathering in the ceremonial area Apona said to her father, "Father, tonight I have a story that I want to tell."

"No. Women do not tell stories about our people," Ranibir said firmly.

Sopi said, "Husband, daughter has something to share with village, you let Apona speak."

"You can speak."

"Father, my story may take a long time. I would like to go first."

"You can go first, daughter," Sopi smiled.

People were beginning to talk among themselves as never before had a woman told stories to the people.

"My friends, I have something very important to share with you," everyone stopped talking. Shelby really wasn't sure what she was going to say. "From the beginning of time our people have come a great distance. When I speak of our people,

I'm talking about the race of Indians. In our legends and stories, there are stories of the white man coming to our land. We all have seen and experienced the good of some of the white race. As well as the bad. Like there are good and bad people among us. I took a white man as my mate, my husband, because I love him so. I wanted no other. This may come to a shock for some of you. Today, I am a hunter and trapper. I have shot two deer and trapped many fur animals." There were gasps of surprise in the audience. "I also clean and keep our lodge, cook and prepare food. Last year my husband talked with a white woman school teacher, who gave me two books to study during the winter. I read and reread and reread and studied both books. One was world geography. About other countries and people all over this world. I understood how small we really are. There are amazing places. The other book was world history. Any of you would be surprised to learn what has gone on for thousands of years outside our little world." She had everyone's attention. "And there are good people as well as bad throughout history of this world.

"Before Kalipona brought Shelby Martin to our village, there were times when I felt ashamed of what I—we are. Here in the village we have all heard about marvels in the white man's world making us feel less than the white man. One day I talked with my husband, Shelby Martin, how I was feeling and this is what he said. The Great Creator did not put the white race, the black or yellow race here. He put our race, the Indian natives, here to tame this land for other races, people, that would come. The Great Creator needed a race of people who could survive the elements and the beasts of nature: the mountain lion, the wolf, the black bear, the grizzly bear, the polar bear and the wolverines. Our fortitude and courage tamed this land for those who are coming now. Just because we do not yet have the material things that the white man has, does not mean that we are any less of people than the white man. Indian natives everywhere have so enjoyed our lifestyle we have failed to change. Change is hard to accept when we do not understand. But if we do not change, we will be left behind and all memories of us will be rubbed out until there is nothing left but dust.

"Studying those two books this past winter opened my mind. Education. Education is the only answer that will keep our stories and memories from disappearing. I'm not saying we must become like the white man, but we do need education. All of us, not just the children. I see there is a schoolhouse. That is good. That is a step in the true course of our existence, our survival as a people.

"Do not ever feel that you are less of a people. Do remember our people tamed this land." There were tears in her eyes.

When Apona started speaking Kalipona was standing in the background behind Shelby. She was dressed like any other woman in the village and no one paid any particular notice of her.

She listened pleasingly to Apona. When Apona had finished speaking, Kalipona placed a hand on Shelby's shoulder and said, "You have crossed your bridge, Apona."

Shelby felt something like a hand on his shoulder and when he turned to see who was there, Kalipona had already left.

Apona walked back to Shelby and he hugged her and said, "That was great, sweetheart. You had their undivided attention for two hours. Listen, you still have their attention." No one was talking.

Ranibir and Sopi came over to see Apona. Sopi spoke first, "You really hunt and trap?"

"Yes, Mother, I do."

Ranibir said, "The greatness of Kalipona—tonight, I think—was in you, daughter. You gave us all so much to think about. And I agree, the answer is education for our people."

"Father," Apona said, "there will be many bridges to cross."

Shelby's heart and breathing stopped when Apona said that about the bridges. Somewhere, he wasn't sure, there was something else about crossing bridges. That's all he could recall. There was more to it, he was sure.

People started to wander off to their own lodges. And still no one spoke.

"You were wonderful, sweetheart. They all heard you."

"At first I didn't know what I wanted to say. Once I started, the words just kept coming. I have never talked so much in my life."

"After tonight you will never be forgotten, Princess."

* * * *

For the remainder of their stay, Ranibir would often want to talk with Shelby. And Sopi and Apona were also invited, which had never before happened. Women just did not interfere with subjects men would talk about.

The morning came when they started their walk back to the border. "Did we get enough for our honeymoon?"

"Yes."

"When do we go?"

"We should wait for the warm weather. June, I think."

"You still won't tell me where?"

"Not until we leave."

The road had been graded all the way to Flagstaff and they arrived just before noon. They stopped first at Adalbert's. "Good day, folks, are you heading back now?"

"No, tomorrow morning. Do you have grips?"

"We sure do," Mrs. Adalbert said.

"What is a grip, Shelby?"

"I think you might call it a suitcase. It's something to carry clothes in when you travel. I think we'll need two, Mrs. Adalbert, if we could pick those up tomorrow with everything else."

They stopped next at the bank and deposited their money.

He deposited $3,400.00. "You now have in your account, Mr. & Mrs. Martin, $9290.17."

"Thank you, Mr. Edwards."

On their way to the farm, Apona asked, "Is that a lot of money?"

"Yes, it is, sweetheart."

Rebecca and Sis were still at the kitchen table eating lunch.

Rebecca fixed them a ham sandwich and coffee. While they ate, Apona told them, "Shelby is taking me on a honeymoon trip next month."

"Where are you going?"

"He won't tell me."

After lunch while Shelby and his mother were talking in the kitchen, Sis and Apona went upstairs to her room. "If you are going on your honeymoon, you should have sexy undergarments."

"I do not understand this, Sis."

"Let me show you." She pulled out from a bureau and held them up to show Apona.

"I understand now. Can you get these at Adalbert's?"

"No, I tried. I bought these while I was in nursing school. I don't dare wear them around here. Mom would have a fit. You take these."

"Do you have any good dresses?"

"I have two with a flower print. We'll see what else Adalbert has. We can go now, so we don't hold you up in the morning."

"We're going over to Adalbert's."

"Okay."

"I do not know anything, Sis, about buying clothes."

"I think because this is a special occasion, you probably should have a couple of skirts with light blouses and two pair of shorts and you certainly need something else for shoes."

"What about Shelby? What does he have for going out clothes?"

"Nothing fancy."

"Well, he'll need two pairs of dress pants and short sleeve shirts and he needs a pair of going out shoes, too."

They found everything they wanted and Mrs. Adalbert put the clothes in the suitcases. "We'll pick up everything in the morning, Mrs. Adalbert."

When Raul came home he was tired and didn't stay up long talking with Shelby and Apona.

The next morning he left the house without breakfast and before Shelby, Apona and Sis. "How long will you be gone, Sis?" her mother asked.

"A few days."

Sis was going to hem-up and shorten Apona's skirts and dresses, so she packed a sewing kit and scissors along with her extra clothes.

Rebecca stood in the doorway watching the three of them walking arm in arm towards town. "Why don't you and Sis look around and see if there is anything else we need. I'm going to start carrying this stuff down to the canoe."

He carried the propane gas tank first and laid it in the canoe. Since the suitcases seemed to be full, one of the girls could sit on one and lean back against the other one.

Apona wanted a fifth of ginger brandy, but they were out, so she bought peach brandy. Shelby paid Mr. Adalbert.

"Mrs. Martin, I received a notice yesterday and your rugs will be in a week from today."

"Thank you."

Sis sat on the suitcase and Apona helped with paddling.

At the portage, Sis was surprised when Shelby lifted the gas tank onto his shoulder. "We'll have to make another trip, so I won't overdo it this trip."

When they were home, all of Apona's flowers had blossomed except for the two rose bushes. "Aren't your daffodils pretty."

Before they could take care of things, Shelby had to pull

the window and door boards off and pick up the nail boards. Nothing had tried to break in. Everything was taken inside and then put away.

"Is this my bed here?"

"Yes, and you can use the drawers under it."

She lay down and said, "I like it. It's comfortable."

Shelby checked the root cellar and everything there was okay.

"How about a beaver meat stew?" Apona asked.

"Sounds good to me," Sis said. "I like beaver now, better than beef.

"How did you like this new cook stove, Apona?"

"We both did. It is so much easier and the cabin doesn't get hot and it's cleaner."

"Sweetheart, would you fix me a cup of coffee?" Shelby asked. "I'm going to take some of this food out to the root cellar. Do you want me to bring anything back?"

"Yes, a jar of beaver, potatoes, onions and carrots."

"Would you two like fresh brook trout and eggs for breakfast in the morning?"

"Sounds good to me," Sis said.

"I make some biscuits now with the stew and there'll be enough for breakfast."

Sis was helping Apona with the stew and Apona was making biscuits, while Shelby went looking for a few grubs. He wasn't long catching what he needed. He cleaned the fish and put them in the root cellar until morning.

Then, with nothing else to do, he sat in the rocking chair on the porch, listening to Apona and Sis talking. *It is good for Apona to have Sis out here once in a while—to talk with another girl.*

He went inside and was going to pour himself a brandy. "Would either of you like a little brandy?"

They both did. "I bought this peach brandy, sweetheart. Adalbert didn't have any ginger brandy."

He gave the girls the peach brandy and he took the ginger brandy and went back to rocking on the porch. And thinking about the gold. He knew even without the gold, he could make enough from trapping to make a good living. But he was worried about the repercussions if it was ever found out. It was a good feeling; Gold Brook would be a reserve bank for he and Apona.

"Supper is ready."

"This stew is so good, Apona," Sis said. "We never had food like this in Waterville."

"It is good."

While they ate, Shelby and Apona wanted to hear all about her training to be a nurse.

After supper the three were sitting on the porch, and Apona said, "Sweetheart, we need a bath. It has been several days."

"I know the water is going to be cold."

"Why not start a fire in the ramdown, so we can get warm after."

"Okay. I do need a bath."

After he had the fire going they took their clothes off inside the cabin and carried their towels down to the river with them.

The water was cold and Apona was the first to go all the way in. By the time she had soaped her hair and body, Shelby and Sis finally were all in. "It isn't so bad after you have been in for a while. You know, as long as I lived at the village, we never had warm water to bathe in."

Shelby and Sis finally soaped up and submerged to rinse the soap off. "Come on," he said, "we have had enough."

They ran into the cabin and huddled around the ramdown wood stove warming themselves.

"The wind is beginning to blow," Shelby said. "We got out of the water just in time."

The wind blew all night and this was like music to their ears, and it stopped blowing at daylight.

While Sis was helping Apona to shorten her dresses and

skirts, she said, "Do you know where you are going yet, Apona?"

"No, he hasn't even hinted."

"Well, if you stay in hotels anywhere south of Flagstaff, you are going to see some modern improvements."

"Such as?"

"For one thing, hot and cold running water in your room. There will probably be a bathtub, too, that you can fill with hot water by simply turning a faucet or handle. When you're done you pull a plug and the water drains. And here's the best thing, when you have to go to the bathroom, you sit on a toilet and when you're done you turn another handle or knob and everything is flushed down the drain . No outhouse. And depending where you go, some cities have electricity and electric lights. That is difficult to explain, but you'll see."

"There are none of those in Flagstaff?"

"No, not yet."

While the girls were hemming, Shelby went out back and worked on firewood. There was still two cord of wood left from the winter. For now he piled the wood up against a tree after it was split.

When he came back for lunch the girls were still sewing up the hem lines. "You keep working; I'll fix us something to eat." And he went out to the root cellar for bacon and an egg and a quart of syrup.

He sliced the bacon thicker than normal. It was just easier to do. The flour was in the back room.

"That bacon sure smells good," Sis said. "It all of a sudden made me hungry."

He started making coffee, too.

"Everything is ready."

Apona slipped the dress off and they sat down. "These are really good, brother. Apona must have given you lessons."

"Yes, I watched to see why her pancakes were better than mine."

"These are good, sweetheart.
"You're all sweaty already, sweetheart."
"I've been working on firewood."

* * * *

At the end of the day no one wanted to bathe in the cold river water, so they all washed up with hot water.

Then they sat around talking and sipping peach brandy.

Just as they were going to bed, a gentle wind started to blow and that blew in rain. And it cleared out again by midnight. It was just enough music to put them all to sleep.

The next day Apona and Sis finished hemming her dresses and skirts and Shelby had worked up more firewood.

The next few days, until it was time to take Sis home, they did a lot of hiking, exploring beyond the traplines. Sis was just as interested as were Shelby and Apona, as to what lay beyond what they already knew.

With nothing to do one day, Apona and Sis took the canoe and went in search of fiddleheads. They canoed up to Long Falls and back down and didn't find anything until Grand Falls. They put in on the east side and went exploring. Behind the alder thicket they found all the fiddleheads they would need.

Shelby busied himself with firewood. There was no hurry, so he took his time piling up the tops and limbs. For some reason they seemed to break up and rot back into the ground faster than simply letting them lay about.

The two girls were back before noon and he was already back and the three of them cleaned the fiddleheads. "Fresh trout would go awfully good with these tonight, sweetheart. Sis and I will make some biscuits too."

Shelby only caught enough fish for supper. Sis and Apona canned six quarts of fiddleheads.

During supper that evening, Shelby said, "I think when we get back from our trip, we should shoot a bear and make some bear bacon and smoke some of the meat and can some. What do you think, Apona?"

"Bear meat is much like beaver, not quite as sweet, but good. I've never had bear bacon, but it sounds good. Every fall our people would shoot two bear and it was good. We used to tan the hides like we did the wolverine and sell them to Pasquale.

"You still won't tell me where you are taking me?"

"Not until we are on our way."

Instead of bathing in the river that evening, they each took turns washing up while standing in the wash tub.

The next day the temperature rose to 90⁰. While Apona and Sis were baking pies, Shelby decided to work on firewood again. "It'll be cool this morning."

But before mid-morning, he took his shirt off and even then he was sweating too much. *I don't need to do this today.* So he walked back to the cabin to find Apona and Sis rocking on the porch with their shirts off also.

The river was their only refuge and they were surprised how much the water had warmed in only three days.

"When will you have to leave for work in Farmington?" Shelby asked.

"I don't start work until August first. I already have a furnished apartment, but I'll need a few days to get settled in. I'll leave home a week early."

"We'll be back from our honeymoon before you leave. Maybe you can come out again before you leave," Apona said.

"I would love to. I really enjoy spending time here with you two."

At Long Falls portage before putting in the second canoe, the three stood on shore hugging each other. Finally Shelby said, "Shall we go."

From Long Falls to Flagstaff there was very little conversation. As usual, Rebecca was happy to see her children and was roasting a chicken for dinner.

Apona said, "Husband, couldn't we have a few chickens to raise during the summer and butcher them before winter?"

"We can and after we get back we'll do that."

"That was a delicious meal, Mom," Apona said.

"Yes, Mom, and yes, we need some chickens."

After the kitchen was cleared, Shelby and Apona had to leave. Their braided rugs were at Adalbert's.

They were loaded light this trip as the rugs did not weigh much. At the portage Shelby carried two rugs and Apona one.

Before putting the new rugs down, they first removed the deer hide rugs and then Apona swept the floor. When the rugs were down, "I like it," Apona said.

"Me too. Those deer hides were getting old."

He folded them and for now put them on top of the wood pile.

"Are you hungry, sweetheart?"

"Not really. I'm still full from the chicken dinner."

"Good, because I have been horny for more than a week. I want you now!"

Chapter 13

Because of Griswold and Gunther Macy's injuries, Judge Norman Hardcore wanted to sentence the two to a maximum security prison north of Quebec City, but he knew the trip would be too much for the brothers in their condition. So he sentenced them to Sherbrook Prison, which was the closest prison.

And even that shorter distance in a stuffy prison wagon was painful. The driver, Jean Lore, was familiar with the two brothers. He had no sympathy for the two brothers and purposely bounced them around as much as he could. They both did a lot of hollering and screaming, but it fell on deaf ears.

When the prison wagon stopped at the front gate to the prison, both brothers had to have help getting out. They were met by two guards who escorted them to Warden Reynald's office.

"Hmm, I was informed a week ago you two were coming but no one advised me how serious your injuries are. It is my policy that all new inmates be kept in solitary for a month. Because of your injuries, I may have to keep you in solitary longer. I'll review your case in a month. You were sentenced to life here and twenty years of hard labor. That hard labor will start in the rock quarry making gravel from larger rocks. You may, depending on your attitudes, progress to cutting firewood or building roads. That'll depend on you, as I said.

"Judge Hardcore said you two are troublemakers. That is something that we deal with very severely here. We will not tolerate troublemakers. Neither will I tolerate inmates fighting.

"Your meals will be brought to you, as long as you are recuperating in solitary. And Doctor Larry Smith will check on you every day."

Warden Reynald only nodded to the two guards, signifying they could escort the brothers to solitary.

Much to their surprise, they were put in the same, larger cell in solitary. It was a sickening feeling when the guards closed and locked their cell door.

"You missed lunch, and supper won't be until 6 o'clock," and then they left.

They both were quiet and subdued for two hours, then Gunther said, "This might not be too bad, Griswold. Least-wise, once we get outside and start working. We'll get fed three times a day. And how many times have we had to go days without eating. We'll have a dry roof over our heads. I bet there are folks on the outside who won't have it as nice as we'll have it in here. I'm not glad we'll have to spend the rest of our lives in here, I'm just trying to look at this differently," Gunther said.

"Not me, brother. I may have to spend twenty years in here, but I'll find a way to escape. And when we do, I don't care how long it takes us, but we'll find that squaw and Shelby and we'll make 'em pay. I ain't ever going to get rid of these scars on both sides of my face. I'll make her pay for doing that to me.

"Until we can find a way to escape, we both have to be model prisoners. That way we won't be watched as closely. Do you understand this, Gunther?"

"Yes."

"If you start any fights or bring the guards or wardens down on us, I'll take it out on you."

* * * *

After a month had passed, Warden Reynald asked, "Doctor Smith, are the Macy brothers ready to transfer from solitary to cell block C?"

"I wouldn't just yet, Warden. Climbing the stairs to level C would be difficult for them both.

"Tell me, sir, did only one man actually do all that damage to the two brothers?"

"That's what the case report says."

"Amazing, simply amazing, that one man could do so much damage to those two brutes."

"Yes, Doctor. I wish we had him on our team. Keep me informed about their progress. By the way, how are they transitioning to prison life?"

"I would have to say very well. They are always very polite with me. Even joking some. I wonder if Judge Hardcore didn't get it wrong?"

"Time will tell, Dr. Smith."

* * * *

Another month passed and their injuries had healed enough so Doctor Smith advised Warden Reynald that the brothers could be transferred to C block anytime. But not assigned to hard labor for another month.

"How is their demeanor now, after two months?" Reynald asked.

"They both are meek and polite. And since the casts and bandages have been removed they have cleaned themselves up."

The scratches on Griswold's face had healed, leaving obvious scars. Now, in amongst the other inmates in the common areas, he was teased some about the scars, and he tried his best not to react to the snide remarks and teasing. This was also noted by Warden Reynald.

Nine weeks after arriving at the prison, the brothers were assigned light duty work to the kitchen crew. They were watched constantly for any disruption in their behavior patterns.

Finally, five and a half months after the injuries, Doctor Smith cleared them both for hard labor duty in the quarry, making gravel. There was ice and snow on the ground and the brothers had to be careful about not slipping and falling.

Even with the day-after-day of laboring in the quarry, none of the guards reported any misconduct. In fact, the two brothers were two of the most mild-mannered inmates in the quarry.

They were being watched so closely, Griswold was beginning to worry if he would ever find a way to escape.

Gunther was happy doing just what he was doing. He now had exercise each day which allowed him to sleep at night, besides having food and a warm bed each night.

There were only a few inmates who would taunt Griswold about the scratch scars on his face and as much as he would like to pound the hell out of them, he didn't. His only saving grace were his plans for revenge against Shelby and his squaw woman. He fell asleep each night dreaming about what he would do to both of them.

Escape from the quarry was beginning to seem impossible. Before leaving the prison compound each day, the inmates were shackled and remained that way until they returned in the afternoon.

As far as Griswold could see, their only hope was if they could join the firewood detail crew. There the inmates were not shackled and the supervision was somewhat more relaxed.

"Gunther, we need to get on the firewood crew if we are ever going to escape. And the only way we can accomplish this—we have to become model inmates, and I think it might help us if we started attending church Sunday mornings."

Warden Reynald called two of the cell block C guards into his office. "I was reading your reports on the Macy brothers and I see they have started attending church."

"Yes, sir, it surprised everyone after what we heard about them. They have become model inmates."

"Even when Griswold is taunted about the scars on his face. Not once has either one of them showed any hostility. And

I think Gunther even enjoys being here."

"That is so strange after everything Judge Hardcore had written in his report. Continue watching them."

"Yes, sir."

This next day the two brothers were taken to see Warden Reynald in his office. The guard remained in the office with them.

Reynald tipped back in his chair and said, "I am certainly surprised how well the two of you have adjusted inside these walls. It wasn't what I was expecting from the reports sent down by Judge Hardcore and Constable Duguay in Lac Megantic. I have only favorable reports about you both from the guards.

"Your attitudes surely have changed. And as long as there are no mishaps, come next summer, I will transfer you to cutting firewood."

"Thank you, sir," Gunther said.

"Yes, thank you," Griswold added.

* * * *

It was a snowy and cold winter that year and often times the inmates did not have to work in the quarry and the two brothers began gaining much of their weight back they had lost. And Griswold was becoming irritable. He needed hard work to keep his mind from dwelling on his hatred for Shelby and Apona.

After the snow melted and the ground had dried in May, the firewood detail went back to work and the Macy brothers left the quarry. Other than the mosquitoes and blackflies, the work was not unbearable.

In the quarry the inmates still had to wear the leg shackles, but not here in the woods. The shackles would be too cumbersome and dangerous. Even though cutting firewood was not as strenuous as smashing rocks all day with a sledgehammer, the brothers were still tired each night when they returned to their cell and slept soundly.

261

The two brothers were being watched more closely than the other two men crews, so once again, Griswold had to prove to Warden Reynald and the guards that they had changed. Hoping the guards would stop being so watchful.

One night when they were alone in their cell, Griswold said, "Gunther, I don't know when it'll happen but when the opportunity arises, I'm going to take it. And when I do you need to be ready."

* * * *

Later that summer, the guard watching over the brothers would disappear for a few minutes and Griswold was thinking that this might only be a test. But he always kept track where the guard had gone. On two different occasions, the guard, after disappearing, sneaked back to watch them from behind a huge pine tree. Griswold noticed, and he sat down on the tree trunk, in all appearances to rest. He knew where the guard was and he didn't look around for him. After a few minutes he went back to work before the guard returned. They were testing each other, and nothing was said.

Griswold thought his best chance for escaping would be in May. At the start of the warm weather. It was now October and he doubted if they would be able to survive on the run during winter. So no, he thought he had enough plans and would make his break in May. The winter would only give him more time to gain more trust from the guards.

The winter was cold as usual but there was not as much snow. The firewood crews had cut enough firewood for the prison and now Warden Reynald was selling the wood to the town residents, school and town office.

When the snow started melting in mid-March the crews did not have to work because of the soft and muddy grounds. One night after lights out, Griswold talked with his brother. "Gunther, as soon as I see a chance to escape in May I'm taking it. By leaving in May we'll have the warm summer months ahead of us and then we can make plans what we are going to do. Are you still with me, Gunther?"

Gunter was quiet, too quiet, before he answered, "I'm not going with you, Griswold."

"Man, what's gotten into you. I thought you wanted to escape from here as much as I do. What in hell is wrong with you?"

"I don't want to have to live my life always on the run. Afraid of settling down somewhere. I'd rather we had us a woods camp somewhere, where we could hunt, fish and live off the land. But that isn't ever going to happen for us, Griswold. I'm different than you, brother. I know we were wrong what we did. I have accepted that, and I'll probably spend the rest of my life in prison. But I'm not going to live on the constant run.

"For me, Griswold, this place ain't that bad. Not really. And it ain't no one's fault but my own for being here. You see, Griswold, I know we were wrong what we did and I have lost all need for revenge.

"I have changed, but the front you put on for the Warden and guards is just that, a front. And someday you'll lose all control of yourself if you are still here and you'll explode.

"I'm not the smartest whip, Griswold, but I do know I'm better off staying here. No hard feelings, brother."

"None, but I can't stayed cooped up in here any longer."

Griswold had played being a rehabilitated inmate for so long even the guards were starting to believe it, and when the firewood crews went back to work in May, the guard watching over the brothers had become slack and a little bit sloppy. He would join in the conversations with them when they rested, joking and laughing.

Griswold decided to make his move Friday after lunch and the lunch crew retuned to the prison. He didn't tell his brother of his plans. He didn't feel as he could trust him any longer.

As the inmates were riding in the wagon out to the wood lot, Griswold was quiet and subdued, while Gunther was very talkative.

Right on schedule, the kitchen crew brought lunches in to the two brothers and their guard, Tony Ouellette. Gunther ate only one of his sandwiches and gave the other one to Griswold, who wolfed it down, knowing he couldn't be sure when he would eat again.

They were still eating when the kitchen crew were on their way back to the prison. Because of the danger of felling a tree on another crew, they were spaced out far enough so Griswold could not see anyone else. Tony had stood up to take a leak and in one swift move Griswold picked up the ax and drove it into Tony's back—so far that the ax stayed in his back when he fell to the ground.

"Holy shit, Griswold, you killed him."

"Keep your voice down. Are you going with me or not?"

"I'm staying."

"Then to make it look good, so you aren't blamed—" just then Griswold hit his brother in his face knocking him to the ground, unconscious. Then he started running. He had studied maps of this part of Quebec and Western Maine, while in the prison library.

He was going east as fast as he could.

* * * *

The day before they were to leave on their trip, Apona packed everything they would be needing in the two suitcases. She made sure to pack enough of her white turtlehead tea, while Shelby busied himself making sure all the doors and windows were secure. Besides nailing a board across each door, he also toe-nailed the doors shut. Even the two doors to the back room.

They also made sure there was no food left inside. He pulled the canoe out and then put the suitcases in; he locked and secured the front door with a nail board in front and another in front of the step. He hugged Apona and said, "Are you ready, Princess, for what I hope will be a grand adventure?"

"Let's go."

Sunlight was just appearing through the trees when they pushed off. They had to move right along if they were going to catch the stage to Bigelow Village by 7 o'clock. They both put their shoulders into each stroke with the paddle.

They were there a half hour early. "That was a fast trip," Apona said.

They arrived at Bigelow Village in plenty of time. They bought tickets for Rockford. "You'll change trains in Farmington, to the Maine Central Line. You'll stay on that train to Brunswick. There will be a slight delay there, but you'll not have to change trains. You stay aboard and it will take you to the Samoset Hotel in Rockford. You'll leave the Bigelow Station at 10 o'clock this morning and you'll arrive in Rockford at 10 o'clock tomorrow morning. Would you like a sleeper berth?"

"Yes."

"And meals? They'll be served in the dining car. And what about a return trip?"

"We'll need tickets for our return, but we aren't sure when we'll be returning."

"Your return tickets, if bought, will be good any time this year."

"How much do we owe, with return tickets?"

"Two people, and return trip, will be $200.00."

Shelby paid the agent. "You can board the train now. Go out to the platform, the car is there now. And have a good trip." They found the passenger car and a seat. "Okay, where is this Rockford?"

"It's where I was born. The hotel sits right on the shore of the ocean."

"We're going to the ocean? I've always dreamed of going.

Before there was so many white settlements, my people would go by canoe every summer to the ocean for the summer. Stories are still told of those trips and how good and varied the food is. The people stopped going before I was born. This will be so exciting."

"It will be exciting for both of us. I can't remember anything of the area. I was four years old when we left. And, like you, I have never been on a train before. I saw one once at the Green Farm, though."

There were only four other people in the passenger car. Suddenly there was quite a jerk and the car lurched forward. "I guess we're on our way."

"Look how rocky that river is."

The train had to make many stops along the way. "Shelby, I have to go to the bathroom."

"I'll ask the conductor."

"Hurry."

"Excuse me, sir. My wife needs a bathroom."

"No problem, young fella. At the backend of this car. I'll show you."

Shelby waited for her outside by the door.

When she came out she said, "This trip is going to be one big wonder. I would never have dreamed you can go to the bathroom inside the car you are riding in."

Shelby decided he would go, too, as long as he was up.

It was two o'clock in the afternoon when the Maine Central Train left Farmington. This time they had their own berth. Already Apona had seen more white settlements than she had ever heard of.

By suppertime, they both were very hungry. They had eaten an early breakfast; the Narrow Gauge Railroad did not serve lunch, and supper aboard the Central Maine Railroad was more than fourteen hours after their breakfast. Supper was a hamburg patty, mashed potato and carrots. "Good, but not like home cooking."

Trying to sleep aboard the rocking back and forth train and listening to the clippity-clap sound of the rails sure wasn't like the peace and quiet of home.

And true to the station master's word, they arrived in Rockford at 10 o'clock the next morning. They were in walking distance of the hotel and they each needed to stretch their legs.

"Good morning, folks, can I help you?" the desk clerk asked.

"Yes, we would like a room."

"And how long will you be staying with us?"

Apona answered that. "Until we get homesick."

"We are on our honeymoon," Shelby said.

"Congratulations! We have a very nice honeymoon suite. Fifteen dollars a day and you get breakfast and supper with that."

"Okay."

"Where are you folks from?"

"Flagstaff."

"Your name?"

"Mr. & Mrs. Shelby Martin."

"Very good. Here are your keys and your suite will be to the left when you walk outside, and the suite is at the end. Room #7."

"Any chance we could find something here for lunch?"

"Why of course. Our cafeteria opens at 11:30."

"Thank you."

Shelby set their suitcases down and unlocked the door to their suite. Then he picked Apona up in his arms. "What are you doing?"

"It is customary to carry the new bride over the threshold, or door. I forgot to do this at home."

"Oh, Shelby, look at this. This is more than just a room with a bed."

"Pretty fancy, isn't it."

"I wonder what is in here?" and she opened the bathroom door. "Shelby."

"Yes."

"Shelby come here. Is this what I think it is?"

"I think so, but it sure is fancier than the toilet on the train."

There was a tag on the brass chain that read, to flush toilet, pull chain. Apona did and the sound of the water syphoning through the drain startled her and she gave a little screech. When the tank filled Shelby pulled the chain. "Well I'll be. I wonder where it goes?"

"Shelby look at the tub. What are these knobs?"

"Turn one and see."

She did. "I wonder what this other knob does?" and she turned that one. "Shelby, this one has hot water. I think I'm liking this idea. And look, this tub is big enough for the both of us.

"How does the water get here? From where?"

"I don't know sweetheart."

"There is no window. When you close the door it must be all black in here," Apona said.

Shelby closed the door and it was totally black. When he opened the door again he saw a switch on the wall. "I wonder what this does?"

"Move it," Apona said.

He did and an overhead light came on. "What did you do, Shelby!" Apona exclaimed almost in a panic.

"All I did was move this button," and he moved it again turning the light off. Then he closed the door and turned the button on again. "This must be electricity. I read about in the newspaper, but I have never seen it," Shelby said.

"I wonder what else we'll discover?" Apona said.

"I want to lie down for a while, sweetheart, before lunch."

"Good idea. You know, sweetheart, from the train to here I have seen many marvelous things. When the toilet is flushed I would like to know where the water goes and why light comes on when you pressed the button on the wall. Like magic. Although it is not magic."

"I don't know any more about those things than you do, Mrs. Martin. It is all new to me, too."

"I like being called Mrs. Martin. It tells everyone I belong to you."

"It is going to be fun bathing together later in the tub. I can't wait."

"We'd better get up and go to the cafeteria."

After a lunch of clam chowder and sandwiches, they went for a walk along the sandy shoreline. "All I know of the ocean are what stories are told at gatherings. I never could imagine anything like this."

"It is big isn't it. Could you image being a seaman sailing across this to Europe? Day after day of seeing the same thing, not knowing for sure if you had traveled far or not. If you get lost in the woods, you'll come out somewhere eventually. But not out there."

"In one of the books I studied this winter, it said the ocean was salty. I want to taste it."

"Okay."

They came to a pool of water caught in amongst some rocks and she dipped her fingers in and tasted them. "Oh—ugh, it's awful salty. How do fish live in something as salty as this?" she asked.

"I don't know. Maybe the fish that live in the sea water couldn't live in fresh water. I don't know."

Apona picked up a piece of seaweed and bit off a piece chewing. "This weed is good. Try some Shelby."

"It is good. It's too bad we couldn't transplant some of this in the river."

They had walked around a point and they were all by themselves and they took their clothes off to go swimming. By the time they were only knee deep Apona said, "This water is as cold as the river after ice out. I don't think I want to go swimming."

They dressed and kept on wandering.

"Look at the waves, Shelby. The water is coming in more and more."

"We should be heading back, anyhow." The closer to the hotel they walked the more the water's edge was creeping closer towards the rocky shore.

"What's happening, Shelby?"

"I have no idea. Maybe we can ask someone at supper tonight?"

"At least we're back in time, so we can have a bath and change our clothes."

While Apona was filling the tub, Shelby shaved. Then he climbed in with her. "Wow, this hot water feels good. It'll be difficult to go back to bathing in the cold river after this."

"Let's enjoy while we can," she said.

"Ordinarily, I'd want to play—I mean we're both in hot water in the same tub. But I don't want to be late for supper," he said.

They dried themselves and dressed, Apona wearing one of the skirts Sis had helped to shorten, and a white blouse. Shelby wore his evening clothes that Sis had helped Apona to buy.

"You are so beautiful, Apona. A real princess."

"You don't look so bad yourself, Mr. Martin."

"Okay, wife. Let's eat."

The hotel maitre'd met the Martins in the lobby and escorted them to a table by a window.

"Would you folks enjoy something to drink first?" the maitre'd asked.

"We are new at this dining out. What would you recommend?" Shelby asked.

"Maybe a light white wine, perhaps."

"Okay."

"Alcoholic drinks are extra. They are not included with your meals."

"Okay." He returned a moment later with a bottle of chardonnay. "The meal this evening is a variety of seafood and you may help yourselves anytime at the salad bar. Bowls are at the end."

"Before we do that," Apona said, "Maybe you will explain something for us."

"I will certainly try. What is it?"

"We went for a walk after lunch along the beach; coming back the water forced us up near the rocky shoreline."

"The tide, ma'am. The tide came in, or as we call it, high tide."

When both Shelby and Apona looked confused he asked, "Where are you folks from?"

"Flagstaff, near the Quebec border. This is our first time to the ocean."

The maitre'd explained all about high and low tides. "This happens every day?" Apona asked.

"Yes, twice a day." He filled their glasses with wine and left.

They each took a sip and then drank it like water. "That was good. I'm hungry," Shelby said.

"Me, too."

They helped themselves to the salad. They finished their salads and had more wine and a young woman rolled a cart up to their table. "Good evening folks, I will be your waitress this evening and my name is Sylvia."

She set the platters in front of them and a basket of rolls and hot butter.

"Sylvia, would you explain what these are? We have never eaten seafood before," Shelby said.

"This is a lobster tail. You break off these tail pieces and then push the meat out the other end. These are shrimp fried in batter and clams also fried in batter and these are escargots. You use that tiny fork there to pick the meat out. They are very good.

The lobster is better if you cut off small pieces and dip them in the hot butter first. Is there anything else I can help you with?"

"No, thank you."

"Enjoy your meal."

Curiosity got the best of them both and they tackled the —

"What did she call these?" Apona asked.

"Escargot."

"Looks like a snail to me. And people say Indians eat strange food."

The meat came out of the shell rather easy. "Hmm, it's good."

"It is."

The food was so good they did very little talking. "I could have a meal of just lobster," Apona said.

Sylvia came over and asked, "How is your meal?"

"Very good," Shelby said. "The escargot are better than they look."

Sylvia laughed and left.

"Have you ever tasted anything as good as this?" Apona asked.

"I like venison and beaver and your apple pies, but nothing can come close to this meal."

When they had finally finished, Shelby said, "Wow, I need some exercise now. We both do."

"Do you remember what you told me married couples do on their honeymoon?"

"I think I can remember saying something like they make love over and over."

"That's exactly what you said. I get you in bed, you won't have to worry about outside exercise. That itch is back."

Sylvia came over while they were laughing. "Would you like dessert?"

"I think I'd rather have a ginger brandy, if you have that?"

"We do. And you, Mrs. Martin?"

"I'll have one also. And no dessert."

Sylvia returned with two crystal goblets with ginger brandy. "Thank you."

Shelby held his goblet out towards Apona and said, "Here's to the most wonderful wife a man could have, Princess Apona."

They sipped their brandy and Apona said, "Thank you. You are pretty wonderful, yourself."

As they sipped their brandy they talked about all of the wonders they had seen since leaving home and Flagstaff. The dining room was filling and they decided to leave to open their table for someone else. He left a dollar for a tip. "That brandy made me feel so happy, sweetheart," Apona said. "And a little giggly." He carried her across the threshold once again and closed the door behind them while still holding her in his arms.

After he set her down, she immediately took her clothes off and when he wasn't moving fast enough she began helping him. Then she lay down on the bed and when he was lying beside her she said, "Let's make this honeymoon one we'll not forget." As she also said, "I"m—"

* * * *

Something neither Shelby nor Apona had ever done was sleep until mid-morning the next day. But as honeymooners do, they made love and played, until they lay exhausted, and with the effect of the brandy, they had succumbed to a deep sleep. They missed breakfast. But that was okay, too, as they had each other.

They did manage to make it to lunch. The claws of the lobster from the previous evening meal was now used in a green lobster salad.

After lunch they were able to hire a surrey and a young woman driver, Rhea, to tour the city and around and along the coastal road. When they came to a bridge over a rough rocky waterway, Rhea pulled over to a wide area at the end and stopped and hobbled the horses so they wouldn't run off.

"Before I drive you across the bridge, I'll walk you over so you can watch the tide come in."

Suddenly, Shelby wasn't aware of much around him as he heard in his head again about crossing the bridge. His wife had also said something about crossing a bridge when they were visiting the village. Now that phrase was trying to loosen memories and images about someone saying something about a bridge he would have to cross. But as hard as he tried to remember and see the clear images, he could not.

Frustrated he let it go and enjoyed watching the tidal surf come through the rocky gorge. Afterwards, they did cross the bridge and took an alternate route back to the hotel. Apona noticed how quiet Shelby had become, but she didn't say anything, until they were alone in their room, "You have had a long face and were very quiet after we stopped by the bridge."

"I know. I heard something in my head and I can't find an answer."

"Tell me what you can," she said.

"Every time I hear something about crossing a bridge, a peculiar feeling comes over me. There's something that I think is important, when I hear something about crossing a bridge. When we were at the village you said something about crossing a bridge and the same feeling came over me. I just wish I knew why. What is there about crossing a bridge?"

"Does it worry you?"

"I'm not worried, but I do find it puzzling."

"We have time before supper; maybe I can help you to forget it."

* * * *

Apona was able to help Shelby forget about crossing the bridge and for supper that night they had baked potato and baked haddock, salad and rolls. "Can we make potatoes like this?"

"Yes."

"Why you put butter in the potato skin and eat. It is very good? I would like to fix potato like this." She tried it and decided the skins are very good.

They had walked along the sandy shore, toured the area, window shopped in the city, ate fried clams and french fires at a sidewalk cafe, and after five days they both were ready to go home.

They paid the clerk what they owed, and Shelby said, "We have enjoyed ourselves so much, we will be back next year."

They had enjoyed their stay there at the Samoset Hotel and were a little sad to be leaving. But they were in agreement that they couldn't wait to get home.

"I wish this train would go faster," Apona said and Shelby laughed.

* * * *

The Sandy River and Rangeley Lakes Railroad pulled up to the terminal platform at Bigelow Village at 8 o'clock in the morning. They had to wait until 11 o'clock to board Raul's stagecoach that would take them to Flagstaff.

As much as they wanted to go home, they both felt they should stay the night at his mother's. No one was outside, so they opened the door and walked in. "Anyone home?"

Sis came barreling down from upstairs and Rebecca was wiping the baking grease from her hands. Sis hugged Apona and then Shelby.

"Are you hungry?" Rebecca asked.

"Oh, yeah."

"How about coffee and apple pie, made Apona's way with ginger brandy."

Apona was telling them all about the new marvels they had seen.

"So what did you do all that time?" Sis asked.

Apona grinned and said, "We were on our honeymoon."

"And a lot of sex," Sis said, shocking her mother.

Shelby and Apona couldn't hold back grinning. This told Sis all she wanted to know.

"Are you ready to go home with us, Sis?" Apona asked.

"Actually I can't. I'm leaving tomorrow for Farmington. I received a letter right after you left. One nurse is out on sick leave and I was asked to come a month early. So I don't know when I'll be able to come with you."

Sis and Raul walked with them to town, and tearful goodbyes were said.

Raul had sold Shelby and Apona four of his chickens and had given them a chicken crate to carry them in with the understanding the crate was to be returned.

"There's home, sweetheart," Apona said. "Look how the flowers have bloomed. They are so pretty."

"What are you going to do with the chickens?"

"For now in the woodshed. I'll have to string some chicken wire across the outside end. It might be a good idea to keep them in there for a day, so they get used to it. Then we can turn them out in the mornings and they should go back in before dark each day."

He set the crate down and checked all the nail boards and then took the door and window boards off and put everything on top of the woodpile for now.

As they lay in bed that night, Apona said, "I enjoyed our honeymoon, sweetheart. It was fun and interesting, but there's nothing like home."

"My feelings exactly. But come next year I think we both will be looking forward to the trip."

* * * *

As Apona was fixing breakfast the next morning, Shelby took yesterday's newspaper that he had bought at Adalbert's and sat out on the porch to read until breakfast.

"Oh, my God!" he hollered and went back inside.

"What are you so excited about?"

"Griswold Macy escapes from prison!" It was on the front page. "Only Griswold. Gunther apparently chose not to escape. Griswold killed the guard with an ax."

"Where is he now?" Apona asked.

"No one knows. This happened while we were with your people in May."

"Do you think he'll come looking for us?"

"I'm not sure. But he doesn't know where we live. We are going to have to be more careful now. Until this guy is caught, I don't think I'll leave you alone here. And we keep our rifles and handguns loaded and reachable. And we lock the doors when we sleep. I wish we had a dog now."

"We'll have to go to town soon. Maybe Raul or the Adalbert's will know someone who has a dog. They are a good alarm."

"For man or beast."

The chickens were doing well pecking for their own food outside of the would-be pen and they were not wandering far away. And on the plus side they were each laying a half dozen eggs each week.

July was an extremely dry month and the water level in the river had dropped the lowest since Shelby built the cabin.

One day after breakfast, he said, "I think we need to pick up all of the gold nuggets on the dry river bottom before someone comes along and sees them. Then we would have nothing but trouble here."

"What are we going to put them in?"

"For now we each could use a Mason jar."

They walked on dry sand along a six foot strip between the shore and the water. They could see gold nuggets shining in the sunshine. They could see some in the water before it dropped off into deeper water. They were on their hands and knees and digging into the sand with their hands and letting the sand filter through their fingers. When they figured they had cleaned up the dry riverbed they moved up into the bushes and the small freshlet still had pools of water. They found more nuggets here than in the river. By the time they figured they had about everything, they had filled both quart jars. "These are heavy, Shelby. What are we going to do with them now?"

"I don't want to leave then around inside the cabin. Maybe we should bury them somewhere?"

"Where?"

"I don't know. Let's put these in the cabin and then find a place."

They walked around outside. "I know," Apona said, "Can you lift that rock beside the path to the spring?"

"I see what you are thinking. I'm stronger than most men and if I can lift it, then most can't. "

He scrunched down, put his arms around it and found two good hand holds. "Oh my word, this sucker is heavy," but he moved it enough so that they could dig out a hole for both jars and buried them deep. Then with a lot of groaning and grunting, he replaced the rock exactly where it had been.

"Will any more nuggets come out of the ground, Shelby?"

"When the water starts to run again maybe. If we sifted the sand between the shore and the water in the river, I think we'd find more. But all I'm interested in now is removing those on top. Someday someone will be coming through. What's under the rock—well, that's our old age investment."

"I bet before we start trapping, once the water starts running in Gold Brook we'll be able to find more under the ledge rock."

Every morning before it was too warm to do much work, Apona would help Shelby with firewood.

By August they had more firewood worked up than they would need, so they walked the traplines, clearing the path of blow downs and branches. Last year they trapped lines number one and two on the west side of the river. This year they would trap on the east side.

By the second week of August, the drought was over and the water level in the river returned to normal. And Shelby and Apona checked Gold Brook, and where it emptied into the river, the flush of water washed sand and clay, exposing more nuggets. They cleaned those up and put the pouch in one of the bed drawers and would sell them in the spring with their fur pelts.

The nights were getting cooler and Shelby caught several brook trout to smoke and put the heads and innards in a bucket and tied it up in a cedar tree across the river.

"And a bear will come to the bucket?" Apona asked.

"Bear live by their nose and they can smell food from a long distance. Those fish remains will smell stronger with each passing hour."

"You know, husband, I have always like eating bear, almost as much as eating beaver. But I have never eaten bear bacon."

"Neither have I, but I think we can make it. Whoever sees the bear shoots, and place a good shot, so we don't have to chase after it. Ah, heck, why am I telling you that. You're a marksman with handgun or rifle."

On the second morning while Apona was fixing breakfast, she said, "Bear," but Shelby had gone out to the outhouse. The rifle was already loaded and she inched the door open and leaned against the door jamb. She waited for a good clean shot. The bear was able to bring the bucket down and now she couldn't see it.

Once in a while she could see part of the back, but not enough to shoot at. She whistled and the bear stood up looking at her and she squeezed the trigger and the bear went over backwards.

Shelby pulled his pants up and ran to the front of the cabin. Apona turned to look at him and she was smiling. With that smile there was no need to ask if she had killed it. "We'll eat breakfast first and then go over for the bear." He had that much confidence in her ability as a hunter.

She jumped out of the canoe and pulled it up so Shelby could step out. The bear was still on his back. "That was a good shot, sweetheart, right in the base of the throat."

She held the legs apart while he dressed it. "While I finish this, Apona, would you empty the bucket in the river and rinse it out and fill it with water so we can rinse the blood off in the inside." He didn't save the liver, but he would the heart.

After the bear was rinsed off, they loaded it into the canoe and pushed off and across to the cabin side of the river. It was too cumbersome to carry it, so they dragged it up to the game pole. "How much would you say he weighs?" Apona asked.

"Two-fifty, maybe."

He began skinning, being careful not to cut through the hide. He knew his wife would want to tan it. When he had the hide off, he said, "These belly sides is what we'll smoke for bacon. Would you bring a pan for the heart?"

While she was doing that, he split the brisket and propped the ribcage open with a stick.

While Apona was cleaning the heart, Shelby mixed a solution of salt and water to soak the bacon sides overnight before starting to smoke them. With that done, Apona helped him to nail the bear hide to the side of the cabin to dry.

"What are you going to do with the skull, sweetheart?"

"Throw it in the river for the fish?" He knew she probably had a use for it.

"I want the brains. I can remember my people would use the brain to soften a deer hide before using hemlock bark. I want to try it. Then I want to set the skull to dry in the sun so I can pull the eye teeth out and make jewelry with them."

He cut the head off and set it aside for now, then he split the carcass using a saw and then he hung them in the root cellar.

Then he cracked open the skull and scraped the brains out

into a coffee can and Apona took that to the root cellar.

"We'll have the heart for supper with onions and mushrooms, if you'll go with me after mushrooms."

"Of course I'll go with you."

They went through the hardwoods first and found a huge bear's head tooth mushroom growing from a rotting wound on a beech tree. They also found inky caps and coral mushrooms.

Before breakfast the next morning, Shelby started a small fire in the smokehouse. Apona fried up the last of the pig bacon with pancakes. While she was cleaning the kitchen, Shelby hung the bear bacon sides up in the smokehouse and then he went out back for a rock maple sapling to flavor the bacon.

While Apona was baking a pie and biscuits, Shelby caught more brook trout to smoke. This smokehouse was big enough to accommodate several racks of meat.

"I thought tonight we'd have a bear roast," Apona said. "Would you go cut off a good piece of meat and bring in some potatoes too?"

"Sure thing."

Even as warm as it had been, he was often surprised how cool it was inside the root cellar. He came back with his arms loaded. "Just put everything on the sink counter for now."

The pie and biscuits were cooling on the table.

"Oh, I need a break," she said.

"Go sit out on the porch. I'll pour us some ginger brandy and I'll join you."

They sat in the rockers sipping brandy and talking mostly about the supplies they would need for the winter.

Apona took another sip of her brandy. "Shelby—there is a canoe coming this way."

"I'm glad we fished the nuggets out of the river when we did."

"He isn't fishing, Shelby, and it's just one person and he is standing up using a long pole and not a paddle. And he looks to be wearing some sort of a uniform."

"I see him now."

"Well let's go meet our visitor." They walked down to the wharf. "Hello, folks. Mind if I pull in?"

"Not at all."

He guided the canoe in towards the wharf smoothly with the pole. Shelby steadied it while he climbed out and then he pulled it up on shore.

"You have a nice place here. And I hope you are Mr. & Mrs. Martin."

"We are, and you?"

"Excuse me, Niles Clayton. I'm a game warden supervisor from Kingfield."

"Would you like a cup of coffee Mr. Clayton?" Apona asked.

"I've never turned down a cup of coffee in my life. Yes."

"Or would you prefer a ginger brandy? We were having one when we saw you coming."

"Coffee will be fine."

"Come on up and sit."

Game warden, Shelby was thinking, *I'm glad that we had removed the deer hide rugs from the cabin. Surely he'd be able to spot the two summer hides.*

"Who shot the bear? I saw the hide on your cabin wall."

"Apona did two days ago. We're smoking the bellies for bacon."

"I've never had bear bacon before, but I bet it would be good."

"We're hoping, this is the first time we have tried it."

Apona came back out with the coffee and Shelby brought out another chair for her.

"What brings you out here, Mr. Clayton?" Apona asked.

"I'm not here by accident. You are Shelby Martin?"

"Yes."

"How would you like to be a game warden?"

"You came all the way out here to ask me that?"

"Yes. I am a supervisor and I need another man to cover the area from Flagstaff to the Quebec border."

"That's a big area," Shelby said. "Why me?"

"A month ago we had a meeting in Augusta talking about hiring more wardens and your name came up. There was a long article in the newspaper a year and a half ago about you saving Apona and her brother's life and about the two burly men you took to Lac Megantic and testified in court that got them both life sentences. For two days I have been talking with people in Flagstaff and it seems you two are a bit of local legend, and everybody I talked with said I couldn't have picked a better man.

"In 1880, the warden service department was created to stop the commercial killing of moose and deer, and to stop lumbering crew camps from killing moose and deer to feed their crews. There has been no enforcement of the laws in this area and that would be your primary concern until it is stopped. If you were to become a game warden."

"And you made a special trip out here to ask me?"

"We need good, capable men who are comfortable working alone and for days at a time in the woods."

"For the sake of argument, if I do decide to do it, I would want Apona to travel with me." Apona was smiling.

"As a rule that wouldn't be allowed, but the rule has been overlooked in another warden's case. A warden south of here in Grafton, Kirby Morgan, and his wife, Rachel, work together and they are a legendary team."

"I know this Rachel. Not personally, but I know about her. She and her husband are one of the stories often told in the village where I lived. She was Carcajou woman," Apona said happily.

"That's correct; she was a legend," Niles said.

"Mr. Clayton, would you care to stay for supper? I am making a bear roast."

"I'd love to. I like bear meat."

"Could I look at your smokehouse?"

"Surely." While they were looking at the smokehouse Apona checked on the roast.

Niles changed the subject. "You have a nice place here."

"Thank you. We have worked hard here."

"How do you make a living?"

"We both trap and we do well.

"On the other side of the cabin is the root cellar." And they walked around the cabin. He opened the doors and Niles walked in only far enough to see.

"How long will food stay good in here?"

"Vegetables forever and the meat will stay fresh for a couple of weeks. We can both deer and beaver meat."

"You certainly have a nice set up here, Shelby."

Niles was surprised to see gas lights and a gas cook stove. "Where does your water come from?"

"There is a spring out back."

"And that door in the back?"

"That's the skinning and stretching room and we store some things there too."

"Supper is ready. Sit down."

"This is a beautiful meal. Baked potatoes, roast bear, onions and mushrooms and fresh biscuits. Do you folks eat like this all the time?"

"Pretty much."

"It's a wonder you two stay so fit and trim."

"Hard work, Mr. Clayton," Apona said.

For dessert they had apple pie. "This is delicious. With a special taste."

"That's a little ginger brandy," Apona said proudly.

"You know, Mr. Clayton, it is too late to think about leaving now. You should stay the night," Apona said.

"After a meal like this—well I think I should stay. I'll go

get my pack out of the canoe and turn it over."

"I'll give you a hand with the canoe."

Later as they were all sitting on the porch Shelby asked, "If I was to accept your offer, would we have to leave here?"

"Yes, you would have to be reachable."

Apona brought a little ginger brandy for them all.

"Are you married, Mr. Clayton?" Apona asked.

"Yes, and two children."

"Do they miss you when you're away from home so much?"

"Yes they do. But I must make a living for them and I enjoy being a game warden, but it *is* difficult for my family at times. When my son is older, maybe he'll want to go with me some.

"This brandy is good. I'll have to tell my wife about adding a little in her apple pies."

"There is another reason for me being here," Shelby and Apona waited. "Griswold Macy escaped from prison in May. He killed a guard with an ax. The prison warden, Paul Reynald, believes he may have been heading for Maine. He has not been seen since escaping. Does he know where you live?"

"No, and we read about the escape in the newspaper," Shelby said.

"You two might want to be careful living out here alone."

"We will, Mr. Clayton," Apona said.

They sat on the porch talking long after sunset. Finally Apona stood up and said, "I leave you two here, I'm going to get ready for bed," and she took her chair back inside.

"I would like a life like you and Apona have here, but it wouldn't be so easy with children.

"What I am going to say next, Shelby, I don't want you to reply to it. But I do want you to think about it."

"Okay."

"A Maine Game Warden is away from home days at a time. You would miss out on a lot of family get-togethers. You'd have to work in inclement weather sometimes and the pay is only slightly better than what you could expect in a mill. You would confiscate enough moose and deer meat so you would never have to hunt for food again. It isn't as much a job, as it is a great way of life. If you like to hunt, then the ultimate quarry is man. A deer you shoot. But if you're after man, you have to outthink, outsmart him. It becomes a great game.

"Now with all that said, if I were you, I would hate to give all this up. Now I'm ready for bed."

* * * *

Niles Clayton was already up and drinking a cup of coffee when Shelby and Apona crawled out of bed. To give Apona some privacy he finished his coffee in the rocking chair on the porch.

Apona was impressed with his chivalry. Shelby poured himself and Apona a cup and joined Niles on the porch.

After a breakfast of scrambled eggs, warmed up smoked trout and biscuits, Niles stood up and said, "Thank you so much for your hospitality, Mrs. Martin. I really must be on my way."

"It doesn't take long to canoe back to Flagstaff," Shelby said.

"I'm not going to Flagstaff. I'm going down river to meet up with Warden Riley at Caratunk. There is a lumber contractor still killing moose to feed his crews. I need to tell him about it and maybe help him. Then I'll canoe my way eventually down to the Kennebec River and onto Augusta. And then hop a train back to Kingfield."

He gave Shelby his calling card, "Think about what I told you last night, Shelby, and a week from today send me a telegram to my home in Kingfield; tell me you accept or decline my offer.

"It's a great life, Shelby, but remember what I said."

Shelby and Apona walked with him down to his canoe. When he was seated, Shelby pushed him off. "Shelby, do you know the difference between a summer deer's hide and a fall hide? Good day."

They watched him canoe down around the bend.

"What do you suppose that was all about, Shelby?"

"He was telling us in his own way, he saw the two summer deer hides on the wood pile."

"Hmm, I liked him," Apona said.

They sat in the rocking chairs talking about Warden Niles Clayton. "Tell me what you're thinking, sweetheart?"

"Listening to him and then what he said about canoeing to Caratunk and eventually to Augusta, I found interesting. But I'd be away from you too much and I'm not ready to give all this up."

Apona was smiling and she said, "I am glad. I, too, would hate to give all this up.

"It's a bridge you didn't have to cross."

The End

About the Author

Mr. Probert retired from the Maine Warden Service in 1997 and began to write historical novels about the history in the areas where he patrolled as a game warden, with his own experiences as a game warden as those of the wardens in his books.

When you work at something that you enjoy, then it never becomes just a job. For Probert, it was more fun than playing baseball. But that doesn't mean that everything was easy because it certainly was not—like having to summons a friend to court or having to pull a friend's lifeless body into a boat.

Mr. Probert now has twenty-eight books in print and the Whiskey Jack series is his favorite series, but Ekani's Journey is the single favorite.

Made in the USA
Thornton, CO
03/18/23 12:44:19

eb44c4e0-bbc3-4efd-9f1c-b441e3a72c24R03